AN ALPENGLOW RIDGE NOVEL

# Whisk til Peaked

## ZEA KAYLEIGH GALAN

Whisk til Peaked: An Alpenglow Ridge Novel

Copyright © 2024 by Zea Kayleigh Galan.

www.zeakayleighgalan.com


All rights reserved. Printed in the United States of America. No part of this book may be used, stored, copied, or reproduced in any manner without written permission except in the case of brief quotations embodied in critical articles or reviews as specified under the U.S. Copyright Act of 1976.

This book is a work of fiction. Names, characters, businesses, organizations, places, events, and incidents either are the product of the author's imagination or are used fictitiously. Any resemblance to actual persons, living or dead, events, or locales is entirely coincidental.


For information contact :

zeakayleigh@gmail.com

eBook ISBN: 9798989899562

Paperback ISBN: 9798301473449

Alternate Paperback: 9798989899579

First Edition: December 06, 2024

10 9 8 7 6 5 4 3 2

To you,
When you receive it, accept and believe it.

# Playlist

Tony Evans Jr. – Somebody's Gotta Do It
George Birge – Mind On You (feat. Kidd G, charlieonnafriday)
Kiana Ledé – Where You Go (with Khalid)
USHER – Caught Up
Alana Springsteen – Me Myself and Why
Tiera Kennedy – Laid Back
Ne-Yo – Miss Independent
Tanner Adel l– Tan Lines
Tucker Wetmore – What Would You Do?
Tiera Kennedy – Gentleman
Tanner Adell – Throw It Back
Bella Dose – Si Me Llamas
BRELAND – Thirsty
Niko Moon – BETTER WITH YOU
Shaboozey – Last Of My Kind (feat. Paul Cauthen)
Don Louis – Watered Down Whiskey
Rodell Duff – Good Days
Hueston – Joy Ride
Thomas Rhett – Star Of The Show
Doja Cat – Need to Know
Rodell Duff – Please Come Home for Christmas
Thomas Rhett – It's The Most Wonderful Time Of The Year
Coffey Anderson – Jingle Bells
David J – DESERVE YOU
¿Téo?–Part Of Me
Mickey Guyton, Kane Brown – Nothing Compares To You

This is a romantic suspense novel that is suitable for mature audiences only.

For a full list of potentially sensitive content, visit my website: www.zeakayleighgalan.com/cw

AN ALPENGLOW RIDGE NOVEL

# Whisk til Peaked

# Chapter 1

## Drea Montoya

"I THINK WE SHOULD break up."

*Sigh.* "Okay, Sean."

He taps on the table once before nodding to himself. I cut my perfectly seared steak and yes! It's warm and red in the center. I've got to tell Chandie and Mom about how well her reverse sear technique worked. I'm seconds from tasting it before Sean interrupts me.

"That's it?" His tone is clipped as his tapping on the table increases in tempo.

Normally I would play into his ego-stroking since that's the only stroking he'll be getting from me, but not tonight. I've been thinking about this meal all day. I began marinating this steak yesterday. The garlic, roasted in organic extra virgin olive oil with fresh rosemary until perfectly golden brown. When I riced those potatoes and added the garlic in, I could already tell how perfect they'd be before I even tasted them. Don't even get me started on how precise my steam and butter baste regime was for the asparagus.

I'm not experimental or Michelin star-rated. I just make good food that makes people happy. Savory or, my favorite, sweet, I'm always excited about creating something delicious.

This meal would be better than any restaurant that Sean could find in town and maybe the state. I am the hidden gem he *thought* he discovered.

But, what he failed to recognize is that my shine sparkled without his buffing. This was my night to celebrate—and he's ruining it.

"Did you expect me to beg you to stay?"

He scoffs and rolls his eyes. "No. I expected you to care about us ending our relationship."

I sigh again, shoulders slumping in recognition that I will not get to enjoy this mouthwatering food in front of me until he finishes whatever this is. I set my fork and knife down. Better to not have literal weapons in my hand. "That's where you're wrong. We aren't ending our relationship. *You* are. I respect your decision to leave. Do what makes you happy."

"See, you don't care! Three months and you cut me off without blinking."

"Again, it's you who's breaking up with me. I wanted to enjoy this perfectly executed meal with you to celebrate the paperwork being finalized and approved for my new business."

"Everything is work with you! If it's not, then it's Mireya. And if not her, then *Tony*. And if not him, then your girls. What about Sean?"

Whenever Sean was feeling particularly petulant, he referred to himself in the third person. It would probably not be a big deal, but it happened often enough in the past few months that I'd noticed... and cataloged it on his cons list.

And another thing to note, Sean Brenford never had to worry about anything work-related because his family owned the steel mill that sat between Alpenglow Ridge and Harmony Hill. He has complained more than once about my work schedule, which included bartending at QB's, my friend's sports bar, and the extra hours baking for events. Not all of us have a silver spoon wedged so far up our asses that we don't understand the cost of living for a single mom of a teenager is high. I have made sure that Mireya never recognized that fact either.

"Sean, I don't want to fight. If you have something to say, please just say it."

"I have a lot to say. I'm sick of these dates that go nowhere! I come over tonight thinking that things will be different and they aren't."

"What exactly did you think would be different? I said I was making dinner for us to share and spend time together. I made dinner. I even changed out of my yoga pants into something nice." I gesture to my form-fitting maroon Ponte dress that makes my curves look more mouthwatering than the meal in front of me. I nearly passed on this one because I thought I'd never have anywhere to wear it. Usually, I'm covered in flour, batter, or seasonings of some kind. On occasion, I have the opportunity to do a little more. There hasn't been a need for new dresses in my life for a while. Much to my friends' dismay.

"See? You tease me and taunt me in these tight-ass dresses. You don't let me touch you. Hell, I'm basically in Alaska on this side of the table. Your daughter is not here. It would be the perfect time... You treat me like I'm some scrub you married thirty years ago, and the flame has died out."

*There it is.*

"Well, I didn't realize that you didn't understand English. *No me tocarás. Soy célibe.* *You won't be touching me. I'm celibate*, I tell him in Spanish. I'm not completely fluent, but I've picked up plenty from my Papi. "I was clear about that from the start. That's not even on the table at this point. You've shown me that before and confirmed it now. It was your choice to leave or stay before, but now—I'm telling you to leave."

"I thought that after we spent these months together, we could move forward in our relationship. Like a normal couple." I'm not sure I would even call Sean my boyfriend. I don't understand why he's got a different perception of this than I do.

"A couple of months? You thought I would end five years of celibacy for a relationship that lasted a couple of months!"

He scoffs, scuffing my floors with his chair when he pushes back from the table. "Fuck this and you. Do you know who I am in this town? I could be with anyone else!" He stomps off, muttering, "Cocktease."

My front door slams as he exits with all the drama he could muster, apparently.

I stare at the wall for a moment, trying to process how this went so downhill. Then, I remember.

Men are shit.

Every single one.

Besides my best friend, he is a special case. Kind of like a unicorn or four-leaf clover.

Back to how men are shit though... They all are too wrapped up in themselves to even think about what our needs are. Not once did Sean ask me what I would need to feel comfortable moving forward in that way with him. He just assumed that by doing the absolute bare minimum, my legs would magically open for him.

And you know what? Maybe with other women, his name and reputation would be enough.

I need more.

I refuse to settle for less than what I deserve ever again.

"Drea?" His familiar deep voice calls out to me from my foyer and I stand up from my chair, walking over to the doorway of my dining room.

*My bestie's here.*

"Yea, I'm in here."

The clomping of Mireya running upstairs to her room is punctuated with a door slam. I sigh, again.

So many of those tonight.

I lean against the door jamb and take in the big man wiggling out of his work boots by the door. His cowboy hat, already hanging on the rack.

His t-shirt is dusty from working today and I take note of the mud on his jeans too. There is a chest of drawers in the hallway that holds more of his clothes than anything else. I open a drawer, pulling out a tank top and sweatpants for him to change into.

Holding them out to him, he takes the clothes, saying "Thanks," before he walks past me to my master bathroom at the other end of the hallway. "I'll be quick."

Nodding, I pour food for his dog, which I already know is playing in the backyard, and fill up her water bowl, too. The moment the kibble hits the bowl, Milli comes bounding in from the doggie door to eat. *At least one of us is.* I scratch her head and she pauses eating for a bit to nudge my leg with her snout.

Washing my hands, I grab the plate I originally made for Sean to add twice as much food to the plate for Ant.

Feeling satisfied with my tasks, I sit back down in my seat. Swirling the Cabernet in my glass, I take a sip.

Finally, I'm going to get the first bite. As soon as the flavor of the steak, albeit lukewarm, hits my tongue, I moan exaggeratedly. That consonant "M" stretches long as the flavors continue to develop with the lingering red wine.

My eyes flutter open when Ant clears his throat in the doorway of my dining room. "I take it that something happened at Mason's then," I say, undeterred from my food. I scoop up the garlic mash and take another bite. I nod and point to the plate across from me with my fork.

"Said she was feeling tired, so I brought her home." He shrugs, walking over to the dining table. His socked feet are still heavy on the wood floors as he nears me.

"Why didn't you call me? I could've picked her up from the Ranch?"

Mason Ranch is the cattle ranch Ant manages. Reese Mason-Whitfield is one of my girls and the new owner. Her kids and my daughter are good friends as well. Mireya often takes the bus with them to hang out after school and I'll pick her up. The bus doesn't come here since my grandparents built this house right on the town's edge.

No one loves to cook as much as my friend Reese's mother, Chandie. I'll often send her pictures of the food I've cooked, and we'll swap recipes and such. And still, between the two of us, *one person* is always happy to taste what we've made. He sits across from me, cutting into his steak. His hum of approval zings down my spine.

I know my food is good, but Ant always makes me feel like I've made something worth blue ribbons and recognition. "You could have... but I figured you'd be busy with *your date.*" We both eat for a few moments more before he asks, "Where is that guy?"

I tilt my head to one side and then the other. "He... umm... Decided that he was not going to be having dinner with me tonight."

"What does that mean?"

"It means that he wanted something else and I was perfectly happy not giving it to him."

He stabs the fork into his mashed potatoes with more force than necessary. I recognize the chokehold he has on the utensil and stay quiet. Ant is not prone to violence or outbursts but I know something I've said has made him unhappy. It's written all over his face. I don't want to defend Sean, but I don't want to lie to Ant about why he left.

Ever since we made that pact of celibacy together, it has received much criticism from people we know and strangers alike. It turns out that men gossip just as much as women. After a few dates gone awry because of the pact, more and more people knew.

I never thought that my best friend and I would be the source of speculation to this degree, but I admire how strong he has been with me. It means everything to me that I have his support, not in just this but in so many other things, as well.

This man knows me better than most, and I would say that he rivals even my girls, on what secrets I've shared with him. That's why what he says next shocks me from the words, down to the tone.

"When are you going to stop dating these boys and get with a real man?"

# CHAPTER 2

# Tony Dupont

I SHOULD NOT HAVE said that.

But, damn. I can't take the words back. They're true and I was thinking them. That's the thing about being best friends with someone you love as more than a friend.

Andrea Montoya is perfect. From her beautiful bright eyes to her luscious body, she is everything I could want in a woman. She's fiercely loyal and her independence is most important to her. There is not a problem that Drea will not try to solve on her own. I admire all the flaws and talents she possesses equally.

I only wish that her eyes worked better.

Everyone sees it, but her.

I'm the one sitting here with her instead of Sean Brenford, the only son and heir to the Brenford Steel Mill. I knew this dinner meant a lot to her. I had a different plan in the works to celebrate her signing the paperwork. That went completely out the window when she said he was going to come over for dinner. After all, she should be celebrating with her boyfriend.

*Best friends don't get the first celebration.*

I brought her daughter home after a long day of work so that she wouldn't have to cancel her date with another man. I'm the good guy after all. If I didn't, then who would?

I'll be sleeping on the tiny full-sized bed in her guest bedroom tonight because I'm too tired to drive back to town after riding out almost forty miles on horseback. My legs and back are killing me and a small bed as soon as possible is more comfortable than veering off the road from exhaustion. Milli's bed on the floor is likely more comfortable than mine, but it's a sacrifice I'm willing to make.

That's why I had to make a change.

Running in circles and hitting my head against a wall that won't come down isn't going to get me anywhere. I don't think she'll like the decisions that I've made, but I know that if I don't fight for my happiness then no one will. It's not their responsibility. I've known that from a young age. If I continue this lie I tell myself, that what she gives me is enough, I'll likely die alone. She's fighting for what she *thinks* she wants with absolutely no thoughts about her and me as more than just friends.

And still, I've said nothing—like the good guy I am.

I should say something now. No, I should have admitted something years ago. Now, it's too late. I moved on. I hope.

"And who might this real man be?" She teases me with a smirk lifting her cheek. It's clear she thinks I'm joking. The fake laugh that comes out of my mouth around the garlic mash is believable enough since my mouth is full.

"I don't know. I guess you haven't found him yet." Each word serrates into my chest as I swallow back the pain of how true and dejecting that reality is. She doesn't think that *real man* could be me. And maybe I'm not because I can't believe I just blurted that. Shit. How can I get my foot out of my mouth?

She cuts into her steak and collects some of the juice onto her small piece before popping it into her mouth. "One day, I will," she says. I keep my face impassive as I eat more of her delicious cooking. *Be grateful you can still be close enough to her for this.* I thought life wouldn't be cruel to me but this seems like a sick joke as I try to not make this weird for her.

Changing the subject, she asks, "Any idea of what I'll be walking into when I bring Reya her dinner?" Drea points toward the stairs with her fork and I follow the movement with my eyes.

"I don't. My guess—something to do with CJ. I saw them arguing when I was trying to get a few of the newer horses through the corral."

Her lips quirk to the side in thought. "You think something is going on there? It's hard to tell. CJ is so quiet. I'll have to ask Reese and see what she thinks it is." Drea stands to grab her phone off the kitchen counter to text my boss and one of her closest girlfriends.

While she's just a bit preoccupied I should just relay the news I knew I would have to at some point. Reese knows I'll be gone and I'm shocked that she hasn't blurted it out like the brat she is. I was kind of hoping for it so that I didn't have to. It's not that I didn't want to tell Drea, it was just that I didn't want her to ask why... just yet. I sip from my water glass, clearing the trepidation in my throat. "I'm going home for the week." She looks up from her phone at me.

"You've been going more recently." She comments. I grunt in response, not wanting to elaborate for fear of what will come out of my mouth. Her lips quirk to the side again and she returns back to the table. Her silence is not unexpected but it's going on for longer than it should. What is she thinking about? Maybe she already knew. Biting the tip off of her asparagus, Drea still says nothing.

"I'll be back for the opening. Don't worry," I say.

"I'm a little worried. You'll be gone this whole time." She shakes her head and waves a hand in front of herself. "I'm being selfish. You're right. It has been a long time. I know you don't like going anyway so I just... It'll be fine. I'll be fine. I'll make it work."

She bites her lip and I struggle to not back out of my plans, but it's time. There's so much I need to tell her that I don't think now is the time. There's lots of reasons why I didn't used to go home often and when I did go, I didn't stay long. My brother wouldn't let either go unnoticed and to keep things cordial with him, I have to at least show my face since I don't plan on being home for any of the holidays coming up.

Besides, I don't know if she is truly upset about how her date went tonight. I didn't want to make it worse with what I was not telling her. As a good friend, I should refocus the night on her instead of what's coming soon. "So, we should toast, yea? You did it! In less than a week, you're doing the big thing, Boss Lady." Reaching my arm across the table, I grab the wine she opened and pour some into my glass. I don't care for the stuff, but I'm not gonna go out of my way to grab the Maker's Mark I know she keeps in the house for me right now. Maybe later.

Drea blinks out of her thoughts and raises her nearly empty wine glass. Her smile glints in the light and I return it. "I knew you would make me feel better. To doing the big thing! To opening my shop!"

Our glasses clink and we both sip the rich wine.

She smiles down at her plate, and the expression piques my curiosity. "What you smilin' about now?"

"Oh, nothing... Just wow. I did this. Everything is about to change."

"For the better." I nod and stand from my chair to walk over to her. She looks up at me and the expression is more dazzling up close. "Joy looks good on you, you know?" I sit on the corner of the dining table, careful not to knock anything over. Never have I been more thankful that this old table was built tough. Something from IKEA probably couldn't take all two hundred eighty-five pounds of my body weight so easily.

"Is that what you call the nervousness I'm feeling in my hands and down in my spirit?" She huffs a self-deprecating laugh, twisting the ring on her index finger. She wears all kinds of rings on her fingers when she's not cooking or baking. The one she spins now is from her grandmother before she passed. Her love for sweet treats definitely came from her. She's told me as much and I think those are some of my favorite stories that she shares with me; her baking with her mom and grandmother. The way she lights up from the inside makes mine shine a little brighter too.

"I think the nerves are natural, D. If it doesn't scare you a little bit, then you haven't dreamed big enough."

"Well, I guess I have definitely dreamed big. I am terrified that this bakery will flop. We've never had a shop like mine in town. What if people don't like what I'm doing and the place just sits empty like a haunted house?"

"Haunted houses ain't empty." Drea turns to me, tilting her head. It's adorable and makes her seem even younger than she is. "They have ghosts that never leave. Sounds like not a bad scenario. If you get a ghost, that might be quite the draw for certain crowds. Halloween is right around the corner."

She smacks my arm playfully. "I'm serious, Ant! I'm doing this all on my own. I can't afford to fail. Mireya is counting on me. I have to be able to give her the life she deserves."

"Shush that noise. You are an amazing Ma. You have given Mireya a fantastic life. I don't think that anything could stop you from doing that." She blinks a few times over her glassy eyes. I cup her chin and force her to meet my eyes. "You're not alone. You have me. I would never let anything happen to my two favorite ladies."

"I don't know what I would do without you, Ant. You are my best friend. I can't lose you."

*Best friend.*

*Lose you.*

I stifle my wince before she can catch it. It hits me twofold. I should tell her now and get this over with. Now would be the perfect opportunity not to blindside one of the most valuable people in my life.

I just can't do it. She's my friend and she'll understand. It might take some time, but I will figure it out later. Tonight, I just want to enjoy the time I have with her before everything changes between us.

"Want me to bring some food up to the teenager?" I ask.

"No. It should be me. Puberty can be pretty volatile. A giant like you might scare her off."

I shrug and stand from the table back to my place and grab an asparagus with my fingers. "She actually asked me to take her home."

"Really?"

"Yea. Stomped right over. She grabbed Milli from the house and every-thing."

"That's... interesting. Well, I'll still bring her some food. It's not likely that I'll get any more information out of her, but I want her to feel like she has someone to talk to...Even if she doesn't want to talk to me."

"I get it," I say. "From memory and recent experience, teenage girls can be scary."

"Tell me about it," she says, walking back into the colorful kitchen.

Drea fixes a plate for her daughter and walks upstairs. I hear the knock before she enters the room where soft guitar music spills out and stops when Mireya closes the door behind her Mom.

I sit at the table for a bit, considering if I'm making the best choice. Can I be happy if I make a decision that hurts either of them? Shaking my head, I start gathering plates from the table, putting away the leftovers as I wait for Drea and Mireya to finish their talk.

We both like the channels that just show endless funny clips from social media or that people have sent in. It started as us just sending those videos to each other via text before we got closer. Now, we could spend hours laughing over all types of silliness that people find themselves in. I get to listen to her carefree laugh and relax after a long day. I honestly look forward to this time in my day more than anything else. Belly full of her food while at the same time aching from all the laughs.

Leaning my head back onto the couch for just a moment, I fall asleep before waking to Drea tapping my shoulder to "move up to the bed at least."

Half asleep, I struggle up the stairs, legs on fire and in need of a good stretch. Millie nuzzles her way into Mireya's room, and I give the mini version of Drea a wave from the hall. She gives me one back before going back to watching something on her TV.

I guess it's just me in the guest room tonight. Staring at the ceiling, I think about what's to come from the decisions I've made. I put my arm behind my head and it's not long before I'm knocked out.

# CHAPTER 3

# Drea

THERE IS JUST ONE week until opening. It was lucky that I didn't have too many structural changes that needed to be made to this space. I am almost positive that there is someone smiling down at me from heaven. I'd like to think that it's my grandmother. I hope that I'm making her proud with what I've done here.

It's only been a few days since Ant went to Louisiana, but I feel his absence like a phantom limb. More nights than not, he's at the house. My refrigerator is starting to pile up with leftovers. I decided to just take them over to my friend Melody's house since she has been a little quiet with her husband still on tour for another week or so. Her dance studio is on the bottom floor of the new house Tyson Abrams, yes—that Tyson Abrams, built for her. She's been busy with her latest bout of dancers, including Mireya, so I thought she'd be grateful to not have to stand over a stove for some good food. Her cat, Wesson, and Mireya get along well, so I'm sure she didn't mind being at Aunt Mel's house for a couple extra hours after practice to eat.

More than just the fact that I've gotten used to feeding a cowboy, I want to talk to him about the little changes I've made so far. For instance, the big sign out front was installed and I sent him a picture, but a text just didn't feel the same as having him here. I want a big bear hug that turns into him spinning me around when he thinks I've done something wonderful.

He'll be here tomorrow and I'm well beyond excited to finally have my friend back in town.

Ten pairs of eyes look back at me from where I stand in the kitchen. The shop is closed today for the remaining improvements and alterations I'm making to the space. It's the perfect time to really touch base with my new staff.

"Okay. Let's start with Ella, Harris, Kristy, Shiori, and Ruby. You all will continue to work primarily the morning and day shifts." Kristy and Shiori wanted to add hours to their shifts by working on some of the more involved baked goods I'm adding to the menu, as well as catering gigs. The five of them nod or agree in some way, so I move on to my next group.

"Next is Jesse, Chris, and Grace. You three will continue to work either midday to evening as the shop will still close at seven PM." Their schedules mostly accommodate other jobs they work, but Chris has also asked to work any catering gigs; staging, and event prep only though. He didn't want to get in on the baking action—his loss. The three of them all agree.

"And now for our newbies. Like me," I giggle, but no one else laughs. "Everyone, meet Lily and Tarah. They won't be working the customer-facing part of Drip and Whip, but you will see them from time to time working on our catering commitments."

My pride about having hires who are going to be working for me solely to help bake and cater events swells in my chest. I'm delighted by the fact I was able to actually have staff specifically for my favorite parts of the business. All mine now.

There are a few waves with *hi's and hellos* that go around.

Everything is feeling more and more real.

I'm opening a bakery and coffee shop tomorrow! *Internal squeee!*

"So, I believe I have everyone's new schedules worked out for the next two weeks. It's as fair as I can be. Anyone who requested to add specialty bake hours or catering events will have hours scheduled individually, and it's also reflected there." I point to the area below the weekly hours on the tablet I'm holding. "Does anyone have issues with theirs?"

A few blinks and the swirling of ice in a cup are the only sounds from the people in front of me. I had spent hours learning new software to make it easy to keep up with everything. It even sent out an email every other week to them with their schedules. It was tedious, but very important to set everyone straight. Less time with me having to mess with the tedium.

"I have a question," Harris raises his hand like we're in a classroom.

"Let's hear it," I say.

"I don't see anything about time off requests. I got the email, and it looks like I'll be working Thanksgiving week on days I won't be here."

"Yea. I was wondering about that too. Walter let me take Thanksgiving and Christmas off." Ruby adds.

Martin, the assistant manager who has worked here for ten years, decided to come in today to add some insight. "I have made note of those requests and they will be taken into consideration as best as we can." He looks at me and I nod. Thank God he decided to come in today too, though we've already talked many times about the opening and further operations. If anyone was under the illusion that owning and running a bakery was only about rolling dough, mixing batter, and dusting icing sugar, they would be so wrong. At some point, I'll be able to play with my ingredients again. First, admin.

Martin continues, "Drea will do her best to honor these requests, but not everyone will be able to take off whole weeks at a time moving forward. Since Thanksgiving is in a few weeks, we'll look at those times first. Know that it may look different from what you asked for. We're going to be as mindful as we can when selecting vacation time. Any other questions?"

No one says anything more and I'm grateful not to have to truly use the conflict resolution course I took online this morning. I'm somewhat gifted when it comes to mediating. It's a strong suit of mine and a skill that I think suits being a small business owner.

Mentally, I brush my shoulders off. Me, a small business owner, with a brick-and-mortar location.

I smile, trying to look as approachable as I can while I wait a few more moments for someone to speak up. I don't want to give a bad first impression. Everyone here is integral to the success of Drip and Whip. "Well, that's all I have for you. I've got my number on all the schedules and I know you have Martin's in case anything comes up. I'll see Grace and Jesse tomorrow for the opening." Turning to where Kristy and Shiori are standing, I pump a fist into the air. "We're getting started on the goodies for tomorrow. You two ready?" They nod.

"I'll get started on croissants, Danishes, and quiches," Shiori says, walking over to the industrial fridge to grab some ingredients. Those recipes I'm not changing just yet because they were a staple on the coffee shop's menu before I took over. They were pretty delicious, so I know Shiori will do a great job with making them for the thousandth time.

"Cookies and muffins for me then," Kristy calls over her shoulder, headed to the pantry I just stocked this morning. She looks over the recipe that I printed out from my catalog. Walter's did have some on the menu before, but I think this is an area where my recipes will suit an update. To be honest, you weren't missing anything with the muffin and cookies they served here before. If it's served here now, it's gotta be up to the standard I can get behind.

Cranberry, double chocolate chip, and lemon blueberry muffins are going to be our new staples. As far as cookies go, I had to choose a classic chocolate chip and a white mocha chip with almonds. All of which pair well with coffee or tea.

"Pies and cakes for me then." I smile again, but this time it's just for me, now that the two ladies are busy with their tasks.

Lemon pound cake and coffee cake were the options I decided to debut. Cake is my wheelhouse. That is what I'm most well known for. I'll start with these basics to have for customers coming in mostly for the coffee. But soon, the fridge on the far right will have decorated cakes that can easily be purchased for special occasions. Quick and easy, but luxurious.

I can see it now. Someone showing up to that birthday party with a cake from my bakery and everyone standing in applause at what a good friend that person was for bringing one of Drea's cakes.

Okay, maybe not applause... but stomachs will grumble in anticipation when they see the little whipped cream dollop on top of my green bakery boxes.

I let out a long breath as the sound of baking surrounds me and the scent of freshly baked sweets wafts into the kitchen. This is why I'm doing it. Being in this kitchen beats pouring drinks at QB's. Being in this kitchen beats anything else imaginable because this is what a dream come true looks like. When the first round of cakes comes out of the oven, I set them to cool and start working on what's next in my task list.

Tart cherry and a silky, smooth chocolate mousse pie are next up. I fall into an easy rhythm of working around Shiori and Kristy as I mix and prepare the dough for the pies and later the fillings. I add coarse sugar to the top of the cherry pies and then spend extra time perfecting the placement of each raspberry on the chocolate mousse pies.

Finally–a round of classic cheesecakes. I'll make several of these as they are so popular from my catering menu. Everyone loves cheesecake. One with raspberry, one with chocolate, and the other plain so people can choose to add sauce or not. I set them in the walk-in fridge to cool and that's my last task for the night.

It's just after eight when we all are wrapping up. There will be more prep tomorrow morning for all the freshly baked pastries that we'll make daily. I can't wait for that four AM wake-up call.

# CHAPTER 4

# Drea

"Mireya, I need you to get dressed. You have to get ready."

"But Mama, I'm watching a documentary on fast fashion. Did you know that more than eleven tons of clothes end up in our landfills every year? It's so sad. Just think, that tank top you made me throw away is now contributing to global warming. It's killing our planet."

I sigh, long and deep. "You will not use global warming as a way to guilt trip me," I swear. Last week, I was raising a five-year-old. Since when was I the mother of a teenage girl? I thought I had more time. "We'll talk about this later. I need you to get ready."

She stomps out of the room and the ever-present slam of her bedroom door lets me know she is at least in the vicinity of the things she needs to get dressed.

The doorbell rings and I rush to the front door to see who is there. "I'm here. What do you need?" Chloe enters my house with a clipboard.

"God, I am so glad you're here." I rush back over to the living room, where there are boxes of flyers and promo materials like our mugs, napkins, and biodegradable straws. The last thing is a specific request from my resident mother earth protector. I have to admit that I'm happy she is interested in something that has a soul to it. It could be much worse.

Like drugs... or boys.

"Umm... heavy lifting is not for me." She turns back toward the door yelling for Quincy. He comes up to the house from where I'm sure he was just sitting in their car. "Honey, please help Drea with her boxes to her truck." He looks over to where I have the boxes stacked up.

"Of course. Hey D." He throws a hand up, doing what his wife asks him. It's quick work for him, as Drea looks me over.

"Come with me," she says. It's not long before she has blown out and curled my hair into a style. My best friend, Chloe, is the only reputable hair stylist in town. She owns the salon above the sports bar where I used to bartend. Her sleek black shoulder-length bob is always perfect because she keeps every utensil and product in her massive purse to maintain it. It's more like a carry-on bag. Flowy ginger-colored pants that match her silk top and cream faux fur vest are both chic and typical for my friend. The woman is fabulously dressed and styled at all times. Referring to herself as *The Gossip Mill*, I think it's the town's secrets that keep her rich brown skin so flawless.

She tsks at the sweatpants and tank top I'm wearing. "We can do better than sweatpants. We can always do better than sweatpants."

I admire her work in the mirror. She picked a mocha brown mock neck sweater with a full pleated skirt that both accentuates my curves while still being low maintenance and fabulous. Thank God for good friends.

The last thing I need to do before we head over to the bakery is grab my moody and empowered teenager. "Mireya, please tell me that you're ready to go. If we don't leave now we will be running behind."

My daughter comes out of her room in the dress I bought for her last week. She looks so pretty. Thank God for small miracles.

It has been months of toiling over this new business. I have been working extra shifts at the bar and picking up any gigs I can find around Alpenglow Ridge and some of the neighboring towns to save up for this. Not to mention the years of working way too hard to make everything work despite Colton and his minions. It finally has paid off.

When Eric Walter decided that he was ready to retire, I was first in line to take his place. It is no longer Walter's Coffee Shop. It's my place now—Drip and Whip, a coffee shop and bakery. I can keep the clientele from his business happy because I managed to get the old man to share all his recipes with me. A fact that my friend, Melody, is ecstatic about. She is kind of a fiend for his lemon Danishes. I was also able to keep most of the employees so that I don't have to worry about who will be working the coffee rush with this being the only coffee shop in town.

The biggest bonus is that I also get to keep my own clientele. My van and I have been hauling around our custom cakes, desserts, and pies for the past three years. The daytime was for baking. The nighttime was for bartending. But now, It's round-the-clock coffee and sweets. A fact I could not be more happy about.

We arrive at the shop and check that everything is going smoothly. It is. Thank God for disaster planning.

"Where's Tony?" Melody asks while helping put up balloons Chloe is unloading from her car. My friend looks nice tonight in her ankle-length knit dress that shows off her dancer's frame. With her long, curly hair twisted into an intricate knot at the back of her head, her dainty features glow with soft makeup. Soft-spoken and usually the quietest of our group, Mel doesn't love being at parties. I'm happy she's come tonight even if she only stays for a little while.

"You know Ant. That man could not be on time if his life depended on it." A fact that I'm grateful has not been made a reality of his. I even told him the wrong time so that he could accidentally get here early. Whoops! Ain't I a stinker? He'll thank me later for that.

The bell on the front door dings several times in quick succession. A blur of curly hair blows past me to get to the glass display case. He looks lovingly at the desserts illuminated in neat rows behind the glass.

Bren. My friend's son is always moving at breakneck speed. "Ah, ah. No sweets until I get everything in place. I, at least, want to get pictures before the inevitable chaos ensues today." He gives me puppy dog eyes. "I know."

I boop his cute little nose. "But I promise there will be plenty of sweetness for you later on, okay?"

"Okay, Aunt D." Mireya and Reese's kids spend so much time together, that we have just told them to think of each other as cousins. He hugs my leg and Reese, the diva herself, comes in with the rest of her family. Her twin girls are happily babbling to each other in matching yellow knit outfits from the stroller that her oldest son pushes. CJ is the more reserved of her sons and tonight is no different as I see him searching for an empty corner of the room. Her husband and youngest son are right behind with more decor from Chloe. Cory matches his youngest in a hunter-green pullover and jeans. They are a beautiful family.

Reese hugs me and takes one look around. "Where is Tony?" She wears thigh-high heeled boots and a turtleneck sweater in a deep wine shade and brown leather leggings that accentuate her light brown skin. Her whole family is coordinated in the fall colors and I know she planned it just so. I'm actually quite impressed that she found those sweaters for her husband and boys that all match perfectly.

"I have no idea, but I need to finish some last-minute details. Would you mind telling him to come find me when he gets here?" She says she will and I work on staying calm since our opening time isn't that far away.

My heart is aglow as friends, family, neighbors, and clients come to celebrate the grand opening. I mingle around and pop back and forth behind the counter to share treats I've recommended to guests. It's all a happy blur, really.

*Life really can be sweet sometimes.*

As a single mom, I'm often the only one doing everything at once. I have all the hats and sometimes I need to wear many of them at one time. I'm blown away by how my little community has come together to really make this night easy and special for me. Still, I can't ignore the absence of one friend in particular.

Where is Ant?

I'm behind one of the registers to keep the line moving when a woman comes up to me. "Hi! I'm Steph," she exclaims. She doesn't look familiar, but it's clear that she expects I should know who she is. I take my gloves off and reach across the counter to shake her hand.

"Andrea Montoya," I say, tentatively. I still struggle to place this woman. "I'm glad you could make it."

"I'm so happy to hear that. I was a little nervous to meet the famous Drea that Tony is always talking about." Her drawling southern accent is more noticeable now and I begin to search my memory for how exactly I know her even harder. "Maybe we could even be friends."

My brows pinch and I laugh awkwardly, the sound coming out a little too forced. "Of course, we can be friends." *Who is this woman?* I look around to see my friends are happily talking with other guests at the opening party. Where the hell is Ant?  How is he still late?

Then, I see him. His broad shoulders and tall build take up all the space in the doorway. A black sweater and dark wash jeans match the black cowboy hat he has on. It's not his work hat that gets dirty and banged up on the ranch. It's the nice one. He looks good. He ducks to miss hitting his head on the bell hanging there. I instantly feel more at ease when he spots me and walks over to the counter *my new friend* and I are standing at.

His long legs make it easy for him to get here quickly. "You are the latest man I have ever met. I'm glad you finally made it though. What took so long?" I chastise.

"There is nowhere to park with all these people here at once. I had to drop Steph off and then walk from the community park. That's no short hike." He shakes his head and I tilt mine to the side.

"Drop Steph off?" I ask.

"Yea..." Taking the hat off his head, he rubs a hand over his waves and then his mouth. No longer is he trying to grow his hair out. He keeps it cut short now and his face clean-shaven. I thought it might make him look young, but somehow he looks more mature. He's not that much older than me. Seven years, to be exact. My thoughts wander off to the first day I saw him without a beard. I snap out of it when I think he says something peculiar. "... my girlfriend."

I blink a few times, "I'm sorry, could you repeat that? I thought you said—"

"D. This is my girlfriend, Steph." His deep voice is firm and there is no wavering in his eyes as he delivers the news.

"G-girlfriend? I stutter.

"Hi... again..." Steph says awkwardly, doing a little hand wave at me. I feel my face malfunctioning because she backs into Ant. Seeking comfort from my—friend.

"Oh," Is all I can manage as my gears start turning and all the ingredients come together. "You're dating someone?"

# CHAPTER 5

## Drea, Five Years Ago

I'M CLOSING TONIGHT AND it's not that busy with it being a Wednesday. Most of our patrons work traditional jobs that require them to get up early. Outside of a few young people scattered on the floor, it's just Tony and me at QB's.

It's not uncommon for me to take the closing shift since Melody is usually over the crowd and people around the time shift cuts for the night are made. I'm thankful for any extra hours I'm able to clock now that Mireya is starting to grow out of clothes like a weed. Any extra money is always a blessing. However, it does leave me at the bar with only the cook and busser, who are both women. Alpenglow Ridge isn't *unsafe*. My wary mama brain can't help but think, it only takes the first time for never to become something else.

Something about this night has me on edge. I've had the usual amount of men hitting on me this week and I've just about had it with all the dating sites. I've got shit for luck or maybe there is some type of pheromone I'm excreting that only attracts the worst the opposite sex has to offer.

Maybe it's the changing of the season that makes me feel reflective, but the thoughts have been brewing in my mind for quite some time.

Anyway, my last bar guest is Tony. The ranch manager from Mason Ranch is sitting by himself at the end of the bar. I would say we know each other since he's in here often enough, but I don't know him that well. He always orders the same thing and usually has only one single neat of Maker's Mark before switching to water. Easy service and a big tipper, though it makes me feel bad so I don't even ring up half the food I'm bringing out to him. And the man can *eat*. I've seen him put away enough food to feed four grown men easily.

Frankly, I'm bored and there's not much to do. That's how I find myself leaning on the bar top in front of Tony. "Hey... I'm Drea."

He looks confused for a moment. "I know..." he says in a baritone that is barely audible because it's so low.

"And you are?" I ask.

Now he really looks confused but he plays along anyway. "Friends call me Tony." Not only is his voice low, but he's got a southern accent I can't quite place, not having left Colorado before. I'll figure that out later.

"Short for Anthony? Right? Or did you just get stuck with a nickname for a name?"

He chuckles. "Nah. If you need my full government, it is Anthony. Anthony Dupont." His smile is straight and white and transforms his otherwise formidable, albeit extremely handsome, face into something far friendlier. He's got a couple of scars on his eyebrow that make him look a little edgier when combined with the tick of his jaw. But when he smiles, it's a completely different story. "Guessing Drea is a nickname too."

I smile back at him. "Of course. But a lady's gotta be safe working in a bar. I don't just go around giving out my full government name to strangers." I add that last bit with a wink.

He crosses his arms over his broad chest. "Am I in danger now?" His eyebrow raises, though my eyes get caught on his biceps bulging from the bottom of the short-sleeved shirt he's wearing.

"Nah," I mirror the way he responded earlier, crossing my arms over my chest as well. "We're friends. No danger from me... For now."

He nods to himself and then his intense gaze lands back on me. "Tony it is, then. Nobody calls me Anthony, but my Ma, and she passed a long time ago."

"I don't like being like everyone else. Don't think I could be even if I wanted to actually... Tony, it is *not*. I think I'll call you..." I think for a moment, tapping my chin. He settles back into his stool, allowing me time to ponder. "Ant! OH! I'm definitely calling you Ant! It's perfect! Ironic and storied!"

His eyebrows pull together. I have a feeling that this man doesn't talk much, but his face sure does a lot of the communicating for him. "Storied?"

"Yea... like when we've been besties for a long time we can tell people about how I put you in danger at the bar I was working at and it even earned you a nickname. Very funny stuff."

"What if I don't want to be *besties*?" His cheek lifts in a smirk that makes me consider how a man like this could end up in Alpenglow Ridge. And alone in the middle of the week. Someone definitely should have snagged him by now. What could be the criteria to be with a man like this and how come I never see guys like him swiping on apps or at any of the clubs I've been to?

Mentally shaking myself, his flirty tone registers in my mind. A laugh comes out more like a cackle from my lips, and I hit the counter. "Sorry Ant, but you missed *that Drea. This Drea* has made something official today."

"What's that?" He asks, clearly more curious than affronted that I didn't play into his flirtation or drop his new nickname.

"I'm officially swearing off men and sex... Indefinitely."

Ant covers his mouth trying not to choke on his water, blustering for a few moments. "Wh-what?"

"I'm done. Men are shit. No offense. I just think it's time that I call it."

"You're what? Twenty-one? How could you call it? You're barely even an adult."

I narrow my eyes on him. "Twenty-five!" I scoff. "I've been an adult since I pushed a tiny human out of my body seven years ago and have been taking care of her ever since." I flip my ponytail around my head to clip it up with one of my massive claws I keep under the bartop. "I didn't make the decision without proper evidence to back it up."

"Such as?"

"Are you sure you're ready for this rant, Ant? This is next-level bestie stuff."

He chuckles again, and I really enjoy the way it crackles across my skin. "Well, take me to the next level then. Not scared of a rant."

"Suit yourself. Many glasses of wine and late-night baking have culminated in two conclusions. One: Dating sites are more risky than gambling in Vegas. Two: My ex is the embodiment of the word 'meh' proving that connections cannot be made on sex alone." I sigh. "What's the point? I give up."

"Just because you've been on a few dating sites and your ex is the embodiment of the word 'meh' I don't think you should give up."

"Not that what you think plays a role in what I've decided... This might be a hard concept to grasp, given your... gender."

He huffs a laugh. "Explain it to me like I'm five then." He's back to crossing his arms over his chest.

"I don't know if what I have to say will be particularly appealing to a single man like yourself."

"How about you try me and I'll let you know whether that's true or not."

I nod several times, giving myself an opportunity to think about how to say this. "I guess it's like this... What would you say if I asked you to finish an entire strawberry cake even though you hate strawberry cake?"

"But, I love strawberry cake."

"Not important."

"Okay. Try again... Don't use food this time."

"Hmm... It's not wholly about the sex really. If you have part of something and it was just okay, what would entice you to take the whole thing?" I bite my lip. "This was much better as a cake analogy."

"Makes sense already though. But there's all kinds of cake. Maybe you haven't found the kind you like."

"Trust me, I know there are all kinds of cake. But what if I'm a pie or cookie person who keeps trying cake?" I shake my head at how muddled this analogy is becoming. "It's about what sex means to each person. For me, it doesn't actually mean as much as it means to the men I've been with.

From what I've seen out there, I'm only as interesting as the chase is to fuck me. Men want all these curves, but they don't want more than to pump and squeeze me, then I'm still left wanting."

"I don't doubt that..." he coughs into his fist. "I mean, about men wanting to..." He rubs a hand over his face and I stifle a giggle at his expense. "There is something about men that leads to some foul ideas about women. Not every man is that way though. I'm sure there are women who are just as foul."

I laugh. "Oh, I'm certain of it. Human beings are largely unique and can have all kinds of ideas about what and how they will get what they want from other people. There are all types of people out there and *that...*" I tap the bar top with my index finger "is what gives me hope. A solid relationship is the goal and with infinite possibilities out there—I will find the one for me."

He leans back in the stool, settling for this conversation in earnest now. "So, how is it that you plan on achieving this goal? Sounds like there is already a plan."

I tilt my head side to side, "I wouldn't say it's a plan... It's a feeling. I'm going to use my intuition. My desire to abstain is more about connection. It's about purpose and intention."

"Purpose?"

"Yes, purpose. Sex has no meaning anymore. Why would I open myself up in that way to someone when I could be just *any woman* in their eyes? My presence could be swapped out and it would make no difference to them."

"That's fucked up."

"I know. But it's the reality of this 'situationship' culture. These dating sites and apps are even pushing for you to hook up with someone instead of just being single. Women are treated like a product to be sold. And what's worse is that it's our job to sell ourselves. It's strange, and I'm over it. It takes a lot of courage to put yourself out there, and it's emotionally draining to become hopeful when you're being love-bombed to only be ghosted in the end. Or worse, only being hit up to spread your legs for them. And this is what I'm putting myself out there for?" I shake my head. "I deserve more than a stream of hookups. All these guys out here have one type—gullible." I pause for a moment because I've been talking for a while and I'm certain Tony has probably zoned out with how quiet he's been. But he's there listening intently, so I continue explaining. "It's not about punishment, power, or preserving some 'magical pussy' from others. I want to love who I am, so when I meet someone—I can be good too. Two people can love each other without losing that love for themselves. I know it's possible. I'm not chasing this Hallmark-branded love that is philosophized so much it's not attainable. Hopefully, that will attract like-minded men, who also love themselves, and then we can build something meaningful."

"And you can't do that if you're having sex with someone?"

"Apparently not. It's the chase to get it, and when you do, that's all they want. No more dating and consideration. It's only about what they can do to get me to the nearest fuckable surface. No more learning and growing together. It's a stagnant step that never progresses."

He nods and sips his drink. I consider whether to keep rambling about what I want from a relationship. But this kind of thing utterly fascinates me, so Tony has fallen victim to a good rant whether he likes it or not. It very well could be a ramble about how sexist and fatphobic acclaim for bakers or bakeries are. He got lucky because this could potentially be useful to him. Maybe...

"There might be *the one* out there somewhere. Hell, statistics say that I have already met this person. What I want is more than physical and fleeting. Connection and compassion. I want something deeper. I want to know that the person sharing my body and my pleasure knows why that's meaningful to me. Someone who understands just how impactful this decision was. I am more than the lust they feel. I am more than just what others want from me and my body." I take a weary breath and lean onto my elbows on the bar. A piece of my bangs fall into my face and I blow it away. "Pleasure for me means what? Can I even tell you, metaphorical you, what I want without it being tainted by your own desires? We can both win. We can both have what we want and compromises can be made in the meantime just as long as in the end, we're both getting what we want." I pause again, biting my lip. "A partner, a true partner, can give me that because I will give that to them in return. Care for them, body and soul."

"That doesn't sound too bad, " he says, breaking me out of my musings. I look up at him to see if he's only humoring me or if he truly means what he's saying. "A fair exchange if everyone is getting what they want."

"Right!" Undeterred, my conviction is indignant about the matter. "It's about sharing and giving. It's not about domination and submission. Neither one of us is greater than the whole of us. As a woman, I'm expected to 'give it up.' It's such a contradiction. The implication is that by having sex with someone, I'm not meant to enjoy it. What exactly am I giving up? And a better question, what am I gaining from giving anything?"

"So is it about men or about the society that they live in? You'll never see me treating women like that. We know men in this town who don't treat women like that either."

"Exactly. There's an exception to every rule. It's not methodical math where you plug the number in and there's only one outcome. It's far more nuanced than that... Like with baking sometimes. All the same ingredients can make completely different results based on any number of factors. Life is the same way. We all come with the same ingredients but have different instructions. I want to find that person who will take time to figure out just what steps he's going to follow to create the best result because I'm more than willing to do the same for them."

"Everything you're saying makes a lot of sense."

I beam at him. "Thank you, Ant." I pat myself on the back in a big show of feeling accomplished. "I think that is why I feel like adding sex doesn't guarantee a connection. It isn't the ingredient that binds. It's the seasoning that improves." I shrug. "Sometimes it does. But look at the couples we know. None of their stories are the same and yet the result *is*. They're happy."

His nod was subtle but final. "Okay."

Now it's my turn to scrunch my eyebrows. "That's all?"

"Yes. That's all. I want that too," he says, simply.

"You do?"

His head inclines forward toward mine. He's so tall that even sitting, I still have to look up to meet his eyes when he says, "I'm honestly the same way. I don't want to go into a relationship where I'm expected to hold up the world for a woman because I am a man when she can offer me nothing in return. Don't get me wrong, I'd do just about anything for the right one. But somebody I'm going to spend my life with will have more for me than just what's between their legs. I want a friend, a partner, and everything in between."

"So are we doing this?" I ask, rubbing my hands together.

He scratches his forehead and it's kind of adorable. "Um... Doing what?"

I wave my hands in front of me now, between us. "A pact of celibacy. You and I are swearing off sex until we find someone who meets all our needs."

"Fuck it," he says, extending a hand toward me.

"No thinking about it first?" I ask.

He shrugs. "Life is just not that cruel. If an idea sounds good, then it must be. I trust what you have to say is out there for us."

"Let's fucking do this," I say, shaking his outstretched hand. "Or I guess not fucking doing this."

Ant laughed, but I knew this was the start of something that would bring monumental change in my life. "Already know you'll be like no best friend I've ever had before."

I smile back at him, certain that he's right.

# CHAPTER 6

## Tony

"YOU'RE SEEING SOMEONE?" DREA'S voice is stilted and detached. It takes a serious amount of control to resist taking the words back even though they're true.

Steph looks up at me, and I give her as cool a smile as I can manage. I knew that this news would not go over well.

Drea has been a good friend of mine for years—my best friend—and it's been amazing to be a part of her and Mireya's life. I panicked and thought that it would be better to just tell her with Steph here.

I might have lost my nerve had I tried to tell her before.

Our relationship had been strained. It wasn't always like that and to be honest, it was likely only strained for me. When she showed me that she was not going to make any changes to her life to include me or make room for me as a real option for her, I needed to move on. Be happy as the best friend and not ruin what we had because I wanted something she clearly didn't.

Years of hoping she would see our potential and years of looking like a simp fool. It was the running joke between our friends that I was collecting stamps for each year I spent waiting for Drea to wake up and see me standing in front of her. It was hopeless.

Now, I stand next to a woman who could understand exactly what that was like. Before I see or hear him, I feel Steph tense next to me. Drea still looks shell-shocked and the air around us is thick with the words that no one is saying.

The bell chimes again and my brother ducks into the door. Mireya spots him, dragging him by the hand over to where Drea, Steph, and I are awkwardly trying to recover from Drea's processing the news I've just said.

"Ant! You're here! And look, Uncle Blue is here too!" Mireya stretches to hug both me and my brother at the same time. Blue rubs her back, and I flick some of her hair off her shoulder. Mireya complains, trying to rearrange her hair again. He doesn't come to Colorado often but the times he has been here, she's seen him since Mireya and I are thick as thieves. She recognizes that someone else is here and pauses. "Who are you?" Mireya asks with curiosity coloring her words as she tips her head to one side. She looks exactly like her Ma when she does it. That makes me smile, though I shouldn't be right now.

Steph is tall and thin. Growing up, she was the only girl who played basketball with us behind the house. She held her own, and I thought for sure that she would try to go to the WNBA. She confessed she didn't because of the pay discrepancy. I don't blame her.

My brother never had plans to be with anyone and that included the one woman who loved him since we were just teenagers playing basketball behind the house. She never let that get to her and still remained friends with him. One thing that I actually like about the woman is that she can hold her own in any environment. As a real estate agent, she is adaptable and quick on her feet. She doesn't miss a beat when she holds out a hand for Mireya. "I'm Steph, and you must be Mireya... Is that right?"

Mireya shakes her hand, but only nods in response. She looks over to her Ma and Drea's smile is brittle as she tries to hide the confusion she feels.

"Well... this is nice and awkward," Blue says into the huddle we've made. "Drea, why don't you show me around? I've never seen the inside of this place..." I lose track of what's being talked about as my brother walks my friend farther away from us. Mireya trails behind them. She turns briefly to shake her head at me.

*What is that for?*

"So, you didn't tell her about me?" Steph accurately assumes.

I scratch my neck. "I was going to..." The words trail off because all the reasons why I didn't were pretty stupid. I think that is the biggest thing that hurts. I made a bad call and it didn't feel like independence from *the friend zone* like I hoped it would. It just makes me feel like a complete dick.

She nods, considering me. "I can see why you waited. I think you broke her face with the news."

I scrunch my face up. This was not the best approach to telling her. I knew that already. "She will come around."

"Are you sure about that?" There are more silent questions bouncing between us as she looks at me from eye to eye.

Her gaze tells me that she doesn't agree. I didn't set out to hurt Drea. I didn't expect to do anything. I just wanted to see what was out there. Was I so blindly infatuated with this idea of a woman who didn't want me?

One night after I found out about Sean, I just got in my car and started driving. I was hurt and upset with her, with myself. Somehow, I ended up in Louisiana the next day. Sleeping on my brother's couch though I had a room at his place. My mood was shitty so he had left me alone and I needed something. *I needed a change.* I couldn't keep trailing behind Drea, hoping she would choose me.

I finally opened one of those dating apps, just to see what was out there. I had been so sick of the friendly rejection that I'd get from Drea on a regular basis. I had enough. I have to cut my losses and move on. I swiped a few times before I got to Steph's profile. I was shocked that she even had an account. I didn't message her on the app, but instead called her to come over. It was easy to pick up a conversation after years of me living in Colorado and barely being back home for long periods of time. We hit it off just like we did when we were younger. I liked how easy it was to talk with her. I figured—why wait? I asked her to be my girl for real. It made sense at the time.

Fast forward to now... She surprised me with a trip up here. Apparently, she and Blue had planned the whole thing, a fact I'm willfully not interrogating her about. They had always been better friends than she and I. As far as I knew, Steph and I were in the exact same predicament.

"She'll have to get used to it. But, it might take a while." I answer her after a few moments of deliberating.

We get some coffee and the spiced coffee cake that was left from the display when it's our turn in the line.

I look around at the turnout for the opening of Drip and Whip and feel a sense of pride. I remember when she thought this was an impossible feat. I remember when she was dead on her feet at the bar, trying to manage it all. But look at how full it is here. Lotta folks here to support her and this new thing. Maybe she hasn't found a real man who could be the one to stand beside her. I wonder if it will be even harder for her now that she has her dream in her grasp. She deserves more and if I've been in the way of her meeting that guy, all of this is happening as it should.

"So, who is this pretty lady?" Chloe asks when she catches us at the table in the back of the shop. I should have known that she would be here soon enough. The woman can smell gossip from a mile away. She holds her hand out toward Steph, "I'm Chloe. I own that salon over there." She gestures vaguely across the street. "And I'm one of the best friends of *Drea*," she says, a little crisper than necessary. I cut a look toward her that she ignores.

Steph tells her, "I'm this one's newest," she jokes. I am obviously not in the dating pool, a fact that Chloe knows well.

The joke falls flat when Chloe brushes imaginary crumbs from her pants. "Oh, don't sell yourself short. You're probably his only."

"Watch out now, Clo."

"What? I'm just thinking about that pact you made with Drea and how it doesn't seem to matter now that you're with someone else right?"

I sigh heavily, tipping my head back. It thunks against the wall as I gather any calm I can muster. "That's enough, Chloe. Please go meddle in someone else's life."

Steph sips her coffee and I gauge just how much trouble I could be in from what Chloe has revealed without my permission.

"Steph—"

"Don't bother. From the information I've gathered, no one knew of me before today, and they don't like that I'm here now."

"That's not true. They just don't know you. It'll take some time before they warm up to you."

"I figured you and Drea had more than you were letting on, but I'm guessing you have a lot more explaining to do." She leans her head to the side where Taylor and Drea talk and I follow her gaze. I turn back to Steph about to say something more, but she cuts me off. "Go. I'll just be over here answering emails."

I stand and kiss her on the cheek. "I'll be quick." She nods, popping a piece of cake into her mouth.

Taylor intercepts me before I reach Drea. "At what point is it appropriate for me to say I told you so?" They raise an eyebrow with all the censure that they can manage. I love Taylor like a sibling, I do. If someone were to ask me who my friends were, I'm thankful that the list is long. Taylor is at the top of that list though. But I'm reaching my reprimanding limit real quick.

"It's not appropriate," I respond, stepping around them. "Excuse me."

"Ah," Taylor's hand presses firmly against my arm, halting me again. "I would think about what you say next. We both know you should have told Drea before today. Watching that was a goddamn train wreck. What were you thinking?"

"I was thinking that it wouldn't matter. I was thinking that I could make decisions without running them by everyone first. What does it matter to you?"

"We've both known her for years. Do you think this was how she should have found out that her best friend was seeing someone else?" I look over to Drea, who has already been claimed by another conversation with an older woman I've seen around town. She smiles though there's a little furrow in her brow. She looks up at me and I see the hurt there.

Hurt that I know I caused.

"Look, I should have gone about it differently. But there is no pomp and circumstance when she's dating some new guy. Why should there be for me?"

"Have you actually thought about the answer to that question? I know you know what it is already."

I glare at them. "Let go of my arm."

Taylor steps out of my path on a beeline to Steph, who I hear perk up at being approached amicably. I don't stick around to hear what they're saying to her.

I have another destination.

If I can at least be honest in my head, she's always my destination.

She looks like she coordinated with the treats she'll serve here. Each dip and swell of her body looks like a dessert of some kind with the sweater and skirt she wears. The older woman I recognize to be Leslie Grunge who lives a few properties down from Mason Ranch. She pats my arm and leaves when I get close enough to see the little freckles on Drea's face. The smile she has for Leslie is no longer there for me.

"This turned out beautifully, Boss Lady. Congratulations again."

She presses her lips together, crossing her arms over her chest. "Thanks for coming," she says, attempting to walk away from me.

"So, you're mad," I say to her back.

She turns quickly and her hair whips around smelling like vanilla and cinnamon, which makes my stomach clench. "Mad? Nah. Hurt? Absolutely."

"You shouldn't be."

Wrong thing to say. I know it's the wrong thing to say and yet, here I am saying it like a fool.

"I shouldn't be mad about my best friend having a whole girlfriend I didn't know about?" She bites out. Her voice is low enough not to attract attention, but when she pokes me in the chest hard enough for me to cringe, I feel a few eyes on us. "I shouldn't be mad about you keeping secrets from me and then dropping this at my feet on my opening? Why not?"

"Alrighty. Let's do this another time." Reese is by her side with her hands on both of Drea's arms. She cuts a glare my way, mouthing *do better* to me before she's ushering her friend away. "Did you see that Carl Ockham was here? He's got the best produce in town and I think you two should definitely talk about a partnership for the future." Reese turns to me again, pointing and mouthing, *do better* again.

I'm doing the best I can. I don't see how I could be the bad guy here.

Speaking of, Blue comes over to me after making his rounds. "Brutal, bruh. You said they liked you in this town."

"I know you can't help yourself, but could you keep your comments in your head?"

"Nah. Am I gonna have to rescue Steph before they get the pitchforks?"

Pulling my brother into the bathroom alcove for a bit of privacy, I glare at him. Since we're the same height and build, I'm looking him directly in the eyes. "Why did you come here?"

"I don't understand what you mean?"

"I left so I didn't have to deal with your bullshit. I wouldn't have to deal with any of this, had you not showed up here with her."

He smirks. "You didn't want to see your girlfriend? How was I supposed to know?"

"By asking!" I lower my tone. "Could have called me and let me know you were coming. You've never been to visit without announcing. And you damn sure never participated in anything my friends have hosted."

"Wait... You don't think me being here is only about you. It was kind of a two birds, one stone type of thing."

Now, I'm really confused. "What does it have to do with then?"

"Well if you were in the biz, I'd tell you. But since you decided to be the 'good brother', it's a need-to-know kind of thing. And you don't need to know."

A sound like a growl comes from my chest unbidden. "Why are you here, Blue?"

He sighs and the sound weighs on my patience like an elephant on a tightrope. "I'm checking on something," Blue pulls on his ear, in thought and annoyance. "I'm checking *on someone.* You know who."

"What did he do?"

"Like I said, need to know basis. You coming into the fold or what?"

"No," I shake my head, vehemently. "Definitely, not."

"Don't worry about it then. Spend time with my best friend, oh I mean, your girlfriend. I'm going to make myself more familiar with Colton's baby moms." He slips out from my hands and into the bakery.

By the time I reach Steph and Taylor, my mind is racing with thoughts of what exactly Colton and Blue are up to that would sanction an in-person visit.

# CHAPTER 7

## Drea

REESE THROWS HER TORTILLA chip down into the basket, saying, "So are we just not going to address the elephant in the room?"

Mel sighs. "Reese, please—" She may not enjoy large parties but Mel has been more forthcoming when she's struggling and wants support. We all brought something to snack on for movies and girl time together at her place. I love that she lets us in more and even if she's not particularly talkative, I know having us close is a comfort to her when her husband is gone.

"No, I also want to address this elephant!" Clo interjects.

Reese points dramatically at Clo. "Exactly! What the fuck was that? Tony has a girlfriend?"

It's my first Friday night off from working in... too many years to count. Martin works the weekend shifts so I get to have time off. My girlfriends have been a part of the "Weekends Off" club for much longer than me.

I'm thankful that my friends are always excited to celebrate just about anything. I'm even more thankful that the past few days have been so busy that I've not been able to spend too much time thinking about how Ant completely shocked me, and apparently the whole town, with the news of his girlfriend.

Something in my gut twisted all funny when those words left his lips. When the commotion of the event subsided and everyone had gone home, I sat in bed thinking about everything that occurred. Did I miss the signs while I was busy making my own dreams come true? Had he mentioned her before? Nothing came up in my memory. I didn't want to be a bad friend since Ant had always been the best friend to me. It was late, but I called him, even though I was nervous about what answers he could have for me. He couldn't talk long since Steph and Blue were at his house and it would have been rude, but he promised we would talk about it soon. I felt so icky about the whole thing, but I couldn't place a real emotion because they all seemed inappropriate.

"They apparently knew each other as kids. Blue told me all about it. She seems nice." I admit, breaking my tortilla chip into tiny pieces instead of dipping them into the queso fundido I brought for Girls' Night.

"She looks like Normani and Justine Skye had a baby. Which isn't even possible!" Reese crunches from a different chip and then points it at me. "You waited too damn long. There goes your Prince Charming... riding off into the sunset with a literal princess."

"Seriously, I'm not getting into this. That's my best friend and I'm happy for him." I might as well have said nothing because the conversation kept going around me.

"If that were my man, I'd beat the breaks off little Miss Pantsuit Barbie," Chloe adds, swirling her wine and Reese agrees with her. The two of them are actually chaos together. If ever there was an issue, these are the prime instigators. Now that they've gotten started, there will be no calming them down.

"Tony is not my man. I've said that so many times. We're *best friends*. That's how it's always been. Nothing is different now."

"Isn't it though?" Reese accuses.

"Isn't it?" Clo piles on.

I hold my wine in front of me, using it to point at the two of them. "No. None of you had anything to say when I dated other guys."

"Yea, because they were dead ends from the moment you took their numbers. That's like asking someone to take a short answer test—in another language." Clo points out.

"What? No, it's not. I thought Sean was really going to be the guy."

Reese's lips press together with a slight frown. "Did you though? Did you really?"

"What does that mean?"

"It means that Sean already missed like three of the boxes you check *before* the first date and you still dated him. It was a losing fight and you know it." Reese says.

"If that were true, why didn't anyone say anything? Could have saved me a lot of time." I cross my arms over my chest. "I don't understand why you all are ganging up on me now."

Clo places a hand over mine and I uncross my arms. "Because we've watched on the side, trying to let you figure this out, but you haven't. Too many of us have come close to losing our person because we couldn't get out of our own way."

"That is not what's happening here," I cry.

Mel touches my other hand, "Isn't it though?"

I squeeze her hand back. "No. He can do what he wants. I really want happiness for him. If he can find it with Steph, then kudos. He deserves it."

"Ohhh come onnn, D! I'm not believing that pack of lies! You're saying you would feel absolutely no type of way about him breaking your pact?" Reese says.

That gives me pause. I hadn't really thought about that being a possibility, but he brought her to my opening. Maybe they are that serious.

What should it matter to me?

It's been years and he's known her for a really long time. She could be the one.

"Listen... You can hear the record actually scratch in her mind." Chloe says, sipping her wine.

I try to fix my face, but it's malfunctioning... again. I wish I were better at concealing my emotions from my face—I'm not. Right now, I'm sure

I'm stuck between confusion, a fake smile, and deep thought. I likely look constipated.

"If he and Pantsuit Barbie actually get freaky, you aren't going to feel any type of way... None at all?" Reese restates in the worst way possible. I fight to relax my fist, but it's proving difficult and that confuses me, most of all.

I'm silent for a few moments as my friends watch and wait for my response. "Why should I? We made it for a reason. He would only break it if he really thought she was the one. And like I said, he deserves to be happy."

"Not to play devil's advocate," something she clearly loves playing, "but him twisting up her legs like a pretzel and showing her what five years of pent-up sexual attraction looks like doesn't do anything to affect you?" Clo asks.

My fist tightens again. "I mean... *gross* is my first thought. Because he's like a brother."

Reese shakes her head exaggeratedly, "I've never seen anyone look at their brother like you look at Tony."

I flinch away from her. "I don't look at him in any kind of way."

"Sure. Sure. And I've never danced on a table naked. Let's get back to the whole pact breaking thing," Reese says.

"Yes, let's," Clo chimes in. "If she's the one, who are you saving yourself for then?"

I stand and bring my now empty wine glass with me to the kitchen. I open the bottle I brought for the night and stall. I knew they never quite understood the purpose of the pact but for some reason, I never clarified for them anyway. We made that choice together and it made us happy. Well, I thought it did. Now, I don't know if I knew anything. "I'm not saving myself for Tony."

They all blink owlishly at me. "I'm not. The pact was about finding someone who would meet our needs... and so that we could meet theirs. Not a poly thing. Each of us, respectively. In individual relationships with other people. Relationships about more than just sex." I snap my mouth shut, realizing that it sounds weird explained this way. I don't get a chance to rephrase before Reese cuts in.

"And... that's not what you have with Tony?"

"It's..." I snap my mouth shut again.

"It is! You two are the most couple-y couple of people I have ever met. One of the first things I ever said to Cory was how much I wanted what you and Tony had because he treats you like the woman who will be his first, last, and only." Reese says.

"He does not. He treats me like you all do. It's the same."

"Are you blind or just delusional?" Clo asks. I cut a look over at her and she holds her hands in front of her.

"I'm neither. Tony deserves someone who can be his everything and that can't be me."

"Why the hell not?" Clo and Reese demand in unison, then chuckle at each other with a high five.

"If the universe wanted it, then it would be. Besides, I have baggage and a plan that doesn't include..."

"Happiness?" Mel asks.

"Partnership?" Clo suggests next.

"Sex?" Reese questions. "You know there'll be flames between the two of you! I've seen the literal fire in his eyes for you."

Mel stands from the couch to join me at the kitchen island. "It's okay if you truly want to be single and if sex is not of interest to you. No one will discount your experience without it these past years, but could you honestly say that you would be where you are without Tony in your life?"

I think hard on her words. Would I? I don't know. He's been such a constant that I can't even reminisce about my life without him in it.

Reese also stands from the couch to join Mel and I in the kitchen. "And just to further this discussion... What happens if he decides Pantsuit Barbie is really the one for him? And he moves back to their beloved, southern romance location of Clayton, Louisiana. And you really do lose him. A man follows his heart... usually his dick, but for arguments' sake, we'll say he's following his heart."

I shudder and cross my arms over my chest again.

"Okay, let's stop calling her Pantsuit Barbie. Seems kind of mean..." Mel says.

"Mel is right. Steph seems nice and successful. She has her life together."

"I'm bringing the cheese in here since we've moved the party to the kitchen." Clo stands from the couch, arms full of food. "Now, what was I going to say?" Her fingernails drum on the stem of her wine glass. "Oh, yea! So do you! You have your life together! You just opened a brand new bakery and coffee shop that people are already loving! You're the best mother and friend. What the hell else do you need for your life to be together?"

I wince. "I don't know..." My shoulders inch up higher before I drop them. "He just..."

"Knows what he wants even though you refuse to accept it?" Reese asks.

"No..."

"Loves your daughter like his own and always has your back." Clo presses.

"No,"

"Cares for you, but respects you the most," Mel says softly into her wine glass.

"Guys, seriously. It's not a conversation. He already picked someone else. He wanted to date his childhood friend, Steph. We are all going to accept that and move on. Weren't there supposed to be movies involved with the evening? The TV is not even on."

"Only because his first choice bowed out of the race," Reese mutters. "Look, I'm picking the movie because Clo will likely put on *Bring It On* and Mel is prone to something sappy. I'm not in the mood to pull my hair out or cry."

"Well, I've got all the streaming services so..." Mel prompts.

The three of them talk over a movie choice, but I barely catch any of it as their words swirl around in my head like sticky dough I can't get off my fingers.

I can't say for certain, but some of what was said tonight really was true. Now, just to sort out which of it I should take to heart. I refuse to lose my best friend over his new romance or any other reason.

My girls want me to feel jealous or who knows what. All I can feel, as I simmer on all the evidence that has been pointed out, is anger and hurt. Why did he keep this secret from me? A whole relationship! How could Ant do this to me, to us?

# CHAPTER 8

# Tony

IT'S BEEN TWO DAYS since Drip and Whip opened and all the messiness of the event. I wanted to go to her as soon as everything was over. But, I couldn't. I couldn't because my brother and girlfriend were still here, unannounced, at my house. I know that Blue could afford to stay at a hotel just about anywhere, but he has to stay at my place for who knows what reason.

I went to work exhausted and unfocused which is a bad combination on a working ranch that sees more danger than any desk job. I might have lost my head if my hat wasn't on it.

Steph was going to be catching up on work, so I figured I'd actually be able to keep my Monday night dinner plans in place. I grab Mireya from the Ranch when I'm leaving work to take her home. My dog is usually riding shotgun, but she's currently at my house with my brother.

There's banging coming from the kitchen as soon as I enter the house and Mireya runs up the stairs to her room. "Drea?" I call, now on alert because what is all this noise?

She calls back, not bothering to meet me at the door like she usually does. "Should I set the table for four or?" Drea's tone is clipped. I rub a hand over my face.

She is pissed. Should have expected that when she had been short with me on the phone. I could even sense the irritation in her curt texts over the past couple of days.

Rounding the doorway into the kitchen, I immediately go into trying to placate her. "I know you're upset—"

She scoffs, throwing a spoon into her sink with another loud clatter. "Me? Why would I be upset?"

"Are you gonna pretend like Steph is not upsetting for you?" She flitters around the kitchen, grabbing plates to put food on each one.

"I'm not pretending anything. If Steph is going to be here, then I just want to make sure I set the table properly. You love to spring extra guests on me. I just don't want to be blindsided again."

Drea whooshes past me and even though I know she hasn't made anything sweet, she still smells like a cupcake of some sort and I sigh. First, in satisfaction because I missed the comfort of her smell. But then, in frustration because I need to let those thoughts go. She's mad and I need to make this right with her. "I was going to tell you sooner," I start.

"Was going to?" she asks, head cocked to the side. I feel like a chastised child in trouble for something I know I shouldn't be doing. Maybe I am. I am well aware of how dumb this was for me to keep all this from her.

"Yes. I had planned to, but I was worried about how you would receive it. You had so much on your plate with this opening and…"

She glares at me from in front of the stove. The plop of charro beans in the pots seems to echo between us as she drops another spoon. "What did you just say?"

"I didn't even know she was coming to the opening. Her and Blue just showed up at the house when I was headed out the door." At her cool silence and frigid indifference, I continue in a different direction. "Drea, you've been stressed. Have a lot on your plate and this would have been a distraction."

"You don't think I would care about you breaking a five-year pact that we made with each other for someone that I have never even met? Never even heard of."

Is that what she is so upset about? "I didn't break the pact," I relay in an even tone.

"Oh." She freezes for a moment before setting the plate she was piling food on down to the countertop. Her emotions flicker from one to the next as I see her processing what I've communicated. For the life of me, I can't see why she is so upset.

Taking measured movements toward me, she grabs my hand. "I shouldn't have said that." I should find comfort in her grasp. *This is comfort.* She is always the first to make contact with someone and at any point in my past I would be grateful for her to hold my hand like that. She shows people she cares in this way. I was one of those people who she touched like she cared for me. Her little hand squeezing my rough one held weight like no other physical touch could. She communicated support, understanding, and compassion to me silently in that little bit of contact in the past.

But right now? I don't feel comforted. There's an ache that's raw and ragged in my chest with her assumption of me.

"There's someone new in my life and you assume that I would just disregard something so important to me? Years of my dedication to something *you* made me believe in and that I still stand behind." Now, it's my turn to scoff, the sarcasm to hide my hurt pouring out just as acidic as my chest feels. "*Wow.* It's good to know where I really stand with you." She stutters a couple of times before biting her lip. "I'm just another dude then, huh? Just like all the other men who are the scum of the earth in your eyes."

"Ant, I didn't say that." In a smaller tone, she says, "I don't think that."

"And I suppose I'm the ass because I heard you incorrectly? You thought that I broke our pact. How is Steph any different from Sean or Michael or Darren?"

She flinches away from me, finally dropping my hand. It falls to my side, cold and unwanted. More rips in my chest.

She presses a palm over her heart. Squeezing her eyes closed, she rubs the spot for a few moments. I instantly feel like shit, but then I don't. "It is," she whispers.

"Tell me how. You're dating other people. I'm dating someone else. It's the same." My voice is too loud in comparison to her small one but I don't know what this conversation is doing to me.

"No, it's not." She shakes her head. "I don't like what you're implying."

"I haven't implied anything. I think you forgot what this whole pact was about. What we agreed to."

She faces me, eyes narrowing. Her voice was soft before but now she stands with her arms crossed over her chest emphasizing her full breasts, chin jutting indignantly. "I do remember. You wouldn't even know about them if you weren't always at the house. Or if Mireya didn't tell you all my business, and all the things that she doesn't tell me. I don't bring any of these guys to our special events, ever."

"But you'll go out with them and flirt with them?"

"They don't matter! None of them are important enough to be introduced to our friends, let alone come to such an important event. They never last."

"Well, I've met almost all of them. They mattered to me."

She blinks up at me rapidly. "Why?"

"Because you're so blind. You can't see anything."

"What does that mean?"

"It means what I said." I take a step back from her. Needing the distance but also because I need to stop smelling how delicious she is with each of my rapid breaths. Allowing that to upset me even more. "I tried to come here so we could talk like adults, you aren't listening and you can't see what is so obvious to everyone else."

"Please just tell me what it is that you're talking about."

I'm already pathetically destroyed by this woman. What could make it any worse? "You didn't want me. I moved on. I'm letting go of you and this idea I had, that we were working toward something when *you never were*. You just find more and more ways to be independent. No one is good enough to be more important than your obsession with self-sufficiency. You need no one, no man. Especially not me. No one fits into your future but you and your daughter. And I'll have to accept that."

"That's not true," she whispers, but I'm still backing out of the kitchen. "I do need you. I—" She clamps her lips closed and nothing else follows.

The sudden silence hurts too much. I bite my lip and stare at the ground for a moment. "Still, you're not hearing me."

"I don't understand what I missed, Anthony. Don't..."

"No. Gonna just go."

I did. I had to get away from this feeling. I'm torn between protecting myself and protecting her peace–like she wasn't hurting me.

"Anthony," I don't turn to see the confusion on her face. I leave and I don't look back.

What did I expect would happen? The truth is always ugly.

***

WHEN I PULL UP to my house, Blue is already leaning over the balustrade out front. The end of the blunt he's smoking glows for a moment and he holds the smoke in his chest. Blowing it out when I get to him. The earthy scent of Dupont's finest wafts around us and I wave my hand to disperse the smoke from around me.

"Don't start," I say, stomping toward the front door.

"No one ever listens to Blue. I told you to lock that down from the moment I saw her. You're a fool."

Turning, I march over to him and flick his blunt. It skitters to the wood floor. "I know... I said don't."

He chuckles, flipping me off before reaching down to pick the blunt up. He dusts it off and inhales again. I roll my fist over my forehead trying to find it in me not to cuss my brother out. "Well, you better get your shit together because your real girlfriend is still in the house thinking you were running errands... Not having a fight with your play girlfriend."

"She's not my play girlfriend. We didn't have a fight."

His lips twist to the side, immediately calling me out on my bullshit. "That's what it looks like to me."

I huff and head for my door again. "Watch how you talk to me in my house."

He inhales again, holding it in his lungs while still talking. His chest puffed up like a damn bird. "I'm outside though..."

"I don't need this right now," I mutter.

Throwing my keys on the table by my front door, Milli greets me as soon as I'm in the house. I rub her face and ears as she whimpers with excitement to see me even though I've barely been gone an hour. Kneeling so that I'm on her level I ask, "How did things take such a steep turn?" Her big brown eyes look me over before licking at my face. "Maybe you could have been a better peace offering. Never leaving you at home again, okay?" She whimpers again and we make our way back into the house.

I'm not the one in the wrong here. I showed her what it feels like. How I have been feeling.

That's all.

*I'm not in the wrong.* I have to take a stab at happiness if it can't be with her.

I have to.

I shower and change into clothes that don't smell like her house and it's a small but jarring detail I notice. Staring at my reflection in the mirror, something else has changed there too. My grimace is out of place. With my hands on the edge of my bathroom counter, I hang my head.

What if in my search for happiness, I lose my best friend?

A knock on my bathroom door startles me out of my pitiful thoughts. "Did you eat already?" Steph asks me.

I rub a hand over my face. It's not that I forgot she was here, but there is something unsettling about her being here when I want to be alone right now. *When I didn't invite her here to begin with.* I couldn't explain it to her without hurting her either. It's bad enough that I had to explain exactly what the celibacy pact was after we left Drea's shop the other day. Fixing my face into a neutral expression, I open the door, walking out in the athletic shorts and tank top I brought in with me. "Nah, I'm starving."

She follows me out to the living room where I flop onto the couch and Milli takes the spot next to me. Steph perches on the arm of the couch, scrolling on her tablet. "Is there really no food delivery here? Even in Clayton, they have DoorDash."

"I wish. Best we can do is pizza and it might take a while."

To make matters worse, I'm missing out on whatever Drea was cooking. Now, I'm settling for pizza that will probably be cold before it gets to us.

"Fine by me, I guess." Steph looks at my brother coming inside from the patio. Milli's nails click along my floor when she hustles over to greet him at the door. "You're loud, man." Referring to how strongly Blue smells of weed and tobacco leaves.

"Heard that before." He shrugs. "Game's on," Blue says, grabbing the remote off of my coffee table and turning it on.

I'm grateful for the white noise of football to drown out my thoughts right now. Steph reads on her tablet next to me, still none the wiser of where I really went tonight. I need to keep it that way. I didn't do anything wrong but I would not like to explain to Steph about why I was in an argument with Drea.

My phone vibrates in my pocket and I check it, not expecting to hear from her so soon.

> **Drea: I'm sorry.**

> **Drea: Can we come over?**

I read the messages, but don't reply. Is her *sorry*, good enough to make years of useless pining worth it?

> **Drea: I'll bring dinner. There's enough for everyone.**

I roll my eyes. She knows that I can't resist her food.

But honestly, it's her that I can't resist. And even though her words hurt me tonight, I still want to spend time with her.

# Chapter 9

# Drea



HE HASN'T SAID ANYTHING to my apology. Not "it's okay" or "don't worry about it". Absolutely nothing. I hate it when people are upset with me. I don't want him to be mad at me. There has to be a conversation where the two of us can figure it out. A text is not going to cut it.



Each step of packing this food up is taking all my focus. I feel so... icky. I don't know why. This persistent icky feeling has been following me from my opening. Quite frankly, I don't know what to do with it.

*Mierda.*

He kept this whole relationship from me. Sprung a whole girlfriend on me! How is he the one who gets to have a temper?

The first satisfying snap of the food container startles me. I need to calm down. My hands shake as I scoop shredded chicken into the next container.

"Where's Ant, Mama?" That's the question, isn't it? Mireya's finally come down from her room. She secluded herself as soon as they got home. Well, Mireya was home. Ant was... Semantics!

"He went back to his house."

"Is Milli here?" My daughter walks into the living room, looking for the brown lab.

"Nope. She's also at his house."

Coming back into the kitchen with her arms crossed, she asks, "But why?"

"I don't know," I say, lamely.

She narrows her eyes at me. There is nothing more unsettling than having your own face scowl back at you. Mireya looks so much like me at times that people often say we could be twins. I'm happy that she got my face as opposed to Colton's. But, it's moments like this where I don't particularly want to look at the scowl that I have perfected, and she mirrors expertly, looking back at me.

I huff. "We got into an argument and he left."

Her scowl deepens as one of her hips juts to the side. "What did you do?"

Now it's my turn to frown. "Me? Why would you assume that I did something?"

"Because Ant doesn't get mad. If he left, you had to have done something real bad." I roll my eyes at her assessment.

Tony never gets mad, not at me anyway. He's curt and grumbly with just about everyone else. I've only seen him truly upset a handful of times and never at me. This feeling is so foreign. "Will you help me pack this food up or not? I'm taking dinner over there."

"Sure," she says, grabbing the largest container to scoop the arroz con maiz inside.

I chance a look at her and lean onto the counter with my hip. "And if I were to have done something to upset Ant, it was only because I was confused."

"You mean about his girlfriend?" She asks, guessing much too accurately for me.

Shooting a glance her way, "No..."

"C'mon, Ma. It's obvious by how awkward you were for the rest of the opening that you had no idea who she was. Aunt Reese and Aunt Clo had a bet going that you were going to have a meltdown in the back."

"They did not!" I exclaim.

"Definitely did. Reese won because you managed to pull it off, but after what clearly happened tonight... maybe they should tie."

"Mireya give your Mom some credit. We're two adults. I was surprised and that's all." My last container is full of pico de gallo with extra onion because that's exactly how Ant prefers it. I snap it closed.

"Mmm-hmm," she says, snapping her food container closed, too.

"Whatever." I turn to lean my butt against the countertop again and text my friends in our group chat.

> Me: Why am I hearing from Mireya that you two had a bet going about me?

> Clo: I had every faith that you would keep it professional.

> Clo: But just in case, I wanted it to be known that I called it.

> Clo: I love you (red heart emoji)

> Reese: What she means to say is that *I* knew you were going to keep it classy. (nail polish emoji)

> Me: I think that everyone should just let me handle things however I choose to. Good or bad. No more bets. That's not cool ladies.

> Reese: Maybe now Drea will pull her head out of her ass! (eyes emoji)

> Me: I don't know what you all are talking about.

Tony's clearly not happy and I know that it has something to do with me. And I hate it.

**Reese: Bullshit.**

**Clo: Bullshit.**

**Mel: Drea, I think that maybe I should give you the advice you gave me.**

**Me: I'm scared to ask what that is.**

**Mel: And I quote: Being that close without sexual action is like a deeper connection. Not everyone can do that.**

**Reese: Oooh we've got you now, D!**

**Clo: Boom! Deeper connection! (Woman dancing emoji) Go get your man, Drea!**

Nope. Not ready for this at all.

I close out of the group message and put all the food into a large tote.

"Are you ready to go?" I ask my daughter.

We drive to Ant's house and Mireya stares out of the window the entire time. I wonder what could be on her mind. It's been so long since she and I had a conversation about what's going on with her.

"Sooo... How-How're things?" Why do I sound so awkward?

"What things?"

"I don't know. School or your friends?" I haven't forgotten how she came home early from the ranch and has been coming home early ever since. If I were on better terms with Ant right now, I'd be able to ask him. Reese has no idea and thinks I should just leave it alone because it's teenage stuff.

All this angst is gonna kill me though. She looks miserably out the window. I lock the door just in case she accidentally falls out.

"Fine, I guess. Normal like it is for any other freshman."

"Okay, okay… cool. It's Thanksgiving break soon. Are you staying at the house or are you gonna spend time at the Mason's?" Reasonable. Very regular conversation.

"I'll be at the house." Her tone is terse and I detect the sadness in her voice. Just a tinge.

"It's gonna be lonely. I bet Reese wouldn't mind having you at the Ranch. You'd be able to play with the horses first thing and—"

"I don't want to stay at the Ranch, Ma."

"Okay… Well—"

"Can we just listen to music?"

"Sure, baby," I say, allowing her to zone out even further but still be worried about what could cause a rift between her and CJ, her closest friend.

Ant is already waiting outside to help bring the food in when we pull up to his house. The large tote bag that I struggled to get into the back of my van is picked up easily as he walks to the house. Milli is hot on his heels to greet Reya and me.

"Hey, Blue," I call over to him on Ant's couch when I walk in. Ant's house is a one-story ranch-style rental on the south side of the Ranch. Blue looks over to me from his spot. He gives me a knowing look before Steph comes into the kitchen. I should have prepared better for seeing her but I didn't.

Her hair is pulled up into a ponytail, which makes her look chic and sophisticated. She has a loungewear set from a brand I recognize Reese is a huge fan of. It's cropped at the waist but baggy on her slim hips. Steph looks like one of those supermodels at leisure with her trendy little outfit. Pantsuit, long gone. Her face glows in the kitchen lighting with all the makings of what someone would consider glass skin. Not a single blemish or spot to be seen. She smiles at Ant who is right behind me with the tote bag of food. When he sets the bag on the counter, she kisses his cheek and sets her tablet next to his hand. My eyes catch how she subtly brushes his hand with her pinky finger before he touches his with hers. My stomach twists. *Stop staring at their hands, Drea.*

Instead, I look down at the crumpled t-shirt I'm wearing with holes and stains from age or multiple attempts at trying different recipes. I had changed out of my clothes from work, into something comfortable. Cute was not even a factor in deciding what to wear. This tee might even be older than my daughter.

My yoga pants have stretched out at the knees and I pull up on the waist of them to try and disguise just how stretched out they are right now. Bottom line, Ant's girlfriend could walk the runway right now where I could, and should, be in the kitchen still.

When she walks over to where I am to help unpack some of the food, her warm scent assaults my senses. She even smells good lounging around. "Thank you for bringing this over. I was just telling Tony how I was willing to settle for pizza tonight." Her smile is genuine and I instantly feel worse. *How dare Pantsuit Barbie be nice?*

"It's no problem. I always make dinner on Monday night for Ant." I bite my cheek, then add, "The more the merrier."

She smiles back at me, returning to where she was before I guess, as I plate up the dinner I made. It's soothing to plate everything and focus on something other than the virtual stranger staying with my best friend.

*She wouldn't be a stranger if you took a chance to get to know her. Ant deserves that much,* a little voice in my head tells me. I agree with the little voice and call everyone over to the table once I've gotten everything set out. We eat without conversation, which feels very awkward though I can't make myself say anything, like I planned.

"So what do you do, *Steph?*" Mireya asks, with a sneer at the woman's name. It sounds more accusatory than conversational.

"Mireya," I snap.

"What? That's not rude. It's the beginning of the week and she's still here. Can't be a regular job." *She does have a point.* It never occurred to me to ask Ant that question myself.

"It's okay," she says to me after exchanging a look with Ant. "I work in real estate. Louisiana is booming right now. I work with mostly commercial properties, businesses, and stores, that kind of thing. I do dabble in residential, houses and dwellings, from time to time." Of course, she does. It's easy to imagine her in her high-power suit and heels every day. She probably has a briefcase and everything. Her stupid little contracts and—

"Drea?" Ant's voice cuts into my thoughts.

"Huh?" I ask, looking up from my fork on the plate.

Blue chuckles and Ant gives him a look.

Steph does this airy little laugh, putting a hand on Ant's. My eyes zero in on the second time she has touched his hand in front of me. "It's ok. I would get distracted by this food too. It's so good." She smiles at me again. "I asked why you decided on a coffee shop slash bakery instead of a full restaurant because this food is really delicious."

I feel my cheeks flame. She was complimenting me while I was tearing her apart in my mind... I sip some water and clear my throat. "I have just always loved sweets. Ever since I was little I wanted to make them. I like creating the kinds of desserts that feel like a treat and are meant to complement a celebration. It calls to me."

Nodding, she says, "I saw your website. You really do make beautiful food. That cake you made for your friend's wedding— the detail! Those frilly bits... I wish I could have tried it. It was almost too pretty to consider eating."

"I've told her that many times. Too bad one of Drea's desserts hates to see me coming. I couldn't resist them if I tried." Ant supplies his glowing review and it just feels different to me somehow. I know it's no different from any other time he's complimented me, but it is.

"When someone says that what I've made is too pretty to eat is a huge compliment." I hate that I kind of like her. "Thank you," I say, trying to remove as much malice as I can from the words. It comes out a little stilted, but I change the subject. "So how long will you be here?"

"Well, I flew in with Blue and I know he can't be away for too long. Just another day in town before I've got to get back to the grind, you know?"

I let out a breath of relief in my head, but only nod on the outside. "I definitely know about the grind. I run a coffee shop now."

She laughs and this time, it's just a little heartier, "I suppose you do," she says.

The conversation that follows over the meal I've made is easy and I fall back from a speaking role. Mireya and Ant banter while Blue and Ant bicker. It's not an uncomfortable mess like I would have predicted because Steph banters with the brothers too. She even shared a story about how she and Blue were on the same team against Ant and a different kid who lived in their neighborhood. Apparently, they won so easily that Ant never played basketball with them again if Blue and Steph were on the same team.

Before long, I say, "Well, I have to be up early for work and to take this one to school," motioning to Mireya. "I hope you get home alright," I say to both Blue and Steph.

I start working on gathering dishes to clean but Ant stands from the table abruptly. "Hey, don't worry about it. I'll just bring them over tomorrow."

"It's no biggie. This will just take me a few minutes."

"No, D. Just get Mireya and I'll drop them off after school."

"Are you sure?" I look over to where Steph watches our exchange.

"Yes," He steps in front of me so that I have to look up at him and no one else can read his lips or hear what he's saying easily. "It's the least I can do. You came all this way to feed me even after I was being kind of a jerk earlier."

I twist the ring on my index finger. "You don't have to do this. I'm sorry that I upset you. I—"

"It's fine." He says though a muscle in his jaw jumps. "Look, we still have things to talk about but it's late. You still have to drive home. Tomorrow?"

"Tomorrow," I say. Hugging him around the waist like I always do, I freeze and step back just as quickly. Over the years, I have gotten too comfortable with this kind of thing. I should stop doing this when I know he has someone else.

He pulls me back into him, apparently not caring about setting a boundary. "Text me when you get home."

"Okay," I whisper into his chest, secretly smiling with our connection still in tact.

# Chapter 10

## Tony, Ten Years Ago

"Listen, Pa is not gonna let you sit around the house all day. If you don't want to be put to work, you're gonna have to find some other job." Blue says.

"Like what?" I sit at our dining table in the biggest house on our street. My family has done well for themselves and my Pa will never let me forget that he earned the right to the biggest one. I'm not interested in earning the way he is.

"I don't know. You could go into Lake Charles and work at the mall or Burger King. Fuck if I know." Blue perfectly slices the cigarillo he produced from his pocket with a fingernail. The contents emptied into the kitchen trash can. The tang of tobacco and spice hit my nose.

"Nah. I don't want to do that." Being cooped up like that makes me itch. I'd rather be outside, doing something in the sun.

"Well, be prepared to learn what it really means to be a Dupont, and quick. Life is about more than what you want." The crumbled little bits of green sprinkled into the paper get rolled up and sealed with a slide of his tongue over it. He sets the blunt on the table. I can feel my older brother's eyes on me like that will clue him in on what I have going on in my head.

I save him the trouble, saying, "That's not me. You're meant for this. I'd just be in the way and hating it. It'd be my fault that everything went wrong."

"I don't think that's true. You're smarter than you give yourself credit for. We could use that."

"So it's *we* now?" Blue had turned twenty just a few days ago. It had been two years of him learning everything Pa had to share with him about business. Next in line to take over the empire.

I'm not dumb. I knew that they were selling enough green to get locked up and never see the light of day again. Our lives were comfortable because of it. And still, I knew I didn't want to get involved in anything that would put me away like that. I didn't know if my Dad and brother, or any of the others involved, were bad people, but I knew that their life choices weren't ones I'd make for myself.

"It's been *we*. You're lucky I'm carrying the weight for both of us, but I won't be able to keep him off your back forever. You and me are the third generation to carry the name. They all know it's ultimately up to me." He taps his chest and my eyes focus on the gesture. "I'll be better than Pa or Big Papa Dupont before him. But everybody has to start at the bottom." Blue grabs the blunt and puts it behind an ear. "Your time will come."

Not if I have any say in it.

***

THE NEXT DAY, I set out to find someone, anyone, who would hire me. I'm not a desk job, fast food, or retail worker kind of guy. I'd rather pluck my own teeth out of my head. College was not ever in the plans for me though I probably could get in if I applied. But, I can't see myself being happy to do that either. I want to work with my hands. I like to be outside.

I tried a few houses in our neighborhood to see if they'd let me cut their grass at least. I had luck with just one house whereas the others had turned me down. I was far from my own neighborhood when I got to a little blue and gray house that very clearly needed the yard work done.

My Charger kicked up plenty of dust in the gravel driveway. A small woman was already watching me walk up her overgrown lawn before I got to the door. I didn't even have to knock to be turned down if she wasn't buying what I was selling.

I didn't need to make any money. There was plenty of it at my disposal for my needs. I never wanted to take too much though. Making anything would be just the right price for me. I had an alibi for why I couldn't be involved with Pa's business and something to do besides rot in my house with everyone else doing something they were passionate about.

I hold a hand over my eyes to shield myself from the glare coming off her many windchimes hanging. Once I got close enough to her, I declared, "I see you've got a bit of overgrown grass on your property. Could I cut it for you?"

"I don't care about the grass much, but I've got a couple horses out back and they could probably use a good ride." The older woman looked me over for a bit from behind her screen door. She could have been sixty or older, but it was clear she wasn't in any shape to take care of her horses day in and day out.

"I'm not too familiar with horses. If you show me, I'd be happy to." I walked around to catch a glimpse of the stables on the side of her house I hadn't seen yet. The gray structure looked sturdy but the horse inside it didn't look too happy. I didn't actually know what a happy horse looked like though. I'd ridden before but I was much younger. Walking back over to her, I say, "Staying on? That's about all there is to it right?"

"More than just that," she grumbled. "Have you ever tended before?"

"No, ma'am," I responded. "I'm no professional, but I don't have any-thing but time on my hands."

"Yard does need some upkeep. Fence too."

"I can do that. No problem."

She considers me for a bit, her russet skin showing its age but her eyes showing their wisdom. She wasn't to be taken for a fool. "How much, youngin'?"

"Whatever you can spare me. I'm just looking to keep busy."

"Alright. You get hurt—I'm not paying for it."

She walked back into the house, coming back with a ring of keys. "What did you say your name was?"

"Tony."

She nodded. "I'm Lynn. The speckled one's Ronnie and the black one's Jolene. They're both a bit headstrong, but they're pretty good at telling who's right and wrong. C'mon back. I'll get you started."

I followed her out to her land in the back. It took me about three days to get the hang of riding the horses though they were as she said, headstrong. I thought Jolene would buck me off the first few times so I spent more time with Ronnie that first week.

It didn't take much time to figure out that these horses were restless with nothing to do. They were playful and at times mischievous but I loved spending time with them. Lynn would tell me stories of her time with them. Both had been a present from her youngest daughter before she passed. Though she spoke fondly of her children, I couldn't help but wonder why they never came around to care for her or the horses. It would be a long time before I learned that they had all moved out west because of unsavory dealings with my family.

I spent the next week mowing the overgrown lawn, which took me three long days. Cleaning and clearing out the stalls had become easy with how much I practiced the skill on my own. It wasn't like they had never been done, but it wasn't being done as often as it should have before I came along.

Lynn would bring me lunch and water, claiming that she didn't want me to die on her watch. The woman was pricklier than a cactus. I kinda liked her. She was nothing like my own mother and I liked that too. Sometimes it was hard for me to not become sad over losing her. Lynn made me see that there were still strong women who didn't need a man, good or bad, to have a good life. In my life, men, my Pa especially, told me that women only had two places. When I was young, I never thought twice about that. But being eighteen now, I knew they really didn't understand how women could and are more vital to our world than we are sometimes. Respecting a woman was disrespectful to the "earners" in my Pa's eyes. If they weren't making money for him, they weren't worth the time for him to care about them. I wondered if my brother would be the same way. They were similar but not exactly. I knew Blue was smart enough to keep his mouth shut when he disagreed with something Pa said or did, so it's hard to tell.

That next week, she decided to sit under a big Sycamore tree near the house and watch me ride Jolene instead of staying in her house the whole time. The dark beauty loved to ride fast and show off for Lynn. She'd take direction well until she caught sight of her owner standing outside, like then. She'd bolt and then sidle over to the older woman. Lynn would rub her side and eventually Jolene would be satisfied to take direction again. I tried to wrangle her in to no success but I kind of love how wild she could be at times.

Ronnie was a completely different story. She was never in a hurry and hesitant to go any faster than a trot. Lynn told me it was because of an old injury she had. Even though Ronnie was healthy and healed, she didn't like to do much more than that. Often, I'd catch her under a tree either laying like a cat on her side or reaching her neck over the back property fence to eat from the wild grass growing there. She was curious and cautious all in the same breath.

It was the first time that I really knew I loved working with horses. I love their personalities and being around them. It made me feel like I had a purpose and it was then that I knew I wanted to be around them for as long and as much as I could. Jolene and Ronnie would always be my first loves though.

I enjoyed spending my summer there. Horses got me and had no expectations of me. It had been a long time since I felt so comfortable. So at ease.

When Lynn handed me an envelope, I wiped the sweat from my brow and ripped the side of it open. My eyes bugged out of my head at the number of twenty-dollar bills in it. "What's this?" I asked.

"Your pay. You keep coming back and they'll be more where that's from."

I went home that night and put the money away in a box at the back of my closet. If I stood any chance of escaping what a Dupont's responsibility to the family was, I'd need to get out of Louisiana and fast. I'd save whatever I could and leave at the first chance I could get.

<hr>

"Listen. I'm not stupid." Lynn's raspy voice came to me from the other side of the stables.

"Excuse me?" I stood there brushing Ronnie's coat. The horse began to knicker at the abrupt halt of the brush on her side. She had proven to be quite the pampered thing.

"You think I don't know you're one of them?"

My heart sank.

I didn't know what to say so I kept quiet. I thought I had more time to build up a bigger savings. I started calculating what was left over after I had bought proper work clothes and boots. It had been two months of diligent work on Lynn's land and with her horses.

A family name can mean nothing. A family name can mean *everything*. I learned to never share my last name in mixed company. I never would find out how Lynn found out mine. It wouldn't matter anyway since she had and she was upset but also worry creased her face in a grimace.

"I can't have a Dupont on my property. I'm old and have no way to protect myself from the mess your family causes. "

"You're not in any danger. They don't even know I'm here. I'm not like them."

She waved her hands around, ushering me out of the enclosure. "It's all the same. Your folks took my babies and I won't let you take me next!"

"Please," I put the brush down on my stool and stood. I was tall enough to cast a shadow over her. "It's not the same. I just wanna make enough to get out of here. Whatever you heard about them is not what I want for myself. I'm not like them."

She seemed to look at me, really look at me. Her expression changed from being upset to remorseful and then her furrowed brow deepened in a scowl before she nodded. "And what's your plan, Tony? It's only a matter of time before they pull you in too."

"I don't know, ma'am. I'm gonna get as much money as I can and get gone."

"Where are you going?"

I looked down at my boots. "Got no idea. Anywhere is better than Louisiana."

"You're a good boy. So much life in you. You finish out the summer and then get gone. Take Jolene and Ronnie with you."

"Take them where?" I shake my head. "I can't. I don't have a plan."

"Let me work that out." Lynn placed cool fingers on my arm, "Can I trust you to take care of my girls?" Her eyes flicked back and forth between mine.

"Without a doubt," I answered with no hesitation.

She nodded again and went back into the house.

Two months later, I was towing my Charger behind the horse trailer to a state I had never been to before to work a job I'd never really known but was eager to master. When I arrived in Alpenglow Ridge, Colorado, I was greeted by a woman who glimmered in the sunlight with a personality just as bright and inviting.

"You must be Tony. Welcome to Mason Ranch." She gestures to the area around her. I followed her gesture with my eyes to take in the large expanse of land behind her that had horses all milling about. The mountain line I followed on my drive here is even more beautiful with the sun setting behind them. "You hungry? I just made dinner," she says. "I'm Chandie Mason, by the way. Danny is in the house eating already. You'll be working under him, but business talk tomorrow." She pats my shoulder. "For now, come meet everyone."

I followed her into the ranch house and quickly felt at ease and at home. I never looked back.

# CHAPTER 11

# Tony

"I THINK WITH HOW things are going with Mr. Danny, I can do about five clients a day if we need to. I can't keep up with clients and horse maintenance if I'm taking that many people on per day though. Maybe you could spare me some cowboys..." Cammie, Reese's newest addition to her ever-expanding plans for the Ranch looks over at me. "Or ranch hands. I don't really know what you prefer to be called."

Danny, Reese's Dad, watches his daughter with proud eyes as she sits at the head of the table holding this meeting. It's been four, maybe five, years of her running things and I know it was his plan all along to give this ranch to her. After a small period of running it myself, I am glad to no longer hold the title for her. She's constantly talking and arranging. It's too much human interaction for me, and what I do now is plenty. Nothing wrong with people, but like Danny, I prefer the horses and kiddos. Much more fun than the adults in any of these meetings.

This particular meeting came about because Reese had decided to add hippo therapy to the list of services Mason Ranch offers. We offer boarding for horses, kids camps, and riding clinics. Plus, it still functions as a cattle ranch like it did when Danny was running it and I first came to town. There's more staff than ever and now more people managing all the different parts of it. The newest addition, Cammie Clyfford, a hippo therapist from the Pacific Northwest who is surprisingly new to cattle ranches of any kind. She was working with Danny exclusively until Reese decided that partnering with Cammie to add another branch would be an amazing idea.

"Don't care what you call me. I've been a ranch hand and a cowboy. Now I just do whatever I need to around here. Making sure the boys are where they need to be and the issues or work that comes up gets handled."

"Well, if you don't mind me asking... What is the difference exactly? That might be a factor in deciding who would be best for the program. Even if it is just short term."

I scratch the stubble coming in on my chin. "It's pretty easy. Cowboys work with the cows and the horses. Wrangling, herding, feeding, watering—all that." I take my hat off, tossing it on the table and placing a hand on my knee. "Ranch hands work the ranch. If the fences need mending, tractors acting up,  or maybe light carpentry, mucking stalls, et cetera. If the ranch needs 'em, they're doing it. Sometimes it overlaps, but not much around here since we've got plenty of staff. To make it easy and because nobody cares about the distinction, everybody is a hand in my eyes. Them boys don't call me that though. Kind of a... respect thing. It's me, Mack, Ellis, and Taylor who mostly work with the cows. But they'll pitch in with the others if we've got a lot that needs doing. Me, not so much. I earned that."

"So, no barrels or roping?" Cammie asks.

I just look at her and then turn to Reese. "I thought you said she had experience."

"Tony, she's not from this life. She grew up in Seattle. Give her a break."

I turn to her, lacing my finger in front of me and leaning in. "Honey, these aren't rodeo games. Those are performers. Just like what I said that overlaps. Some of them might actually work a ranch for real and use those skills but there's not a person out there working with the cows who don't know how to rope. Part of the job. But what we do here isn't for show. It's labor. Hard work. If we're roping, it's for a reason. Not some athlete trying to look pretty and get some..." I gesture in front of myself looking for the word. "Ribbon."

"Anyway," Reese cuts a glare at me. "Will you be able to spare any hands?"

"I can spare a couple. It's gonna be a little bit slower around here now that the last of the hay has been baled for the season."

Reese looks over to Cammie who is studiously writing something on a notepad. She clears her throat and Cammie looks up to acknowledge us at the table. "Perfect. That's perfect. I really only need one person, but two would be fantastic."

"I'll let Ellis and Taylor know that they'll report to you. Probably would love to get a break."

Cammie stiffens in her chair. She shoots Reese a look that I catch, though I know it's not meant for me.

"Is that a problem?"

"No... No problem. I'm grateful." Her tone doesn't bear a sense of gratitude as it comes out through a fake smile.

Looking back at Reese, she shakes her head quickly. My brows pinch. What is this nonsense? There's a lot of looking around at this table. I'm ready to get back outside. Danny makes a sound somewhere between a grunt and cough that breaks the tension in the room. Reese looks over to her dad, sliding the water closer to him and picks up the conversation again. "Well, that settles that. We'll just have to work out how to make sure there is adequate space for ranching and hippo therapy to occur, simultaneously. We can, of course, put up a corral and I know you like to go on the trail for a more tranquil ambiance since it can get rowdy—"

"I trust that you two can work out the scheduling of all that. I put in everyone's schedules. You can just update Ellis and Taylor with the locations there." I tap the table twice, rising from my chair and putting my hat back on. A smear of dirt from my fingertips lingers behind me on the cream-colored dining table. I swipe at it with my hand, making it the spot worse. I dust my palms on my pants before I make a bigger mess. "Text me if you need me again. I'll be out making sure that alfalfa is being allotted the way it's supposed to."

Reese agrees as I throw a hand up, ducking under the dining room door frame to the parking lot.

**Blue: Are you gonna see your real girlfriend before we leave?**

Me: I'm working. I saw her before I left for work

**Blue: At 5 AM. No one is alive at that time.**

Me: I was

**Blue: So that's a no then?**

I put my phone into the holster clipped onto my jeans since it's more likely to fall and get lost in just my pocket. But it also makes it that much more difficult to be distracted by problems I shouldn't have to be dealing with right now. Like the clusterfuck of having my girlfriend and best friend in the same small town.

Even saying that makes me seem like an asshole.

But I'm not.

I had a plan that involved telling Drea after her opening and potentially allowing the two of them to meet... It was less of a plan and more of an... educated wish.

I like Steph. I wasn't completely trying to hide her. I just needed to figure out how to introduce her to Drea, while also finding separation from my two favorite people. God. It still sounds bad. Sooo much for that! Blue came into town and blew up any plans I could have had as far as that goes.

The worst part is that I know who Blue was here to see. The only added benefit for him was that he got an opportunity to be an asshole and create unnecessary drama. Probably to deflect from the real reason he's here. He knows I don't like it. I like it even less because I don't know how far all of that has spiraled since I first clocked his twisted scheming.

I sigh, mounting Daisy, my working horse, and heading over to the east field the alfalfa hay has been stacked up on. I need to get back to work and stop thinking about how much damage control I might have ahead of me.

⸻ ✦•••✦ ⸻

I'M A SIMPLE MAN. I have simple wants for my life.

Work hard and make an honest living.

Surround myself with good people and make good memories.

Come home to a good woman and... make even better memories.

I've crossed off two out of three of those things. The third, I'm doing, in a fashion I guess... I spend way too many nights at Drea's house with her daughter—but Drea is not *my* good woman to make the memories I want with. *She's not mine.* I would give my left nut to sink into her. Not because she's sexy and strong and my every wet dream, but because I know, *knew*, that she is the woman I could see forever with.

At one point, I'd give anything for it to be that way though. I want—wanted—Drea. I fucked up somehow, somewhere along the way. I can't make her see me as more than that.

Maybe I'm an asshole really, because it made me just a little happy to see Drea's reality crack when I brought Steph into that bakery. Was she thinking about how I meant more to her? Was she thinking about how I found someone who could think of me as more than a friend?

Chandie piles some pasta onto my plate. When she reaches for another plate, I tell her, "It's okay. I'm not really feeling that hungry." She gives me a puzzled look.

In all the years I've worked for this family, I've never turned down food. She often had to limit what I was taking, since I could actually eat any living person out of their house and home.

"Are you feeling okay?" She asks, pressing a hand to my forehead.

"I'm feeling fine. Just wanna get back out there so I can get home."

"Ah," she says. "Steph."

It does not shock me that my old boss's wife knows about the change in my relationship status. She has become somewhat like a mother figure since I don't have one of those myself. Plus, small town gossip travels faster than a rain cloud around Alpenglow Ridge.

"Nah. She's probably already on a plane back." She waits for more but I don't elaborate. "Does everybody have their own scolding for me on this? I'm single. I can date whoever I want."

"But, do you really *want* to date her?" Chandie asks with a wink.

I shovel pasta into my mouth so that I can't respond and she nods, already getting her answer. She packs away the large container and pats my shoulder before she leaves the kitchen. "I trust you'll figure it out."

"He won't," Reese clomps in with her red boots. "I'll take it from here, Mom."

I roll my eyes. "Should have known that you'd be in here soon enough. Don't you have another addition to make to the Ranch? Lots of work that is more pressing than getting on my nerves."

"I take it very personally that you think I would slack on my duties as *an annoying little sister type.* You knew this was coming. I gave you the weekend to get your shit together."

"My shit is together. I'm dating someone. Not committing any crimes."

"Like hell! You dropped the damn ball. What kind of knight in shining armor are you? Getting a whole new princess? C'mon, Tony."

"Drea is no princess," I respond, drolly. She's a queen.

"You're right. She's the queen." She pushes my plate from in front of me. I narrow my eyes at the dark-haired woman looking at me expectantly. She is like a little sister to me. When I got here she was so young, I feel like I watched her grow up into the woman she is today. She was gone for a while, chasing glamor and maybe fame. I don't know. Though years had passed, she came back with the same amount of annoyance if not more. I still love her for it. Not right now though.

"You think I don't know that?"

"Yes!" She smacks the fork out of my hand next.

"What's your problem? Last time I checked, Drea and I were still friends."

She huffs and stomps her foot before crossing her arms over her chest. "What is *your* problem? Last time I checked, you two were still made for each other!"

"In your eyes, sure."

"In everyone's eyes, Tony." She shakes her head. "How could you give up on her? On them."

I grind my teeth. "I didn't give up on her. I'm still here ain't I?"

"Are you? How long before you decide that you don't have time for them anymore because you want to be with *your girlfriend*?" Reese sneers "girlfriend" at me, looking more juvenile than a thirty year old woman should.

"Look, Reese, I get that she's your friend. But it's none of your business. Drea has made it clear that she doesn't want to be more than friends." I stand from the stool and grab my plate and fork from the counter. "Despite what any of us want."

I leave out the back door, giving her a wave over my shoulder.

When I get over to the barn, I call out, "Taylor. Ellis. Left door!"

They both lope over. Taylor looks me over and crosses their arms over their chest. "What's up, boss?"

"You're gonna be reporting to Cammie for the foreseeable future. She needs the help until they hire on staff specifically for the hippo therapy stuff."

"What are we gonna be doing?"

"I don't know. Just maintaining the horses Reese wants to delegate to the program. Don't know past that, not my business."

"And you didn't ask?" Taylor asks.

"For what? You work for the Ranch. Cammie is running a program at the Ranch. So you'll be working. All I needed to know."

Taylor leans over to Ellis, pretending to whisper behind their hand but not actually lowering their voice. "You'd think he'd be in a better mood. Girlfriend problems already?" Ellis chuckles at Taylor.

"What is everyone's fascination with Steph? That has nothing to do with you two chuckleheads. Get back to it. You'll wait for Cammie in the main house, starting Wednesday."

I stalk off, still trying to eat my lunch before the flies get to it first.

# Chapter 12

## Drea

Fall is hands down the best season. Especially in Colorado. Nothing could make me change my mind. The way all the leaves go from rich green to gold and brown and all the shades from peach to red, it's like a canvas that was made for me. The temperature is perfection. Not too hot, not too cold. Snuggling in a plush blanket becomes an actual pastime instead of the cry for help it would be in summertime. And the standard outfit of an oversized sweater, leggings, and boots is all around me. A season of twinning because we all have the bright idea of comfort, even Reese and Mel participate in.

Not only that, it's when all the best eating holidays occur! One of my favorites—Friendsgiving! Not to be confused with the other holiday that happens on Thursday.

Friendsgiving is a special time for all of us. It's on the last Friday of November. Over the years it has looked different but there are some things that have never changed. Reese and Chloe are in charge of decorating. It has gotten more and more lavish since Reese moved back to Alpenglow Ridge. Much to Chloe's excitement since neither Mel nor I really have a desire to be a part of that part of things at all. Reese's Mom is in charge of the bird, now birds, with all the guests. Chandie and I work together to create the sides. Tyson is in charge of the music so it inevitably leans more towards country and indie guitar instrumentals. I, of course, am in charge of desserts. This year I have created mini whiskey sweet potato pies, pumpkin spice conchas, and two of Ant's favorites—double chocolate cake and strawberry cake.

What started as a twenty or so person event, has morphed to serve nearly a hundred. It's far larger than most expect and we still end up with plenty of leftovers to send folks home with. It's one of my favorite times of the year. A holiday that has the worst history, is transformed into something different in the massive ranch house on the Mason's property.

This was the first year that Ant didn't sit in the kitchen with me as I baked all this stuff, talking about everything and nothing. I actually had not seen him very often since that night I brought dinner to his house. We'd talked plenty. As much as we usually did on the phone which turned out to be not much at all since we spent a lot of our time together.

But there he stands in the doorway looking like a sight for sore eyes.

Ant is cleaned up for the event. His dark eyes run over the crowd of people gathered and I feel when they find me. He smiles and it's small but not without excitement. I've seen this plenty of times. Per usual, Mireya finds him first, hugging him around the waist. Now his smile stretches his cheeks as they talk before my daughter drags him through the crowd of people. He's too busy greeting others and excusing his way through that I'm able to scrutinize him uninhibitedly.

His strong jaw, stubbled in that way that begs for a hand to run over it. Tan Stetson and Chambray shirt on that screams Marlboro ad. I know he doesn't smoke but if he were to pull a cigarette pack out of that breast pocket, I might lose all function of my knees.

Is it true what they say, that with absence the heart grows fonder?

It must be, because all I want to do is climb this man and the urge is strong enough that I have to press my thighs together. It's a foreign sensation because I haven't thought about things like this since I first talked to him in the bar.

Finally, they reach me. Mireya finds a friend in the crowd and leaves us just standing there. I wait for my big, warm bear hug, but it's not big or bear-like. He puts an arm around my shoulders and I'm left colder than I was before he touched me. That stings, but then I remember.

"No Steph tonight?" I ask, feeling like a lame. And I don't understand that either.

"Nah. She's with her family for the weekend."

I've not once seen Ant go home for the holidays. He usually spends it with the Masons or, more recently, with us. It's on the tip of my tongue to ask why he didn't join her. I decide against it since I'm not a glutton for punishment.

"Shame she'll miss all the potluck. I saw some really yummy stuff over there. Not just my desserts either," I laugh and it falls a little flat.

He eyes me curiously before responding. "From memory, her folks throw down, so I'm sure she's still eating good."

"Right… Well, how have you been? I feel like I haven't seen you in a while."

"Good. I've been good. Every time I drive by the shop, it's been busy. Makes me real proud."

I smile, allowing his compliment to soak in. It's been a while since I heard one from his deep baritone. I reach out and grab his arm, pulling him close to me. "Well, why didn't you stop by? I wouldn't make you wait in the line." I hope, more than the times before, that I don't sound desperate and fake as I cover the confusing mix of longing and, still absurdly, arousal.

He looks down at my hand on his arm and I drop it. It feels inappropriate and strange to touch him because…

Well, because he's not mine to touch. He's taken.

That thought clangs around in my head. Like metal on metal colliding over and over again. He's *taken* quickly becomes *he's gone* and that hurts a little too acutely.

Reese and Clo were right. And now that I can see it in front of my face I feel the deep flush rising on my neck and heating my ears.

I could lose him now that he's seeing someone.

"Are you okay?" Ant asks me. There's concern in his eyes and I can't really bear it right now. For some reason, I want to cry. My eyes are stinging with it.

"Yea, I just need some air. I think—" Turning, I run into another person. "Colton, what are you doing here?" I was upset before, but now I'm just shocked that Mireya's Dad is here.

Colton and I never had a romantic relationship really when I got pregnant at seventeen in the back of his car. Look at me, the cautionary tale of what happens when you're young and dumb. Pregnant with the boy I had known almost all my life because our mothers spent a lot of time together. I was curious about sex, but not very safe so I ended up pregnant on my first time experiencing it.

He and I are cordial, but he's not as big a presence in Mireya's life since I chose to stay in Alpenglow Ridge and he still lives in Harmony Hill. He's actually one of the county's sheriffs. He's fully dressed in his uniform and though no one is doing anything illegal here, I feel how everyone creates space around him and in turn, me.

"I need to talk to you for a second." I stand there waiting for Colton to continue, but he glares at Ant until the tall man rolls his eyes and excuses himself. I don't want him to leave so my eyes follow the path he takes to the grand table of food.

Turning back to Colton, I ask, "What is it? And why are you being rude to Ant? You could have at least said hi or something."

"I need a favor."

I scoff. "Are we the kind of people who give each other favors? I must have missed that part of the relationship." Okay. So... *cordial* may have been a stretch. Though Colton lives just under an hour away from me, I have been every bit the single mother because he does nothing for our daughter. He uses his badge more than ever on me as a reason for why he can't do the little he was doing before like watching Mireya while I worked or picking her up from school on days I needed to work a double to support us.

He completely ignores my tone and proposes this favor to me anyway. "Well, I sort of talked you up to my boss and I need you to be in Breckenridge for our Christmas Retreat."

"What?"

"It's not that bad. The retreat only lasts five days, the twenty-third through the twenty-seventh, and you'd have your own room."

"What does that matter? Five days? What did you promise them, Colton?"

"I said that you could cater the desserts for the event and it would impress the departments in attendance."

My mouth hangs open. I can not believe him. "Just how many people are going to be at this event?"

"I don't know something like three hundred. It's just the sheriffs and sheriff deputies and their plus ones"

"Three hundred?!" He nods "What the hell? Five days? Have you lost your mind? You can't spring that on me." The thought alone is making my pits sweat. But in the same swirling ball of self-doubt is the idea of how amazing of an opportunity this could be. The connections I could make...

Colton continues talking and I listen more interested now. "I know you can do this, Drea. It would be great publicity for your shop and it pays well. They have the budget for this event."

I cross my arms over my chest. Five days over the Christmas holiday... Could I make this work? Would it be worth it? I don't know if I will even have enough people working around that time to help me make all these desserts. Especially not that close to the actual holiday.

"Please? It would mean a lot to me." He looks so desperate and I don't know what to say, what to choose.

"But you're asking me to spend that time away from the family... I ca—"

"That's the other thing. Mireya sort of asked to stay with me over the break."

"She what?" First Ant and now Colton? She's having conversations with everyone about what she wants in her life besides me. With Ant, I understand. With Colton? I'm utterly flabbergasted and even more hurt. She barely even sees her Dad. His choice, not mine.

"I know. I was surprised too." I roll my eyes to keep from saying what that comment deserves. "I think it will be good for us to spend at least Christmas together. She's always at your house for the holidays since I've been working them. It's kind of perfect. I've got some vacation time. Maybe we'll go stay at my parents' cabin and—"

"Back it up. I haven't agreed to any of this. You're throwing way too much at me way too fast."

"Okay." He blows out a breath, running a hand over his head. "You're right. Take some time to think about what I've said and let me know. Okay?"

"Yea." He tries to hug me, but I keep my arms crossed. *We are not there. Not even close.* At my discomfort, Ant is by my side again, quickly.

"What is your problem, Colton?" His voice remains calm but there is an edge to it.

"Think about what I said," is all he says before walking through the throngs of people who part for him on his way through the Mason's house.

"What did he say?" Ant looks me over with concern like I'm coming out of a boxing arena. No physical damage, just many emotional ones being reigned, unfortunately.

Giving him a weak smile, I say, "I think he just wanted to talk about a job."

"What kind of job?"

I tell him all that Colton has told me and it's the kind of thing that makes me feel a little queasy. Could I pull something like this off? When I was working as both a bartender and trying to hustle gigs like this on the side, maybe not. My hours could never allow for it.

But now...? This could be the kind of event that could be a stepping stone for Drip and Whip to be put on the map! My mind whirs as I think of just how to make this happen. I have three weeks to figure it out and potentially pull this off.

"So you're gonna do it, right?" Ant asks.

"Of course. I'd be so silly to pass up an opportunity like this one. This is why I opened the shop, right? To cater events this size. To be taken seriously as a baker, as a business. This is a serious event."

"It would sure make Colton look good."

"Why do you say that?"

"Nothing. No reason."

"You really think I should? The universe kind of plopped this right into my lap."

"It only seems scary because you haven't done it before. I know you can do anything that you set your mind to and this is just another step towards what you've been wanting."

I smile and bump into him, "So is that a yes... or...?" I giggle before he bumps me back.

"It's a yes. Don't want you to stress yourself out though. The whole reason you've got this shop is so that you don't end up doing everything yourself. Please tell me that you'll use your people for this." His eyes are pleading with me. He has seen how I've worn myself out in the past, trying to wear all the hats at the same time.

"I promise."

Nodding to himself, he takes a bite out of a dinner roll from the plate I'm just now noticing him holding. "Did you eat already?" he asks.

"Actually, I haven't."

We walk over to the huge spread of food and I start grabbing things from the table. My friends find me amongst the other guests and talk around me with others, but my mind is still thinking.

What if I take this event on and it turns out amazing?

# Chapter 13

## Drea

I WOKE UP STILL feeling frustrated.

Not about the Christmas retreat, well a little bit about that. I accepted the event and continued to think and think about just what I wanted to showcase. The possibilities were endless and I wish I had a little more time to disaster plan. Everything has to be perfect. It would be our first big, big catering gig. No hiccups are allowed. Landing this and pulling it off is essential. I might even be able to take a vacation. What a miracle that would be.

I have employees now, staff. They rely on me to make sure Drip and Whip doesn't capsize. One bad event couldn't do that. But if I don't shake out of this funk, who knows how all of this could manifest in my baking. I can't fail them.

With three full weeks as the HBIC, as Reese would say, at Drip and Whip... I was exhausted. It's not that my staff disliked me or that things weren't working out, I just... wasn't winning them over as easily as I thought I would. *Maybe they did dislike me.*

I don't know how Eric Walker was with them before I stepped in. He seems like a sweet old man, but that could be my ageism showing. Anyone can be a hard ass, regardless of age. I thought that letting everyone carry on with their original schedules as such would be simple. A few of the staff did want more hours so I was able to get more help with the baking than I expected. It was still a lot of work.

Adding to that feeling of frustration is my daughter still being hush, hush about her sudden dislike of being at the Mason's. Now, my work hours really can facilitate her school and extracurricular activities more. I'd have to beg her to come home practically and now she's running to my van when I pull up. She'd rather wait in the car than sit inside while I say hi to my friends, nieces and nephews. It was not a big deal to go and pick her up after being dropped off there. I wish she would talk to me about what happened. At some point, I would have to admit defeat and get Ant to figure out what happened with her and CJ. I just know that it has something to do with him. She is more willing to talk with him than me, it seems. I'm not quite sure how to feel about that fact. What am I doing wrong with her?

With all the new changes happening in my life, there's Ant. He still hasn't been over to our house, like usual. Normally, he'd be at the house after bringing her with him when he was done with work. I've been lonely. Like, depressingly so. I'd call my friends but they all have partners and their own lives to enjoy. Not even my daughter will spend time with me. I've never had free time like this since I first got pregnant and I was a teen then. The house seems colder and emptier than it ever has.

I miss my best friend. I miss our laughs on my couch before bed. I miss how he'd pretend that I plated too much food for him but he'd still want seconds. I miss him and it's been manifesting in strange ways.

Maybe not strange, but unlike anything before.

There's nothing I can do to relieve how much I suddenly wanted to get laid.

I know!

I don't know what came over me. It had been years of my hand, my toys, and my overactive imagination where I never had any worries. It was enough. Something has changed between now and then. I didn't know what it was or what I could do to make it go away.

That overactive imagination I mentioned before was toying with me. I felt like some sort of horny teenager. Everything was fair game for my dirty mind to make sexual. It was annoying and inconvenient. I had more important things that should be getting my attention. My libido was getting in my way! *Mierda.*

His words, *we were working toward something,* play in my mind as I try to make sense of them. He just meant us finding our respective person, right? We both were. I still was, though each date was worse than the last. I was not closer to finding my person. And this need, this ache, inside me was growing with his absence on top of everything else.

I barely slept this past week and I couldn't find any relief. I felt so icky after my dinner with Ant and his girlfriend and it didn't clear up even after she left. I couldn't explain why. I should be happy that he seemed to be happy with his choice. Every time I'd think to call him, I'd hang up and put my phone somewhere out of reach.

*I don't wish my misery upon him by any means.*

Maybe it was my intuition telling me that Steph wasn't good for him. Maybe she was secretly the worst and my friend needed to know.

*It wasn't any of my business.*

I need to let him make decisions on his own and stand beside him in support like he has done for me. And by standing beside him, I mean waiting for him to realize I was missing him through... ESP?

Ugh.

Music will probably help. I click over to my playlist and pick a Tony Evans Jr. song that I think will capture my mood perfectly.

I'm dancing around as I prepare the countertop for the project I have planned for the day. I sing and am so lost in my own world that I don't hear the front door open before I'm startled by his deep voice booming from behind me.

"How come you never ask me to help you when you're making food?"

I recover quickly, drying my hands off on some paper towel. Newfound excitement about his unexpected visit bubbles up inside me as I lower the volume on my music. I smile and ask, "Am I supposed to? I didn't know you were coming over." He leans against the countertop, crossing his arms in front of himself. The thermal henley shirt he wears stretches tight over his shoulders and arms. My eyes catch on the cuts of his muscles. How could I not notice them? I drink from my spiced iced coffee to try and quell the sudden thirst. "Did you want to?" I ask.

"Maybe. Watched you make plenty of meals and desserts and not once do you put me to task."

I shrug, brushing some hair from my face with my shoulder, as best I can. He reaches over to tuck the hair back behind my ear. "Thanks," I say, face heating. "I don't know. It was never like that in my house. My Abuelo and my Papi both stayed out of the kitchen whenever the women were cooking something. I just thought if you wanted to, you would. That's how I learned. I watched and just started doing it."

He looks over the counters with bowls of ingredients and the flour I just pulled from the cabinet. "Maybe I should stay on this side of the counter. My Mom would always end up making me wash all the dishes. I never got to do anything fun."

I boop his nose, leaving a white smudge of flour on his smooth brown skin. "Nope. You said it now." He balks and I add, "I won't make you wash all the dishes, but I'll show you what I'm working on today."

He nods, standing from his chair with his hands out. "Where do you want me?" The veins in his big hands are distracting as he clenches and unclenches his fists like he's waiting for me to put something in his hands. It does something funny to my stomach.

"Let's start with flour," I say.

Ant looks completely out of place in my traditional kitchen. On horseback, wrangling cattle or leaning against the open barn door directing ranch hands on where to go is more his scene. In my mind, anyway.

After he works those long hours, I like to see him fed and seated at my table. Like any friend, I want to help him in any way that I can. I know Chandie feeds him and all the staff there just fine while they're there working, but it's not lost on me that he lives alone. He's likely to eat at QB's every night. Whereas I don't mind bringing him his burger and onion rings,

I know he needs better nutrition than that if he's going to be hauling hay and wrestling colts... Or whatever he's doing all day. Honestly not sure why I can only picture him doing the tasks that are the sweatiest.

*Not going to think about it anymore.*

Point is, he doesn't spend time in the kitchen and I do. I think. *What was my point?*

I'm quiet, thinking about how sweaty he gets and the noises he makes when I've seen him baling hay is not helpful for my brain as I measure out flour.

"What are we making?"

"Oh, right. We're making cream puffs."

"Really?" Ant's face brightens with a smile that I was hoping I'd see.

"Yes... Hopefully. They can be a little finicky, but I have an idea for a filling I want to try. If it turns out good, I'll add it to the menu at the shop."

"Sure, I'll eat it up even if it doesn't turn out." He's looking over the counter at the ingredients I've pulled out and doesn't notice how I faltered with the pot I've just measured water into. "What's next?"

I clear my throat, suddenly feeling both too hot and too cold at my stove with Ant right behind me. "We're going to put the pot on the stove."

"That's it?" His breath fans over my neck and I shiver. Why am I so keyed up? *Get it together, Drea.*

I need some separation.

"No, that's not it. It's just the first step. Baking is about process. Precision. You have to do things in the right way for it to turn out the way you want."

"Baking is about process. Cool."

"I don't know if you're joking."

"I'm not." He laughs. "Where do I come in?" Is everything he says going to be an innuendo? I wish my brain would move past this already.

"Grab that butter from over there and cut it into eight equal parts."

He nods and gets a butter knife from my drawer. The look of concentration he makes while diligently slicing the stick of butter makes me break out into laughter. "Today, please?"

"You said it needed to be equal!" He complains and I only laugh harder.

I wipe my eyes with my arm. "Yea, but you're also not a robot. This is not where the precision really matters. Here we're just breaking it up into smaller cubes so that it will melt faster and easier in the water."

"Okay, well I got it cut up. Equally. Precisely." He sasses. Walking the plate over to me with his butter, I scrape it carefully into the pot with my spatula so that it doesn't splash up on us.

Adding a little salt to the pot, then pointing at him with my spatula, I warn, "I'm gonna put you on dishes duty. Don't sass the instructor."

His cheek lifts with a smirk. "Fine, fine. I'll behave, *instructor*. Now, what are we doing?"

"You see the flour I measured?" He nods. "We're going to combine it into the water and butter once it's boiling."

He brings the correct bowl with flour over to me just as the water gets to the temperature I'm looking for. Our fingers brush the tiniest bit and I am hyper-aware of the contact. It feels too hot in this kitchen. Turning the burner down, I pour the flour in and step back from the stove. "Me?" he asks. "I'm going to do it?"

"Mmmh-hmm. Hurry before it gets thick." Damn. And here I am with these innuendos. He takes the spatula from my hand and peers into the pot with caution. "I mean clumpy. Mix everything around until you don't see any white clumps of flour."

He starts working the dough as I lean my butt against the sink. Each twist of his arms makes them flex and bulge. It's downright obscene by the time his veins are visible. I bite my cheek and it is clear that there is a very good reason why he should not be helping me in the kitchen.

"Is that good?" He asks, showing me the pot.

Clean it up, Drea! *This is Ant.* Act like you know that!

"What? Oh, um... let me see." He steps aside for me to look over his work. It looks good to me and I hold my hand up to him. He smacks it lightly, giving him the high five he deserves. The connection of his skin on mine sends a fizzle of energy down my arm and I look at my hand for a bit.

"Oh come on, D. I barely even tapped you."

I force a chuckle. "You don't know your own strength," I chastise, trying my best to cover how I'm flustered.

"Or you're just weak." He chuckles.

My face flames because I am weak. And I don't know how to handle anything about us anymore.

# CHAPTER 14

# Drea

"Now what, because I've got to admit that this is not looking very much like a donut right now." Ant points out.

"We're still making the dough. Process, remember?" I try to gain my composure again, but it's proving to be difficult. "It's not done yet. It needs some eggs." I grab the eggs and the pot and take them over to the countertop.

I feel his eyes on me as I take time to crack and add each egg into the mixture.

"Still doesn't look like a donut, Drea." He laughs when I set the pot to the side.

"Oh, hush," I swat at him. "We're gonna cook them and then you'll see." Scooping the dough into a piping bag I start carefully creating the shapes I want with enough room between them. Ant watches from the sink and I feel nervous. Luckily it doesn't take long to pipe these and get them into the oven on a timer.

"This already seems like a lot of work," he bends over, looking into the oven at the puffs.

Don't look, Drea. Don't look. Don't look.

I'm weak and I totally sneak just a quick peek at his tight ass and thighs in those jeans and my heart starts to pitter-patter like rain on a steel rooftop. If he was a Marlboro man at Friendsgiving, he's the reason for the invention of Wrangler butt. If I submitted how his ass looks in these jeans, everyone else would have to bow out of the competition. I bite my lip. How long is he gonna look at these uncooked puffs?

"You know looking at them, won't make them cook any faster?" Now, I laugh under my breath.

He stands fully, facing me with his eyebrow raised. "Don't laugh at me. I'm an experienced baker now. I know some things."

"I don't think you can say that until you've actually made something edible."

"Under your wing, I'm on my way." He smiles at me and I smile back.

"C'mon, *experienced baker*. We're gonna work on the filling while those cook." I pour the maple syrup into a different saucepan and put it onto the stove to boil.

"Yes! Now we're talking! Fillings are sweet and don't look like this goopy stuff you had me stirring."

"Shut up. Everything basically starts as goopy stuff for desserts." He bumps into me playfully, softly laughing. His touch tingles against me again and I falter for only a minute before I grab the bowl I put the eggs into. "I'm going to crack and separate these eggs because we only want the whites. We'll pour them into the mixer and let it go."

I take my time, making sure no shell gets into the bowl. Ant is behind me again. He's so big that even with both his hands on the counter, he's not quite touching me. I'm caged in though and the heat from his body presses against me like maybe we are actually touching. I could just ask him to take a step back or move away from me, but I don't.

When the last egg white falls into the bowl, I say, "Start with the medium setting, we don't want to rush this process. Just going to whisk until peaks form."

He reaches over my shoulder to turn the knob on the mixer. The whisk beating against the eggs makes a sound that is more erotic than I have ever noticed before. Neither of us comments on it, watching the mixture begin to get frothy and opaque for minutes upon minutes. The time passes quickly with his warmth pressing in against my back. It's more than just that though. It's him. He is the warmth. He is the comfort that I've been missing and nothing can keep me from seeing that as clearly as I do now. I miss him but it's more than that. I don't know exactly what. I can't explain how this ache came to be, but I wish that he would help me alleviate it.

He reaches over me again to turn off the mixer when the timer I set trills into the hum of the space between us and the clean scent of my own laundry detergent on his clothes mixed with his natural smell pulls me in.

I shouldn't care at all about how our scents mixed, but the baker in me couldn't help but categorize scents. It's how I cook, mostly by smell. And Ant smells delicious right now.

Maybe it's the...

"Oh!" I pop up, breaking his hold on the counter to rush over to the maple syrup which is fragrant and just barely saved from burning. "I forgot about this." Ant gives me a confused look, but I don't miss the way his eyes are slightly hooded.

I turn the mixing bowl while pouring the syrup in and again, it's his presence right behind me, with everything incorporated into the meringue.

Should I say something? But what would I say? Thankfully I don't have to say anything because Tony speaks next.

"I know we have to wait for the puff thing to cool, but can I eat this? Looks fucking good..."

I nod because words are still failing me. It takes him a moment to figure out how to remove the whisk from the stand mixer. When he does, the peak of meringue stands tall between us. "Can I just lick it off from here?"

My heart stutters and my brain works over time. Both in trying to stop thinking about Ant licking and imagining him licking me all at once.

His finger swipes a bit of the fluffy white filling from the metal and he groans at the taste when his finger comes out clean from his soft lips. "Fuck, Drea." Lord, please help me. I can't press my thighs together any tighter.

"This tastes so good. Here," He swipes up more from the whisk and his finger is in my mouth before I can think twice.

Now, I moan. Partially from the feel of his rough fingertip on my tongue but also because the meringue came out just how I wanted. The maple is just forward enough to feel like Fall and will bring something special to the dessert.

I startle out of my thoughts when he finally removes his finger after several moments. Heated eyes meet mine. I don't know what had been happening while I...

Ugh. While I tasted meringue off his finger like it was foreplay!

Saved yet again by my cooking timer, I rush to the oven to silence the timer and remove the baking tray. All the while, I feel Ant's eyes on me. I should say something. I should. But I don't.

I move around the kitchen getting the piping bag I need and start slicing and filling the puffs. It should be distracting me from my horny as fuck thoughts but it isn't. Each swirl of meringue in the puff makes me think dirtier and dirtier thoughts. My cheeks are inflamed and I feel my hands shaking.

Placing the tools down on my counter, I turn and Ant's face nearly breaks me. He's confused and concerned. I know he can sense my change in energy. We're too close for him not to notice.

"Drea, I—" His phone rings and he picks it up. "What?" Then his face changes again.

I take a moment to try and catch my breath as he listens to whoever is on the line. I mouth, "Off day?" to him but he squints his eyes at the phone.

"No, it's fine. I'll be there." He responds to the call and shoves his phone back into his pocket. "I need to go to the Ranch for a bit. Are you... Drea, do you want to talk about—"

"Nope. You should go. I'm good." He moves forward as if he will hug me but I can't take it. "I don't want to have to wash my hands again. I'll just see you later right?"

His brows pull together. "Yea," he says and then leaves the kitchen, taking his intense energy with him.

I spin to grab my piping bag again and finish filling all the puffs. Hands still trembling with need. I can clean up later.

What was I thinking? What am I thinking? All of it needs to stop.

Once.

One time.

I just need to get this out of my system.

As soon as I can no longer hear Ant's truck in my driveway, I rush to my room to bring out the big guns. I'm itching like a goddamn addict. I dive onto my bed, reaching underneath for my chest. The moment I open the lid, my options are all laid out for me. I know what I need.

The little pink rose looks at me and I look at it.

*It's on.*

I have about an hour before my daughter will be home and I need to get this out of my system before then. That's it. I wiggle manically out of my leggings. I'm already wet as hell. My panties stick to me and I shiver when the cool air of my room meets my bare center.

Flickers of the memory of his breath on my neck and those little bits of energy that transferred between us run through my mind. I run a finger through the wetness at my opening. I don't question why it's his rough fingers I'm picturing. I trail a slow glide of my arousal over my clit that's already sensitive and begging for more.

Teasing myself for a moment more, I make sure there is enough moisture around for the flower petals of my toy to form a nice seal when I turn it on.

The toy is still a little bit cool when I place it over me. The stark difference feels good. *So damn good.*

"Just this once," I repeat, pressing the button for the first setting. It immediately hums to life and I shudder at the soft sucking sensation. "It doesn't have to mean anything," I say to no one in my empty room.

The first setting is not nearly enough to get me there. I grab onto my nipple over the soft bra I'm wearing. Gently rolling the peak.

Third setting it is. I need to get there and get there fast.

I want to reach that climax. Maybe if I come with my senses on such high alert, I'll be able to shake this persistent ache in my body.

My pussy clenches on nothing and I consider getting another toy, but decide I'm close enough to just use my fingers. I slowly pump them in and out of myself all the while still imagining it's his fingers. Mine are much smaller than his so I work up to three, all rubbing the top of my channel until I get to that spot I'm searching for.

Yes.

I'm so close. I'm—

"Ant," I pant as I crest the edge of my high.

The front door closes and I freeze.

"D? I left my jacket and I didn't want to... D?" He must have noticed that I'm not in the kitchen anymore.

Shit! *Mierda.* Shiiiit.

I throw the rose onto my bed and search for the leggings I hastily threw across the room. I try to hop my fastest into each leg. I curse again, finally getting them up over my ass by the time Ant rounds the corner and is standing in my doorway.

"Ant..."

He looks me over and his eyebrows lift. I think about how I must look right now. Half crazed, cheeks flushed. Lord only knows what my hair looks like right now.

He looks to the right, behind me, and God I wish he was not seeing what he's seeing right now. "Is that a treasure chest of dildos?"

# Chapter 15

## Tony

I WAS ONLY A few minutes from Drea's house when I realized I left my coat. It tends to get a little warmer when the sun is up and shining in December. But it would be brutal to go without a coat and this is the only one that I work in. No use in dirtying up a perfectly nice one when I could just turn around to get my other one.

Mack called me to come onto the property since we had another two areas of the fence that had been demolished by who knows what. We suspected that it might be mountain lions but this kind of damage makes me think elk are trying to pass through and got into a scuffle with another group of 'em. Could be a territory thing. Again, who knows? Either way, I need to be there to document as this is a recurring thing.

After what was happening between us, I didn't want to leave Drea's kitchen to deal with that shit. But, I need my coat and it'll be easier to get it now rather than later.

Now, I stand in Drea's doorway seeing something I very well should not be. In the chest behind her are sex toys of all sorts. Some I recognize and some I've never seen before.

Her chin tilts indignantly as she tries to fake the bravado against her... embarrassment? I can't tell. She looks that way or maybe...

My eyes flick to the bed. It looks like she was just lying on it. Drea is insistent on making her bed up every morning, so the disheveled appearance is a dead giveaway. If it weren't, the little pink toy still lying on her bed should be.

I look her up and down.

Damn. *I should not be seeing this.*

Why me and why now?

My mind is racing with images of her using any number of those toys on herself in this bed. There's one that I know is a rabbit on top of the pile in her chest. I can easily picture laying her back on the bed, spreading her thick thighs to tease her with the purple dildo. She would squeeze my head between her legs before I gave her any relief, thrusting it in and out of her...

Damn.

*I should not be seeing this.*

I can't do anything from those thoughts right now that would be appropriate. I wish I could but I can't. To say I wasn't already sporting a half chub when she sucked my finger into her mouth and moaned earlier, would be a lie. Though I'm pissed Mack called me, I'm thankful because I don't know what would be happening right now if I hadn't.

Steph. I have to think about her and the commitment I made.

I turn and start walking toward the front door again without a word.

Drea stops me with a hand on my forearm. "Anthony, don't leave."

"I have to." I shake my head, stepping out of her grasp. "You were saying my name and I thought..." I lock eyes with her. "Why were you saying my name?" It comes out accusatory. It shouldn't have but then again, it should.

She flushes a deeper red and shakes her head. "I don't know."

"You do." I grit my teeth. Balling my fist to stop from grabbing her and doing any number of the things I've thought about from a few minutes ago.

"Just forget about that. It was a lapse... in judgment. I've just been frustrated and it was—"

"It was what?"

"It was nothing. I'm sorry you heard that."

I'm not. I won't be able to let this go. "Why were you saying my name?" I shake my head again. Everything is jumbling up inside it. "Not saying, you cried out *my name*. Is there some other Ant you know?"

She looks down at her feet. Her little pink toes wiggling, uncomfortable with my line of questioning. "I don't know."

I nod my head. "Fine." I walk away again and this time she doesn't stop me. I have to get out of here before I do something incredibly stupid.

Swiping my coat from the kitchen table, I slam the door and stomp over to my truck.

The whole drive to the Ranch is a blur as my mind races. Flicking back and forth between the intense longing I've felt for her and reprimanding myself for thinking about another woman coming on my dick when I have a girlfriend.

I have someone, who I can be with, who chooses me.

How could she fuck my head up when I was finally able to get space from my disappointment in our potential?

Weeks that have been hard to stay apart from her. Weeks of wishing everything would be the same when it's not. It can't be.

*I made a choice.*

I park at Mason's and get Daisy ready to ride over to check on what's happening with the fencing. I'm on autopilot. Going through the motions until these guys have what they need from me so I can get back home.

What am I going to do? I need to figure this shit out. I can't keep getting caught up in her.

That's what I am. Caught up. She has a hold over me that I can't shake no matter what I do. All I wanted was to be with her. She didn't.

Said she didn't.

And I believed her.

But then she calls out my name when she's coming?

Why?

# CHAPTER 16

## Tony, Four Years Ago

"IT'S NOT TOO LATE to come back to the boot and be the man Pa wanted. We all have a responsibility to the name and you know better than most what that entails."

I look at my brother and wonder, not for the first time, how we ended up so different. Blue's loyalty has only grown deeper and I know he's been more thoroughly integrated into that life.

I'm glad I got out while I could.

"I'm not telling you that what I'm doing is better than what you're doing with your life. I'm not even telling you to stop doing it. That life is just not for me, guy. What you do is yours, what I'm doing is mine. I like it here."

He scoffs. "It's even more bum-fuck than Clayton. You're doing every-thing Pa worked so hard for us not to do."

"I'm aware," I grumble.

"Are you? He's rolling in the grave right now. You gave up on him. Just think of how this move could be good for us. There's so many opportunities with how legislation is just giving y'all the right to make everything Pa sacrificed for easier than ever."

"Nah, man. Don't start."

I drive us down the road to the house I've been renting on the edge of Mason Ranch. The Masons have been good to me and when they said this house was being built here, I was first in line to plant roots. Best decision I ever made.

We drive down the dirt road until I see the curve of a delicious ass just before the gorgeous face of someone I recognize pops up from under the hood.

Drea.

Her car has an alarming amount of smoke coming from the hood and I pull over immediately.

My brother hisses in the passenger seat. "Damn. She's a fucking sight."

"No," I tell my brother, unbuckling my seatbelt and letting myself out of the car.

"Lock that shit down brother, or somebody else will," he says before I close the door in his face.

Drea startles immediately. She wasn't paying any attention to her surroundings when she let the hood down.

"Thank God." My smile comes easily at her proclamation. I will be her savior if need be. "It's just you," she says, dusting her hands on the back of her jeans. Her deliciously thick hips sway as she walks past me to the driver's side again. I try my best to pick up my jaw and say something that doesn't give away how her words cut me even though they shouldn't.

*Just me?* I roll my eyes internally. We're *besties* now.

"You having some car trouble?" Obviously. Do better, big man.

Blue's chuckle is audible from where he leans on my truck, watching the exchange. I regret agreeing to let him visit me more than ever right now.

"I don't know what happened. It was running just fine... until it wasn't." I look at the beater and it's more than apparent that this hunk of junk was on its last leg before she must have gotten it. I've seen it parked on the Ranch plenty of times to know that. The crumbling paint and missing car make letters are a dead giveaway.

"Uh-huh," I say, scratching my chin. She walks around to the back passenger door and her little girl hops out of the car. Her little ponytails bounce as she comes toward me.

Or so I thought.

My dog barks from the back seat and I see her head poke out to lick the little girl's hand. Drea scrunches her face up at the thorough cleaning her daughter is getting but I cough to cover my laugh at her expression. Blue opens the back door for the little girl to hop into my back seat. "You need a ride or do you have someone on the way already?"

"I don't have anyone on the way. I... Would you mind taking me somewhere and then somewhere else?"

"Yea..." I should have probably asked where before I agreed, but I don't.

She twists a ring on her finger. "I can give you gas money or something."

"Your money's no good. Just get her seat and I'll get you where you need to go."

She eyes me for a bit, ready to argue about how independent she is and doesn't need help. I'm thankful her daughter distracts her before she can. "Mama look at this! Milli has a gold chain. She's a fancy lady."

I got a dog shortly after moving to Alpenglow Ridge. It was lonely in this small town and I honestly had no intention of making more friends. I just wanted to have someone to hang out with when I wasn't working. Milli's big brown eyes stole my heart easily. Years later and she's with me more times than not.

Drea's eyebrows lift. "Okay, honey. Maybe don't stick your hand in her mouth anymore."

The little one agrees and I'm already over to Drea's backseat unclipping the booster seat and putting it into my truck. Blue gives me a look and I tell him to fuck off with my eyes alone. Some odd feeling rushes me at seeing the pink little seat in my truck. An even more odd feeling assaults me when Mireya sits in it and Milli plops her big head onto the little girl's lap.

I don't get time to revel in that new sensation when Blue moves my dog bodily to make room for himself on the bench.

Don't like that picture very much.

"You didn't have to do that. I can sit back there with her." Drea says from outside the passenger door.

"Nah. You're good." She doesn't argue further, but Blue gives me another knowing look in the rearview mirror. I don't like how smug he looks either.

Originally, I was not enticed by the women who hang around the Ranch because most of them are Reese's age. In my mind, I can only see her as the little teenage girl with a crush that I had to set straight when I first got to town. That would be all well and fine until her friends started hanging around more when she came back home. My eye caught on her stunning friend who was always nose deep in a book with something that looked good as fuck on the cover.

When Quincy opened his bar in town, she was one of the first to become a bartender there. I remember that one night when I was the last guy at the bar. She introduced herself even though I already knew of her and we became *besties*, as she says.  It became a routine of mine to go after work and make sure she made it to her car safely after that point. Any time I got to see her was a plus, but sometimes she would make something just for me to take home, knowing I'd be there for her shift.

When I tasted the food she made, I couldn't get enough.

She brought a double chocolate cake for Reese's birthday at the Ranch and I struggled not to moan when I took a bite. Chandie Mason, Reese's Mom, was an amazing cook. She was always feeding the people who worked on her land, but she could not hold a candle to what Drea could do with desserts. Reese had one slice and said she couldn't eat it all so the rest of us could finish it. I watched each slice disappear with the kind of hurt in my heart that made no sense. Fuck if I didn't want to deck every one of those ungrateful dudes who stuffed their mouths with it. It was just cake. You could buy it at any grocery store. It wasn't a rare commodity or something, right?

Wrong.

It has gotten to the point that if I ever see her walking toward the main house carrying something that even resembles a food container, I haul ass to get there before the vultures descend. I may not get to eat all of it, but I get the biggest portion of it. Everyone knows how obsessed I am with her food. It's no secret. But my admiration for the woman runs deeper than just food now that I've spent so much of my free time with her. Only made more intense by the fact that I hadn't touched another woman since I agreed to this pact with her. I haven't even wanted to spend my free time pursuing anyone else if I can spend that time with Drea instead.

"Where to first?" I ask.

She winces and I turn to her fully. "Harmony Hill."

My eyebrows rise. "For?"

"Mireya's Dad lives there. It's actually his weekend and he's having this thing at his house. I said I would stay with her until it's over." She looks over to me expecting me to make some excuse for why I can't take her or some shit. She hates asking people for anything. The bronze glint of her eyes cracks something in my chest because she should know by now that I've got her. Her hand brushes mine before she grabs it more firmly. "Don't feel like you have to stay. I'll find another way home. I know you didn't plan to be anyone's knight in shining armor today." *What did I tell you?*

Knight in shining armor? That—I am not. Either way, I tell her, "It's no big deal. I'm off this weekend. Blue's just here without shit better to do. Right?"

He looks up from his phone, "Yea. What he said." By the tone of his voice, I know he isn't exactly happy about the turn of events, but I don't give a fuck. Drea needs me.

Turning to look into the backseat, she says. "Sorry. I don't think we were actually properly introduced. I'm Drea. That's my daughter, Mireya."

"Blue. Like the color. That one's older, better, brother."

She lets go of my hand and the coldness that surges in her absence is acute. "I figured. You two are kinda like twins." She shakes his hand awkwardly over the seat. Why is this so fucking upsetting? "Jury's out on the better brother business though. Ant is pretty great."

I inwardly preen at her assessment but Blue just chuffs, focused on his phone.

She gives me the address and I arrive at a house surrounded by cars. Noticing how I take stock of the many vehicles, she informs me "I would say that they're Colton's friends, but I think goons is the more accurate term." Blue steps up behind me with Milli in tow. He pats his back to show me that he is carrying his piece and I cringe. We look intimidating as hell walking up to the door. Both 6'5" and big men by any standard.

With the two of us standing in front of the door, the man who opens it freezes. Should have seen that coming, it would put anyone on high alert. He calls for Colton and it's only then that Drea pushes between the two of us blocking her from sight. Her little hand brands my side, but the guy visibly relaxes when he sees someone familiar.

Colton comes to the door anyway. He pats her arm and I tense, ready to maul him. "I've got Aaron on his way to wait with your car for the tow. You should have gotten rid of that thing years ago."

"You didn't have to do that. Call Aaron and tell him to turn around." I like the firmness in her voice with this guy. I don't know how I went from longing from a friendly distance to standing between her and her ex. Well, I don't actually know if they had ever dated, but she certainly has a kid with him. Something had to be going on there even though she doesn't talk about him with me. I admire how she handles this situation though it is nowhere near ideal.

He shrugs, "It's done." She bristles and I place a hand on her shoulder. It's then that Colton finally acknowledges my brother and me. "Who are these guys?" He points to us behind her. "What? You doing some poly thing now? One wasn't enough, huh?"

Blue laughs and enters the house. "Good luck," he says, walking right by Colton. Mireya follows him into the house with the dog.

"Hey." I step up to him, dwarfing his shorter stature.

That heat from her touch returns when Drea puts a hand on my back. It's light, but there. I turn to her and she looks up at me. I don't miss how she's silently telling me to leave it alone. I ignore it, turning back to the boy in front of me. Who does this guy think he is?

"I don't want to hear that kind of shit from your mouth. Don't like what you're implying. You won't disrespect her like that." He takes a step away from me. "Name's Tony. That's Blue. We brought Drea and Mireya here after we found her stranded on the side of the road today." I cross my arms. "Why is it that you couldn't pick your own daughter up for *your* visitation? You could send whoever the hell Aaron is, but it's not you to go get your daughter when she needs you?" I spit to the side of me. "Don't like what she's driving? Fix it. Don't like the methods she had to use to get from point A to point B, then you should have been there, to begin with."

His brows bunch as he blinks a few times. Then a smile breaks out over his face. "Heard," he says. "I like him, D." Stepping to the side, he lets us in unobstructed.

WE SIT IN THE grass away from whatever is going on inside the house. I can see through the big sliding glass door that Blue has found Colton and they talk away from the others. There are only two reasons that Blue talks to anyone for that long.

Sex and business.

And I don't think Colton has the parts desired for the other things Blue wants.

"One year and what have we learned?" Drea asks, distracting me from my scowling.

*That I want to be besties about as much as I want to stub my toe every time I enter a room.* "Happier," I respond instead.

"Yea?" She asks, eyebrows raising with hope written over her features.

"Yea. Gotta admit that I wasn't chasing women like you seem to think all men are. But I don't have those hangers-on who just want to ride a cowboy."

She blushes in the most adorable way, speaking around a giggle. "Ride a cowboy?"

"You know the ones," I confirm.

She blushes harder. "Yea. I know the ones. Is that really all that's changed? What about dating?"

"For what? I work, come to the bar, hang out til you get off, and go home to pass out. When would I date?"

Drea pulls at some grass in front of her, twisting the strands and then letting them float off in the breeze. "I guess that makes sense. But you said you were happier?"

"Yea…" I hedge, but not much. "Are you?"

She looks at me, and I'm blinded by how she beams. "I am. I've been on a few dates but nothing to write home about. I like spending more time with my friends and fostering those relationships more."

"See, happier."

Nodding, she says, "You don't have to keep the pact going, you know? I'd understand if you wanna… You know…" She wiggles her eyebrows.

"Nah. I'm in this."

"Good. Me too." She smiles. I shouldn't take it to mean more than it does but I do. I trust that she will see that I'm here for her. That I have her. The last thing I want to do is push her into something that she's not ready for. I'm old enough to know that an independent woman has to want it for herself. No matter what it is.

"So how long do you plan on staying here, playing babysitter?" I ask, tone wry.

Mireya plays in the yard with Milli. She tosses a ball around with her. Milli loves little kids and it looks like Mireya loves her too. They're fast friends.

"Until it seems like things are calming down. It looks about that way now." I take a look at what she's seeing and it's a lot less busy. There are fewer men that I can see in the house and the cars lining the street are far fewer.

"I gotta admit, I don't like the idea of you being here by yourself. What would you have done if I hadn't been driving by?"

"I would have been fine, Ant." She's still the only person who calls me that nickname. I can't say that I mind having a name that only she calls me. Well, now her kid too. "None of these guys will give me any trouble while Colton is here, especially with Mireya around."

I frown, throwing the ball that's rolled over to me far and wide for Milli. She bounds after it and Mireya is right behind her, giggling. "I like it even less now."

"It's fine. Colton's always been like that. Twenty guys hanging around is no new thing. It was less when we first got together. Nothing to worry about now."

I glance over to my brother, who is still talking to her ex. There is no indication that Drea knows anything about what that could mean. I'm not certain she even understands why all these men are here. If I know my brother, he's working hard on getting Colton into the fold. My family's business is built on the model of expansion. With twenty guys already under Colton's wing, I can only imagine how the dollar signs are popping out in bold font for Blue.

There's nothing else I can or want to say about her assumption of the situation. Blue came here with a mission that I refused to help him in. It looks like he might have achieved that goal anyway. I stand from the grass, dusting the dirt off me. I hold a hand out for Drea and she takes it. "We should probably get on the road since it's getting late."

The lab and the kid are a-ways away so I call out to them. "Come on M&M. You need to get ready for bed and I've gotta take your Mom back home."

They both trot over and Drea talks to her daughter before we all re-enter the house. Drea crouches, kissing Mireya's forehead and they hug for a bit before Colton makes his way over to us. There is just something about this guy that I don't like. Maybe it's because I know he's been with Drea, but I think it's more than that.

"Come little ray of sunshine. It's bath time," Drea says, and Mireya pouts, rubbing my dog a few times.

"Goodbye, Ant," Mireya tells me before hugging my leg. "Thank you for bringing me to my Dad's house and letting me play with Milli."

I pat her little shoulder before she lets go of my leg. She is a miniature version of Drea in every way. They have the same face and striking amber eyes. Mireya hugs my dog a final time before walking down the hallway with her Dad.

Drea finally stands from her crouch and crosses her arms. Her full chest is pressed up by the gesture and I don't miss it. Nor do I miss how misty her eyes look. I can't help but put my arm around her shoulders, rubbing her shoulder. "We should go," she says. She doesn't shrug out of my arms and I take that as a win.

I nod, "Yea, we should."

# CHAPTER 17

# Drea

Why me?

Why am I the only person alive who can be simultaneously too uptight and too horny? I kick the lid to my trunk closed and slide it back under the bed where it belongs.

I flop into the bed face first, wishing it could swallow me whole. I'm so embarrassed. Not only with what I did but the fact that Ant immediately caught me.

*Mierda.* Shit.

The rose pokes into my side uncomfortably and I huff and kick into the bed, realizing that he must have seen it too.

Shiiit. *What am I doing?*

I lie on the bed for as long as I can stand it before I hear the front door opening again.

"Mama?" Mireya calls and I slide off, putting the toy into my night-stand drawer. As much as I wish I wasn't, I will definitely be revisiting it later tonight. This time in the safety of my shower.

Walking out to the kitchen, my daughter is already devouring one of the cream puffs with no remorse. "Can I have one of these?"

"Think it's a little late for that, honey. You're already having one." Using a kitchen towel, I wipe some of the filling from her cheek. "How was practice?"

"It was good. Aunt Mel said that she couldn't stay because she needed to pick up Uncle Ty from the airport. She says hi though."

I nod and send Mel a quick thank you via text before turning back to my daughter. "Are you feeling ready for the recital?"

"As I'll ever be. I got a seat for you and Ant to be next to the Mason-Whitfields." She nods and then laughs. "It's gonna be my whole family in the second row if everyone shows up."

Something in my heart warms when she says that. If you had asked me what motherhood would be like when I was still pregnant with Mireya, I would have had a very different answer than the reality of what I have now.

I never wanted her to feel like she was missing anything with me being on my own. But I'm not. An abundance of love and support surrounds her. There are so many people in our lives who are more to her than just my friends—they're her family and mine.

Mireya has learned that family is more than just blood.

My eyes sting with the pride I feel and the gratitude I have for my amazing daughter. I place a hand on my chest, attempting to revel in this moment.

"You okay, Ma?" She grabs the hand at my side and squeezes. I squeeze her back.

I blink a few times, clearing my throat. "I love you. You know that right?"

She laughs and picks the puff up again. "And I love you." She takes a bite and chews while I try my best to remember her at this moment. She narrows her eyes at me. "You're not gonna start crying, are you?"

"No..." I start wiping up the bits of sugar falling from her snack on the counter. "A Mom can be emotional about her baby."

"I'm not a baby."

"I know. You're so grown up and I'm proud of you is all. You make me so happy to be your Mom." The words are watery by the end and I'm blinking hard.

"Ant will be there so at least you'll have someone's hand to hold when you cry at the recital." The mention of him again, or maybe it's just how emotional I've become, makes me think back to how he left earlier. I know that won't keep him from showing up for Mireya, but I hope things won't be too awkward between us. He didn't actually see me doing anything...

That's another problem for a different day, so I change the subject. "How about we go see grandma and 'buelo? Up for it?"

"Sure, let me just go shower and change."

<hr>

I PARK RIGHT OUTSIDE of the luxury new builds that house only seniors. And I don't mean the high school kind. My Mom and Papi are currently living in the Maple Grove Assisted Living Community just between Alpenglow Ridge and Harmony Hill and loving it.

When Mom approached me about moving out of my childhood home, and the house I now own, I didn't know what to say. You never expect that your parents will ever get older as you are, but I guess mine are a special case. When Denise and Luis Montoya adopted me from my birth mother, they were already forty-seven and fifty-two, respectively. I don't remember much of that time since I was only three years old, but this town never let me forget just how unfit my mother was.

I'd get pitying glances every now and again until I started to show with my own pregnancy at seventeen. That's when the hushed whispers became more pointed and only recently have I been able to move out of the vitriol that gossip can spread faster than a wildfire. And Colorado has been known to struggle with several of those in the past few years.

I think that's why Tony started going to the grocery store and running errands with me, even when I knew that he was dead on his feet from riding all day or wrangling all evening. Less and less people had negative opinions when they thought a man was coming in to complete me and my family.

That's where they're wrong. Mireya and I are a family with or without a man in our house. Family has no set number or look. Besides, blood is no thicker than water in terms of support and familial loyalty and love. I've been blessed with so many in my life who have shown me that. Whether I have one kid or none, a range of skin tones in my clan or we all look the exact same, I shouldn't be held responsible for the faults of a mother I've never even known.

My birth mother disappeared shortly after I was adopted and no one has seen her since. I have no idea who my birth father even is.

As far as I'm concerned Denise and Luis are the only parents I've known and that I acknowledge. With my light brown skin and silky hair, I very well could be their daughter. People who don't know our history, assume that I am their biological daughter. I don't really know what my true heritage is, a mix of this and a bit of that. My birth mother was Afro-Latina from what my Mom has told me.

All I do know is family is what you make it. And I will never forget all the things that my family has given me.

I knock once on the condo door that reads "417" and open it with the key I have.

"Mom? Papi?" I call into the house to further announce myself.

I said they were older... not dead. I've learned the hard way that multiple announcements are necessary for a couple who still loves each other this much... especially after my Papi's hip replacement. I've also been scolded that *family* doesn't knock.

Quite the conundrum.

Their small chihuahua mix comes barreling into the entryway, skidding and sliding on the laminate flooring when Mireya calls for him. "Quito, slow down!" She says, scooping up the dog and dropping her bag on their front table. Taquito is blind in one eye and thus his depth perception is not the greatest. He has hurt himself many times out of excitement for my daughter. Mireya has such a way with animals everywhere she goes. I don't understand it, but I love it about her.

We meander around through the living room and kitchen before we see the puff of my Mom's fluffy white hair poking over the patio chairs in the back. As soon as she hears the slide of the door, she gets up to greet me. She hugs me close to her and then goes for Mireya and Quito next, who circles around Mireya's feet with his little bone, waiting for her to play with him.

My daughter obliges the little animal and then it's me and my parents on the patio. I pull out one of the extra chairs after hugging my Papi. Before I have a chance to sit, my Mom asks, "Oh baby, what's wrong?"

I jerk back, incredulous. "There's nothing wrong."

"And the sky is green today. Don't lie to your Mom. It'll send you straight to hell."

I shake my head and smirk at the ridiculous line my Mom always used on me as a teenager. Her brown face is only slightly creased from years of smiling and not taking herself too seriously. The only sign of her true age is the curly white afro she wears with a colorful scarf tied around the edges. "You know that line doesn't work on me anymore."

"It's worth a shot. Does it have to do with this new girlfriend Tony has?"

Now, I really am shocked. "How do you know about that?"

"How would I not know? What did I tell you, Andrea?"

I roll my eyes, but she continues to wait for my response. With a sigh, I monotone, "Scoop that one up before he's gone."

"And did you listen?"

"Mom. That's my friend. Plus I think the girls already beat you to this conversation."

"Oh did they?" She smiles to herself, a fact I'm sure she already knew as well. "So what happened there? What's she look like?"

"What does it matter what she looks like?"

"Because if she's not pretty, then *my daughter* might still be able to salvage this."

"What does pretty have to do with being in a relationship?"

"Everything, baby. You got all the blessings one could bestow in that department. You can thank me and Papi for that." She bumps into me and I laugh with her. My Papi still lounges, soaking in the temperate weather of Fall. Their patio has a great view of the mountains and trees on the other side of the building. They're all turned warm colors of the season and I love how the leaves still rustle in the breeze blowing softly.

"Would that have made you happy? If I was coming here to tell you that I was in a relationship?"

"Not if that's the reason." My mom looks affronted. "I—We—just want you to be happy. You and Ant are good together. I just don't want you to miss out on a good thing."

Papi reaches over to me to squeeze my hand. "A man who loves your daughter as much as he loves yours is a rare thing, mija. A man who is willing to wait for you is even more special." My Papi's light brown skin is also creased with how happy he has been in life. The two streaks of silver in his salt and pepper hair make him look distinguished and polished. My parents are such a beautiful couple. My standards are likely too high because of them.

Holding his hand was always a source of strength for me and I think it's where I got the habit from. His hand still feels strong in mine and I give it a squeeze back.

"We're friends. He's not waiting for me. He's there for us because he's our family in that way."

"Ah. But we see how he treats you and how he treats your friends. If you wanted, he could be more than your friend."

I wave him off. "Papi, I'm good. He's with his new lady and I'm happy for him."

"Okay, but is she cute?" Mom chimes in again.

"Will you stop?"

"She is," Mom gasps. "Looks aren't everything! You could still fix this."

I stand from the patio chair, just about done with part two of this intervention Clo, Reese, and Mel started. "Alright. How about we get started on dinner?"

She allows me to change the subject and we leave Papi on the patio with Mireya and Quito.

"So, Mireya will be staying with us for Christmas?" She asks after searching for her pots. The large heavy soup pot clangs on her stove top followed by a smaller sauce pot.

"Yes. She asked to spend it with Colton, but I would just feel more comfortable for her to spend most of the time I'm gone with you two." I cut bell peppers next to my Mom as she measures out seasonings.

We work in tandem as I cut more veggies and she measures out rice and caldo de pollo into the sauce pot. "That boy was the biggest disappointment. Lydia is such a sweet lady. Never thought her son would be so... uninspiring."

"Colton has his strengths and weaknesses. We were young."

"So what? He's barely around now. It takes two to make a baby and somehow you are carrying most of the weight." Her truth rings true in my mind. Colton was never a good partner for me, that much is obvious to me now.

"Mom, I won't trash talk him. We both know who he is. Besides, he seemed happy to spend the holiday with her. Maybe it's a turning point. And he got me this event. That counts for something."

"I guarantee you that it serves him more than it serves you. He looks good with you showing up and showing out like only Montoyas can."

I just chuckle and shake my head at her. I slide the veggies I've cut up into the soup pot and my Mom is right behind me seasoning the mixture.

"Well, I won't turn him away if he shows up, but can't stay long."

I nod, even though it frustrates me that they give him a hard time. I have my issues with him but that's that. They're my own issues and I hope that my Mom isn't sharing her opinions of Mireya's father with her. "He'll just be by to pick her up. He's going to stay in their cabin until New Year's. I still think it's a good idea for them."

"Are you going to have some fun with Mireya taken care of?" She nudges me and I pretend not to be worried about the time away from my daughter.

"Probably not. I'm going to be so busy, I'll likely sleep through Christmas."

"Agh. Tell me that's not how you're really going to spend the holiday."

I shrug, washing my hands in the sink behind us. "Rest is a treat that I think I deserve, Mom."

"Sure, sure." She gives me a look and I know she's going to say something I won't like next. "Maybe Tony is also going to be alone on Christmas. You should check on that."

I grimace. "Mom!"

# CHAPTER 18

## Drea

CAN I BE THE only one who stresses about being good enough to do it all? And by it all, I mean just functioning.

It's my day off and I should, by all means, be cleaning my house, or I don't know, relaxing. But something is pressing into my frontal cortex like a hot poker. I know I should be worrying about something...

Possibilities are endless, so I take a deep breath as I lay my head back on the headrest outside of Drip and Whip.

First priority, Mireya. She is at rehearsals. I just dropped her off. Recital is coming up, I've notified everyone who matters.

Second priority, me. I had breakfast. I'm stressing but that is an *in-progress* thing.

Third priority, friends and family. All are healthy and fine. Just talked to Reese about her potential outfits for the aforementioned recital on FaceTime. Which turned into a three-way FaceTime to include Clo, so they both could pick out what I was wearing to my daughter's recital. I'm now expecting a couple of dresses they've agreed on to be delivered tomorrow. Mel and Ty are wrapped up in each other since he's home from the tour. And I just saw my parents, so they are also good. Ant... Still awkwardly keeping interactions limited after the whole treasure chest and crying his name in ecstasy thing...

*Moving on before my face burns any hotter with embarrassment.*

Fourth priority, work... Then it hits me. Schedules went out today. I hurry from my van into the building and to my office. It's not huge, but the two wood desks sit in caddy corner amongst a filing cabinet and a few cork boards on the walls that have the newest recipes, procedures, and the like. Wasting no time, I log onto my computer and pull up the program I use for scheduling. The breath that whooshes out of me fogs the screen momentarily.

*Found the source of my stress.*

I look at the schedule for the fourth time. Each time I check it over, there seems to be less and less people on it. Thankfully, I have my regular staff working their hours as decided for the front to serve coffee and sell food. I thought I would be fine giving half the bakers the time off right before Christmas with only Kristy and Tarah on the schedule for prep on the twenty-third.

I don't know what I was thinking. We'll still be open that day and we need to have fresh-baked menu items available. Even if I designate Kristy to focus on that, it still leaves me with just one baker to help me with the prep for the Christmas retreat.

If this were a smaller-scale event, it would be fine.

But it's not and right now I'm screwed.

Martin knocks on my office door and I tell him to come in. He takes one look at me and steps into the office, closing the door behind him. "What happened?"

"Nothing," I say with as much calm as I can.

"Okay... I haven't known you for long, but this looks like a 'we should collectively panic' face."

I sigh, letting my shoulders slump with the weight of the realization I made. "I think I'll be understaffed for the Christmas retreat."

"You think? Or you know?"

"Pretty sure I know. If I honor everyone's time off requests, then I'll still be short."

"So figure out who is not getting that time off. You're not even supposed to be here today. It says very clearly on your schedule that you're not."

"It's not that simple. And I don't want to be that kind of boss who just lets things be chaotic. I'm already disappointing some people because I didn't give them the full-time they requested. Eric totally let everyone do what they wanted. If anyone has questions, I want to be available to them."

He fixes me with a look. "Drea, if you need people to work this event, you need them. You never said everyone would get the time off. It's not like you're asking them to work the holiday. Our scheduling is already more generous than most places."

I know what he's saying is true, but I can't help but think about when I wanted more time off to spend with Mireya during the holidays. I was running myself thin.

*I'm still running myself thin.*

"I'll figure it out."

"Do you want me to tell whoever it is that you need them to come in?"

"No," I let my face drop into my hands. "I'm going to do whatever needs to be done. I can work something out. Finding common ground is my strong suit. This will be a piece of cake."

"If you say so..." Martin drops his bag on the filing unit behind the desk and rolls me in my chair out of the main desk. "I do actually have reports to get to today so I'm gonna need you to trade desks with me."

"You're right," I say. "I'll just bang my head on this one instead."

He chuckles at my joke but adds, "I will be the big bad, just remember that."

I'm grateful for Martin being here and giving me options. That's something I didn't have before. Work or be without, that was my reality. Kind of feels like I'm walking back into that hole again.

It's important to me that I create an environment that doesn't make my staff feel the same. If I can do it myself and allow them to have a relaxing holiday, then it's worth it. Mireya will be with my parents and then with Colton, so I have the time.

I spend the rest of the morning planning out the strategy for preparing the dessert menu for the Christmas Retreat. It's somewhat calming to lose myself in the possibilities of what I'll serve. Holiday desserts can be whimsy and fun. This is the best part outside of actually baking, dreaming up the desserts, and planning how to make them efficiently.

Time flies and I'm still in my head when a hand presses on my shoulder. Martin is there, ushering me out of the office for real this time. I go and pick my daughter up and head home. I'm cycling over and over again through how I can make this event go off smoothly.

I miss how often my best friend would talk me off the ledge. I knew that he was there for me but it was more than that. I had not realized how much he really did keep me sane. I told him about how much I wanted from life and he never made me feel silly. To me, starting this business was always the goal. I *always* had this goal. When I worked the bar and took outside gigs on top of getting Mireya right with school and trying to keep her busy with activities that she enjoyed, it was a lot but guess who was there to help me?

Ant.

I didn't have to ask him most times either. He showed up for me and at some point, I just assumed he would always be there.

Walking into my home that's missing the friend I was just thinking about on the drive here, I hang my purse on the empty hook where his hat should go.

Mireya lies across the couch, compelled by the documentary she put on and I'm only partially aware of what we're watching. The gaping hole of where Ant should be is nagging at me more than this whole scheduling conflict.

Making everything all awkward with the cream puffs and then him walking in on me crying out his name seems pretty irredeemable. What was I thinking?

He has a girlfriend and I was the one who insisted that we just be friends in the first place. And now what? I think things will be different because maybe I wanted more from him than I have allowed myself to have.

That's what's happening, isn't it? If I hadn't stuck my foot in my mouth, then he would be here now, watching TV with us. Or if I hadn't insisted that my life was too hectic and too much for him, taking that next step of admitting that I like him as more than just a friend wouldn't have felt so outlandish and simultaneously hypocritical.

He might have a girlfriend, but I miss him. I can be respectful. I will be because I can't lose him. He's too important to me.

"Mama, just call him already."

I blink and look over at my daughter. "I wasn't..." I trail off instead of finishing the lie I was about to tell.

"You were and it's obvious. I miss him too."

My heart cracks a little bit and I wish my decisions weren't affecting Mireya like they clearly are. Did I expect he would be happy with no one in his life to fill that role forever? Did I truly think that I would be happy without a special someone myself? No. As made obvious from my failed relationships I have all but stopped since finding out about Steph.

My daughter reaches out and squeezes my hand. "Make the call, Mama. I'm gonna go get ready for bed." She clomps up the stairs to her room and I stare down at my phone.

Why does this feel so daunting?

Finding his name, my thumb hovers over the contact. I nearly drop my phone when a call comes through before I'm able to press that tiny phone icon.

A giddy smile stretches my cheeks and I answer, settling back into my couch cushions.

# CHAPTER 19

## Tony

MILLI PLOPS HER HEAD into my lap. Her big puppy dog eyes tell me everything I already know but need to hear again.

I wish I could say that I am doing better with more space between me and Drea. I wish that I could say that trying to fall for someone new was working.

Wishes are all they are.

I've got to man up and admit that I was wrong.

I was wrong to think that I could get her out of my head. Her breathy voice saying my name has played on a loop in my mind ever since I left her house.

As a grown man, I should be able to move on and just write it off as nothing like she said it was. But every moment where I'm not actively working, I'm thinking about it. The separation from her hurts like nothing else could. I miss her and still, I can't have her in the way that I want.

I need to call it.

I'm not ready to move on.

I want to have that time with her, even if it feels like torture to be so close to her and yet not close enough. I miss being there with her and her daughter so much. I feel frustrated sitting at my house alone when I could be there with them instead.

I could be mad at Blue, but I can't be. If he had not been the asshole to throw this wrench in my plans to move on then I wouldn't see now that someone new was not the solution.

Flicking to her contact, I press the call button before I lose my nerve.

"Hey, do you have a minute to talk?" I say when she picks up.

"Spare me the conversation. I get it." Steph says and I blink in surprise.

"You do?"

"You're a good person, Tony. I, honestly, wish you the best. If I were smarter, I would have broken things off when I saw you two in Alpenglow Ridge. We've been trying this long-distance thing and I know that you're unhappy. It's not because I'm not there either. I just think it's because I'm not her."

I curse, feeling like double the jackass. "I'm sorry. I didn't want to lead you on. I just..."

"Like I said, I get it. But can I give you some advice?"

"Am I gonna like it?" Rubbing a hand over my face, I wait for her response. "Maybe."

"I've been getting it unsolicited by the bucket load lately. 'Preciate you asking first at least."

"Don't fuck this up with her. I saw how she reacted to my presence. And everyone else did too. Kinda thought her friends might burn me at the stake for just being there."

"That's not—I wasn't... We aren't—"

"If us being together didn't ruin things too much, you might have a shot with her. I like her for you. Truly. She could make you happier than I could."

I let out a breath, heavy and exhausted. "She doesn't want me like that, Steph. I'm back to square one with or without you in my life."

"I think you never tried to get past square one. Give yourself some credit. I know a woman waiting when I see one."

"Steph, I'm sorry."

"It is what it is. I've gotta go. Friends?"

"Yea..."

"Great." She hangs up and I look at my phone.

A weight lifts from my chest as the status of my relationship crumbles.

I'm a single man again.

The first thing I want to do is talk to my friend about it.

"Hey," her voice comes onto the line and makes my heart race a little faster. She sounds happy and I don't want to bring up something that I know will upset her.

"Hey," I say back and feel how awkward things are between us now. What do I say back? Before I'd probably just tell her I was on my way to her house. But I don't know if that's a good idea or not now.

"What are you up to?" She asks at the same time I ask, "What you doing?"

We both laugh and I say, "You first."

"I was just lying on the couch. We were watching TV, but Mireya went upstairs. Her recital is tomorrow, you know?"

"Oh, I know. Talked to Cory earlier about what flowers I should bring for this kind of thing. We can't let those other moms outdo us." Reese's husband, Cory, has gained a bit of a reputation for being a flower snob. I've gotta admit that he does have an eye for this kind of thing. I was beyond relieved when he said he'd help me out the other day. He's dropping the arrangement off before they start getting ready for the recital.

"Right? Mel told me her parents used to bring a cowbell and like a whole sash with ribbons and such. Like a homecoming mum... I don't know, it's a big thing in Texas."

I chuckle, "I know what she's talking about. It must be something they only do in the South. We had those too for homecoming." Scratching my chin, I add, "I really don't think I have the time to do something like that. A big as fuck bouquet will have to do."

Now Drea laughs, "I'm sure if you had time you would." She trails off and I think again about going over there. "I miss you, you know?"

"Miss me?" My racing heart stubbornly picks up pace feeling relieved to hear the words. I'm going to need as much elaboration as I can get.

"Yea. I feel like you should be at the house right now." How does she know what I was thinking without me having to say it? This desire to be close to her isn't one-sided.

"Me too," I say. "Life's been different for both of us… You know I'll always be here for you. Right?"

There's a moment of silence on the line before she replies. "I know, Ant. I'll always be here for you too."

---

I SHOW UP TO Mireya's recital just in time to miss the pomp and introductions. I'm definitely not here for all that. Ballet and theaters are not my scene. Who knew that I'd be in a fancy ass theater watching Mireya perform? If it weren't for the teenage girl who told me, not asked me, to be here—I would have just caught them for the celebration afterward. My tardiness will just have to be excused.

The spot next to Drea is open and I do my best not to disturb the other people there for the show. Unfortunately, I'm six foot five and well past big man status, so there is no way I'm going to sneak to the middle of the second row without disturbing anyone. From the looks of it, it's only people I already know in this whole row so they don't give me any flack besides a few quick *hi, heys.*

Drea's lopsided smile meets me when I squeeze into the theater seat next to her. "I'm gonna have to find another way to trick you into being on time." She whispers.

She moves her arm from the armrest and my shoulders are still encroaching on her seat and Chloe's next to me. I settle at an angle to try and take up less room. Finally, I give up on that and put an arm over the back of Drea's seat to split the difference in how tiny these seats are.

"Your trick didn't work because she gave me the invitation." Lowering my voice and leaning into her ear, I add, "An hour earlier than the recital was wild, even for you, D."

Drea pulls her chestnut waves to one side and leans against my arm. Her dress shimmers in the low light as she puts her arm back on our shared armrest. The vanilla and cinnamon scent of her hits me and I breathe a sigh of relief. "And it still didn't work. You missed the young kids. They were so cute."

I am a little bit upset that I missed the little kids. Would have either been hilarious to see them trying or impressive to see them pull off the choreography. I'll have to ask someone about that later. "I only came here to see one special girl dance her heart out."

"She was so nervous. The boys are all here." Drea gestures with a head tilt down to her left at Reese's three boys who are on the other side of Reese and her husband. He catches my look and waves. What a dork, but he's good people. I nod back at him.

There's hushed whispering all through the audience while the curtains are still closed. My eyes zero in on the pendant she's wearing that glints above her ample cleavage while they prepare for, what I'm guessing is, the next performance. The soft slope of her neck to her shoulder is bare. The tan knit fabric draped over one shoulder and off the shoulder entirely on the side pressed to my chest. It's then that I actually look at what she has on. The sweater dress hugs her body, showing each dip and curve. Her hips and thighs are pressed against the sides of the seat and I have to tear my eyes from them before I reach out and squeeze her closer to me, though only the divider of the armrest separates us. My mouth waters with the combination of her bronze skin and delicious smell. I shift to adjust myself as discreetly as possible. She doesn't know that I'm no longer dating Steph but that doesn't mean my brain isn't thinking about her toy chest or suggesting she show me which is her favorite.

Melody comes onto the stage in a pastel suit with a microphone clutched in her hand, giving me something else to pay attention to so I don't act on any of these thoughts I'm having right now. "We have our junior company performing next. Please hold your applause until the end of the performance and enjoy."

The music is slow, like a lullaby, but I don't recognize the music. Behind the dancers is a large white Christmas tree with big red candles all lit up. Large snowflake cutouts and fake snow decorate the back of the stage. It doesn't take long for me to spot the young girl I would recognize any-where. Her slicked-back hair makes it easy for me to see the focus in her amber-colored eyes. I know Drea finds her too, because she grabs ahold of my hand, shaking with anticipation and nerves. You'd think it was her up on the stage.

There is nothing to be nervous about because Mireya makes every move and keeps in time with the other dancers easily. Before I know it, the routine is done and we all get to clap and cheer for her. She makes me so proud. The kid has more talent than I do in my left thumb. From picking up everything I've taught her on the ranch to schooling me on earth-conscious choices, I'm always astounded by what she's capable of.

Much to my chagrin, there are four more performances to sit through after this one though. They aren't that bad, but I only pay attention to the ones where I can see Mireya is in them.

Once they're finally over and we give a final clap for the performers, I excuse myself from the mingling to run back to my car. Thankfully, the December chill has kept the bouquet I grabbed intact. When I return to the lobby where all the dancers are now exiting to join the audience members, I feel the arms wrap around me before I see the teenager in her sugar plum fairy outfit. I hug her back and make a big show of revealing the full bouquet from behind me.

"Oh my god! Ant this bouquet is bigger than I am!" She hefts the flowers over her shoulder exaggeratedly.

"You were amazing up there, Reya. I barely fell asleep," I joke.

She laughs, leaning into me for another hug. "I'm glad you came anyway," she deadpans, which is only made more comical by how fairy-like she is in the costume.

We talk about how long it took her to get into costume with her adding, "You won't believe how nervous Mama was just putting the wings into the back of the van. I don't think she was breathing."

"She was still a ball of nerves in the audience." I stretch out my fingers in emphasis.

"Yikes," she says, and another girl dressed like Mireya comes over to talk to her.

Something shimmers in my periphery, and I turn to see just what it is. I didn't have the full effect before, but now my jaw drops momentarily before I clench my teeth together. Drea and Chloe talk as they make their way over to where Mireya and I are waiting.

She looks like a goddess as the lights sparkle and dance off of the dress I'm getting to see in all its sinful glory. It must be new because I've never seen her in this before. She wears tall skinny heels that only amplify how sexy her legs are. I don't know what to look at first. Drea is stacked. Each layer from top to bottom, I want to eat and leave no crumbs... like cake.

Fuck. Cake is my favorite.

I take a moment to thank the stars that I put my long coat on before I went out to my car. It's hiding the chub that is growing harder the longer I watch her hips sway in opposite time of her full chest.

Goddamn. I need to focus on something else.

Fully turning to face Mireya who waves at the women walking over to us, I ask, "So where are your pointy ears?"

Her face twists up. "What pointy ears?"

"Aren't you supposed to be a fairy?"

"Yea, but it's not like that. See the glitter in my hair? My wings?" She flaps her arms which makes the wings on her back move. "And the tutu? Obviously, I'm a fairy."

I pinch my chin. "Right, right."

"Aunt Mel even liked my idea about making the set mostly recyclable. All the parts that can't be recycled are gonna be used for the show next year. The entire show was relatively low impact. Isn't that cool?"

"Very," I say. "Always finding a way to make a difference, huh?"

"Each bit counts," she beams. Then she spots her Ma close behind us and hugs her tightly. When they break apart, Drea squeezes her daughter's hand.

"You were amazing up there! I knew you would be!"

Mireya hugs her Mom again, careful not to mess up her costume. "Thank you, Mama."

"I'm so, so proud of you, honey. Ant barely fell asleep."

Mireya elbows me this time, "Yea, he already told me." We all laugh together and it doesn't surprise me that things feel right like this with the three of us.

I press my hat a little more snugly to my head. I have to find something for my hands to do. Normally, I would have already pulled Drea into my side but now I don't trust my hands to stop on her shoulder. Instead, they're likely to somehow end up on her waist where the dramatic flare of her hip calls for my hand.

Chloe finds her way back over to us with her husband, Quincy, and the rest of the crew telling us that they're ready to head back to QB's for the celebration if we are.

After a lot of agreements from everyone, I'm forced to let Mireya and Drea out of my sight even though I wish it was all of us doing this as a single unit.

A family, like I always felt we were.

# CHAPTER 20

# Drea

Something's changed.

I can't put my finger on it and I'm too scared to call out what it is because I like how things have changed.

Let me rephrase that. Everything is returning to normal.

Mireya has been at the house more and so has Ant. It's like there has been some freaky reset or something.

I don't like it.

I'm happy that the awkwardness of nearly crossing the line is only a small walk around instead of the big elephant in the room. But! There would have been more to say. There would have been answers to this new realization that I've just been holding my tongue about. He isn't here tonight after a week of eating at my kitchen table, looking like he is fitting into the picture that was missing something. He's the finishing touch that just makes everything come together.

Thank god that my foot-in-the-mouth innuendo horniness has passed.

I don't want to make Ant any more uncomfortable while he's still in a committed relationship with Steph. *I'm not that woman.*

My teenager is letting me know about her plans with her Dad coming up. "We're gonna hang with grandma and 'buelo before we go up to the cabin." I knew already but I find no need in informing her of that.

"That'll be nice. I know they'll really like that. I know I've enjoyed having you here with me more and actually getting to see you. You're having a new kind of holiday break."

It's my short break between all the prepping I'm doing before this retreat. I've got to get onto ordering any ingredients I'll need more of for the desserts I have planned. After a quick conference call with Bill Shaw, who is coordinating the event, we came to an accord on which of my confections he wanted to be served. There were only three nights where there would be dessert served as a part of the evening so I lucked out in that regard. Over-prepared doesn't even begin to cover what I am right now. We have room to store all the extra products, even if I don't use it.

I wish I wasn't like this though. The holidays are supposed to be about baking for joy.

I'm so stressed. I'm destined for a hot bath before everything is said and done. And hopefully, I can soak in it for a few days.

"Yea. It'll be just me and Dad. Are you sure you're gonna be okay?"

"Of course. I trust your Dad." *In theory.* He's an officer of the law so I'm sure she's as safe as she can be with him for a few days.

"That's not what I mean." She sits on the kitchen stool next to me. "You're gonna be alone for the holiday. Not just alone, but working. That's not what the holidays are about."

"That's life, kid. Sometimes it doesn't look like the movies."

"I still hope you get a Christmas miracle." Looking over at my daughter, I sense her concern. If I could tell her something different, I would. I've never been one to lie to my daughter about anything. Anxious energy must be rolling off of me in waves if she is hoping for a miracle for me.

"I might need one to get everything done for this event." She grimaces. "Kidding. I'll be fine. It's just nerves. Your Mama is gonna be fine. Don't worry.."

"Promise me that you will at least try and rest when it's over." Her eyes, which are so similar to mine, hold my gaze.

I kiss her forehead. "I will. I promise."

<hr>

THERE ARE THINGS THAT you learn how to manage as a single mom that comes without a handbook. It goes a little something like this: Be prepared for the absolute worst because there are no replacement children.

As you can imagine, this applies to many instances, going to a theme park, doing a road trip, moving to a new house, slumber parties, et cetera.

Today, it applies to the Christmas retreat I have been ever so diligently preparing for the absolute worst to happen.

Here I am, standing in Drip and Whip's kitchen, looking at how empty it is.

In the midst of the holiday season, both Kristy and Tarah caught the flu and are at home.

I have exactly zero desserts started for tomorrow.

By some miracle, Shiori was able to come in to at least cover the bakery staples, but now it's just me.

It's *always just me.*

There is no more time for a pity party. I need to get started now if I expect to get everything done before I must get it all loaded up into my van. I'll be packed in like a sardine to accommodate everything I'm taking.

The first dessert I need to tackle is the cake rolls. The cake itself is not challenging, but it's the designs that I, regretfully, suggested and Bill decided on. Some will have tiny Christmas trees and others will have holly berries decorating the outside of the rolls. It's a piping technique that involves a lot of time and concentration to get right so that once they bake up, they'll look like the intended design. I make the batter for the designs first, choosing to get the batter piped and frozen on the cake pans. The red velvet cake will cover the trees and a spiced cake will be the main base of the holly berry design.

The rest are not nearly as time-consuming. I'm glad they chose mini pies and gingerbread police people, and finally a three-tiered cake large enough to feed almost two hundred.

Time management is usually my strong suit. But it's five thirty AM and I'm dead on my feet when the very last cherry goes onto the piped border of the double-barrel top tier.

"Did you sleep at all last night?" Shiori asks, hanging her coat on the hook by the back entrance. The shop is about to open again, and I haven't even been home yet.

My tired eyes take her in. She definitely had rest after she left yesterday. I have not. Ella is behind her talking to Chris, who picked up extra hours for the holiday.

"No, I haven't, but I'm definitely going to go home and crash now."

"Umm… okay. Please be careful. You look like a zombie right now."

"Thanks for that assessment. I feel like one," I shuffle out of the building on my sore legs and my arms cramping from how many mini shells I rolled out, the gingerbread details I piped, and lugging the tiers of that massive cake around before I got the cake on wheels.

When I finally make it home, I crawl to my shower. Each flaky bit of pastry or flour and sugar, scrubbed off and down the drain. My bed has never looked better as I slip under my sheets, thankful that my daughter is at my parents' house. I'm about to be beyond dead to the world for a few hours.

# CHAPTER 21

# Drea

"SHIT." I COUNT THE trays in my travel cart again. "One, two, three... nine..." I flipped the door back and forth to see if maybe I just left it on top of another tray. A very unlikely possibility...

*Nada.* Nothing.

Shit.

Okay. Don't panic.

I stomp the entire way from the loading bay to the kitchen. Thankful that it's in between lunch and dinner service, so there is no one in the resort kitchen. I march directly into the walk-in freezer.

As soon as the door closes behind me, I let out a scream. And I mean, the scream of all screams... because this cannot be happening!

But it is.

This is what occurs when you have not slept because you were up all night and took the smallest nap possible before you had to wake back up to continue preparing for an event and continue to not get any rest because you need to drive five hours up a mountain with delicate cargo and then end up at said event missing an entire tray of rolled cakes!

*Mierda!* Shit.

My fingers and nose begin to feel numb and I give up on the dramatics, pushing the freezer door back open.

"Are you okay?" A woman, who clearly works here, asks me as I step from the freezer.

"Yes," I say quickly. My false laugh rings absolutely false in the space between us. She looks uncomfortable and I probably look deranged, but there's not much more I can do about that. "I was just... umm... testing out the acoustics in there. Not great."

"You're not the first to scream in there... Are you sure you're okay?"

"No. Not sure. Gonna have to get back to you on that one. Thanks for asking," I respond, walking back to my van in a hurry.

I managed to get all four carts rolled into the kitchen. Two go into the walk-in refrigerator and the other two go into the storage pantry until I need to get them baked up.

I plop down onto the bench outside of the kitchen, banging the back of my head against the wall. I check the little watch on my wrist and exhale a shaky breath. I have to get everything in the oven in the next hour before dinner service truly starts and I won't have time or space to get everything ready to go.

I dial the number from my favorites. "Please pick up. Please, please..."

Tony's voicemail comes onto the line and I wait for the automated message to finish before I begin talking. Closing my eyes, I hold my forehead in my hand. Slumped in defeat. "So... you were right. I bit off more than I could chew and still ended up doing everything myself. I should have owned up to that and just accepted defeat. I was so close to making everything and getting it here on time, but I messed up. The *pinche* tray is still at Drip! I'm going to have to show up to the Christmas dinner with less than I said I would. Maybe it's not a big deal, but I don't want to admit that I'm not ready to do it all. I need help."

"And you'll always have it from me." I startle at his voice. Looking down at my phone it shows that I'm still leaving a voicemail. I look up again and there stands Ant.

"You're here!" I yelp, jumping from the bench to hug him. He wraps his arms around me, his hand on the back of my head. I didn't know how much I needed one of his hugs. It's been too long, and I instantly feel much lighter in his arms. There is no better place than in one of Ant's hugs.

I bury my head into his strong chest before I realize that I likely shouldn't and break out of the hug. "You're here," I say again. "What are you doing here?"

"I went to the shop to check that you had left already. Lights were off since y'all closed early today. Peeked inside anyway, and I saw a tray on the counter. It was clearly for this thing. I packed it up best I knew how and it somehow survived the drive up in the Charger."

"You did? That's a five-hour drive." I pinch his arm, shaking my head. He chuckles, rubbing the spot where I got him. "You should have told me. Where is it now?"

"I took it to the kitchen. They have it."

I hug him again this time, just a quick one. I have got to remember boundaries with him. "Thank you, Ant. You saved my bacon. You have no idea."

"Oh, I think I do..." He points to the bench, saying, "I just followed the sound of head thumping to find you."

My face flames under his accurate assessment and I twist my ring. "You saw that?"

"I caught the end of it. When I felt the call on my phone I knew you were calling me." He tucks a bit of hair behind my ear and I lock on to his sympathetic gaze. "You didn't fail. My intention was never to make you feel like you couldn't do this. Just didn't want you to do it alone. You don't ever have to shoulder the burden of everything by yourself."

"It's not appropriate for me to ask these things of you... Ant, you have someone. She deserves all your time. You can't—"

"Why don't you let me worry about what I have time for?"

I look into his eyes, searching for any small bit of uneasiness. I have to trust what he's telling me. He can make his own decisions. "Okay," I say, after a while. "Where's Milli?" His brown lab is usually in tow so it's a little strange not seeing her trotting behind him.

"Dropped her off with Reya before I left. She's probably already being spoiled rotten by your daughter and Ma."

I chuckle. "You're probably right." I twist my ring again. "Do you have time for dinner?"

He takes his phone out of his pocket. "I should probably get started back down the mountain. It's late and I'm already tired."

"You need to eat. We'll just grab it from the kitchen and eat in my room. Then you can be on your way. Please," I beg. "I feel horrible that you drove all this way! At least let me feed you."

He tilts his head from side to side. "Can't hurt, I guess..."

<hr>

I'M SO GRATEFUL ANT is here. More than him saving the day with the missing roll cakes, I get to see my room for the first time with my best friend. With me being so busy, I haven't had a chance to feel how alone I am right now. It's very strange to be somewhere without my daughter and also without Ant. For the last few years, I've had one or both of them with me for just about everything. Even if he can't stay, I have him for a little while.

The desk clerk tells me all the policies and such before handing me the keycard and pointing us in the direction where my room is located.

When we step outside, the temperature has dropped quite a bit from when I was first out here unloading everything I prepared for the event. Shivering, I button my coat up before grabbing the duffel I packed. Ant takes the bag from me before I can fully grab it from the van.

"What am I? Some chump? I don't even have bags. I'm not letting you carry this." He throws the strap over his arm. "You pack a dead body in here? You're going to be here all of four days."

"No dead bodies. I brought some wine... maybe a few bottles." He gives me a look. "What? It's my first Christmas without Mireya. I needed something to be my company!"

"Uh-huh."

I narrow my eyes on him. "I'll carry the food then."

Ant follows me to the third floor, which is coincidentally the top floor of the main building. I lucked out in getting a suite somehow, so there is lots of space here. There's a full kitchen and a sitting area with a couch and recliner. A tiny Christmas tree sits in the corner of the room with festive mini ornaments on it. I suspect they have some kind of incense sticks because it smells like pine as if the tree were real. It really does feel like a luxury and not a bad way to spend the holiday even though I'll be alone.

I've never had a holiday alone. It makes me wonder what my family and Colton are doing.

Distracted by my thoughts, I heat up the dinner that the kitchen prepared. I re-plate the food on the dinner plates from the room and even manage to pour some wine from my duffel bag into the wine glasses.

"D. Are you good?"

"Huh? Oh, yea. I'm fine."

"You know I don't like wine," He makes a face. "Did you pack some Macallan in there too?" He nods his head over to the duffel.

I throw his napkin at him. "No, I didn't. I had no idea you would even be here, remember?" We sit at the small dining table across from each other. "You could probably order some with room service."

"It'd get here after I ate." He shrugs. "It's whatever. I'll have a glass tonight, I guess."

"Poor baby." I pat his hand. "However will you go on without some brown?"

"Don't know. It'll be hard but I'll give it my best shot."

I laugh at him and sip from my glass. "Nothing better than a Cab Sav after a long day of work."

"Speak for yourself." He cuts his chicken and takes a bite. "You could've made this better."

I take a bite from my own chicken and nod. "It's still good though." I take another bite. "After how mushy my brain feels, I don't know if I could get anything else done without a long night of sleep first. The chicken might have burnt black by the time I remembered I was cooking something."

"Even in your sleep, you'd still do better than this."

He's always complimenting my food. Whenever I try something new, he's the first person I want to taste and give me feedback. "You know, I'll still cook for you even if you don't blow smoke up my ass."

Ant coughs and chokes, sipping some of his wine before breaking out in a big belly laugh. "If all I had to do was compliment you to get some good food. I don't think I'm doing enough."

"What do you mean?"

"This," he gestures to the room. "is just the beginning. I see you going far with your food. Your desserts should have been rewarding you like this long before now. I'm not doing nearly enough. You should know that you deserve this and more. A full staff and trips to beautiful places because they want what you have to offer. A compliment is the very least, Drea."

"Aww, Ant." I place my wine glass back onto the table and wipe my mouth with a napkin. This table is tiny in comparison to my dining table at home, but it feels just as familiar to be sharing a meal across from him. This man is always encouraging me. "That's..."

He raises his glass toward me, "Mean your scheduling and priorities do need a bit of upkeep but hey, she can't be perfect in all things."

"Well... there you go. Keep me humble." I clink my glass on his.

"I'm serious. All that's true. You're strong and independent and you can achieve anything you want in this world. You know I believe in you and in this dream you have. But you need help sometimes. You don't become an amazing businesswoman off your own back. If you're going to grow you have to allow that to happen. It takes more than one woman and now more than ever you're in a position to ask for what you need."

"What do I need?"

"A team. A reliable team. One who will show up for you when you need them."

"I have a team."

"You have a lot of Walter's people. Sure. But you need more of your own."

I look down at my plate. "You're right."

"You're learning and... Fuck, I don't know everything. You're just starting this thing and it's the holidays so maybe it's just a mix-up." He reaches across the table to grab my hand. "I'm not trying to get on your ass or preach, but I see your potential. You're destined for more of this. You deserve it."

I GRAB MY DUFFEL and change in the bedroom area. The sound of the TV reaches me from Tony watching something in the sitting room.

I look down at my tank and sleep shorts for a moment longer. Not quite something I'd wear in front of him but I wasn't expecting him to be here, and I want to get comfy before I pass out tonight. And that is going to happen sooner rather than later. I'm ready to crash after the past forty-eight hours.

*He shouldn't be here.*

Why does that make me feel warm and fuzzy inside that he is?

I can't say that I don't know that Tony is both attractive and a good person. I do know that. He doesn't bullshit me or let me feel the weight of my mistakes. He cares about me. Cares for me and my daughter. He's always there for me.

Every time.

I shouldn't have any other feelings for him besides immense gratitude. That's all. I should only have friendly, platonic feelings.

Only.

So... What about the lines of his strong shoulders are making my neck heat as I walk back into the sitting area now?

I take notice of his eyes on me the moment that I'm in the sitting room with him. He looks me over from my bare feet to the little stack of macarons tattooed on my thigh. He bites his lip by the time he reaches my Terry shorts. I don't fidget though I kind of want to when he takes in where my tank top dips low over my ample cleavage. For him, I didn't take my bra off because that would definitely be too much for friends to just be sitting and watching TV. I'm thankful for that because my nipples are rigid peaks right now.

He leans in the opposite direction when I take the one spot next to him on the couch. "What are you doing?" I ask, wiggling my toes underneath his big thighs, searching for warmth.

Ant settles his thigh more firmly over my feet. "You are freezing, woman."

"It's getting so cold now. Maybe I'll get a white Christmas this far up the mountain..."

Turning to me Ant asks, "Is it snowing?" I nod. He stands from the couch, taking his warmth with him. Walking over to the window, he curses under his breath. "I should probably go before it gets bad."

My heart sinks. "Right, you probably should." Ant shoves his arms into his coat and pulls a beanie out from his pocket to pull on. He gives me a side hug that feels awkward. He's out the door while I stand there keeping it open, feeling empty somehow. "I'll text you when I make it home. Don't finish that bottle tonight, okay?"

I nod, crossing my fingers behind my back. He makes his way down the hall. I let the door close on its own. It slams and I wince. *Alone again.*

What was I expecting?

Anthony has a girlfriend. Steph, who is perfect and everything a man could want. Not a single mom who is still kind of a train wreck. He's my friend! I shouldn't put him in this kind of position. Strutting around, mostly naked.

*Ugh.*

Drea.

So inappropriate. I roll my fist across my forehead in frustration. *What was I thinking?*

"I can't keep that promise," I say as I pour myself another glass of wine and turn the heater up in the room.

# CHAPTER 22

# Tony

WHAT AM I DOING?

Why am I leaving the room?

*You know why*, that little voice in my head tells me. It has nothing to do with the snow.

It's not until I'm in the lobby of the building that I notice the snow is coming down much faster than I originally thought it was. The fat flakes land on the ground which is already covered completely in a thin layer of white. My boots crunch as I make it over to where I parked my car.

I get into the car to realize that the pattern of the snow is shifting. The flakes swirl about as icy rain thunks against my windshield. The wipers are able to clear the fresh snow, but it's hard to see this time of night with the precipitation picking up. Still, I start the engine and back out of the parking spot. A truck is already clearing snow as I creep down the frontage road. There's hardly anyone out, but it could just be this time of night with the weather.

How could I be in this predicament? What was I thinking?

I can't just pounce on her like I had every thought to. When she changed out of her jeans and sweater to those tiny shorts, thighs bare and taunting me. I could barely manage to not touch her when she slid her feet under me. We always sat that way at her house. Something about the energy in that hotel room is different.

Crossing a line and ruining our friendship for my building lust for her is not in my plans today. Or ever really.

Fuck.

I get a few miles down the narrow highway until I hit traffic and see the car in front of me turning around, and heading in the opposite direction.

There's a barrier on the road to prevent us from moving forward. The sign reads "HWY CLOSED TIL 8AM" and I slam a fist on my steering wheel. The weather is definitely too unpredictable to be slipping and sliding down the highway when I don't have snow tires.

No.

This can't be happening.

Drea talks often about how the universe will make a way for what is meant to be. But this is not how it's meant to be.

I turn around with the other cars and dial Drea on the car's hands-free assistant. It rings a few times before she picks up, sleep already thick in her voice.

"H-Hello?"

"I'm headed back up there. They closed the highway for the weather. Apparently it's gonna be a big storm."

I hear the rustling of what I'm guessing are the sheets and the click of her lamp. "Oh, I saw the snow, but I didn't think it'd be that bad."

"Me neither." I tap the steering wheel a couple of times. "I'm gonna call the resort to see if they have any other rooms available for the night."

"What?" More rustling, "I mean, why? You could just stay here. I have the pullout couch."

"Yea... I'm not really interested in fucking my back up trying to squeeze my big ass on that thing."

"Oof," she says. "You're right," I hear some more crinkling as she moves around. "Let me just put some clothes on and I'll go ask if they have any other rooms."

My mind instantly draws up the picture of Drea in those little sleep shorts again and I hope like hell she's wearing more than that in the lobby or I might have to break someone's nose.

"Are you sure it's okay if I stay there if they don't? I can just look somewhere else."

"Of course, it's okay. Don't be weird. I'll see you when you get here. You need to drive safely." She hangs up before I can respond and I'm met with the silence of my car. The rain isn't as heavy as before but the snow is steadily picking up.

I hydroplane enough to scare the shit out of myself, exiting off the highway. The accumulation on the ground is so thick that I can't make out where any of the lines on the road are supposed to be.

Sighing in relief when I see the familiar sign for the resort, I park in the spot I was in previously and get out. I didn't pack any clothes since I didn't plan on staying, but I do have some extras in my car for after work. I put the spares in my coat, under my armpit, and tug my beanie down tighter on my head to face the cold.

By the time I enter the lobby, I'm covered in snow. I stomp my boots on the rug just inside the doors to shake the snow off before it soaks through my clothes. Ripping off my hat, Drea is already there brushing snow from my shoulders. Her warm hands swipe snow from my lashes and stubble. "God, your face is already frozen!" I nuzzle into her warmth on my face before I can stop myself. *What are you doing, Tony?*

"I know. It's only getting worse out there." I gruff.

She wipes her hands on her pants to get the moisture from my face off of them. She opens her mouth and then closes it before crossing her arms over her chest. She's still in that tank top so I know she must be getting cold at this point. She opens her mouth again and rushes out, "I'm so sorry you got stuck here. It's Christmas Eve and you're stuck here just like me."

"It's not your fault." I rub her arms with my bare hands that managed to stay warm in my coat pockets. Or maybe I'm just running hot now that I'm near her again.

She stomps on a clump of snow with her fuzzy boot, never taking her eyes off the destruction. "If I would have just taken a second to check everything again then you wouldn't have had to come and save the day like you always do."

Shaking my head, I tilt her chin up to look at my face. "Stop beating yourself up. Nothing serious."

"Are you sure?" Her eyes flick to mine, begging me to answer honestly.

"Yea."

Her head bobs from side to side in indecision or maybe just apprehension. Finally, Drea winces, "Well, they don't have any more rooms available for the next two days, so you're stuck with me and the pullout couch." She fiddles with the drawstrings on her sweatpants before she looks back up at me.

"Oh, well," I shrug.

"Oh, well?" She repeats.

"What am I going to do? It's a snowstorm. I'm guessing anything is better than being stuck out in that. C'mon." I tug her by the arm for several moments before she relents and walks back over to the room with me.

The second we both step into the room again, the sweltering heat hits me. My toes are already tingling as they defrost and Drea races over to the heater. "I think I turned it up too high after you left. This thing is way more sensitive than the one at home."

"It feels like a sauna in here." I take my shoes off propping the door open to try and let the heat out. I'm already sweating.

Drea takes her sweatpants off, fanning her face with a room service menu. "It should cool down now that I turned it off, but it might take a while."

My traitorous eyes take the opportunity to devour the sight of her shapely legs on display again.

"You should take your coat off. You're starting to sweat."

I gulp.

Maybe sleeping in my car is a better option. I'm only so strong. We've been in the same house, same room alone plenty of times. I sleep at her house almost as much as I sleep at my own. But this...

This is completely different. I don't want to make something happen that shouldn't. If I were thinking with *the big man*, then it definitely will.

Goddamn. I want to be between those lush thighs more than I want my next breath.

Just a taste would likely do me in. Laying her down on the bed. Nipping and biting my way to the apex of them. Her fingers on my head, nails scratching. My name on her lips just like I heard her the other night...

She said it was a slip-up. An accident. But fuck if I haven't beat my meat to the memory of her calling out my name while she—

My coat slips off my shoulders. "Seriously, I think you're about to overheat. Wool and the eighty degrees of intense heating in this room could make you pass out."

I shudder when her hand skims my wrist to pull the rest of my sleeve off. I'm bricked up and that is not the best way to avoid pouncing on her in the room. Her hips sway the whole way to the coat rack and it's distracting as hell since I should be going to sit somewhere and disguise my stiff dick in any way possible.

I manage to make it back to the couch and quickly tuck my shit in the waistband. Wiping the sweat from my brow like I am a fucking sinner in church.

Drea plops down on the couch beside me, tits bouncing. I realize that the couch was a bad option. I should have sat in the recliner. But it's too late and I'll just look weird if I move now.

Her toes wiggle under me and again and I say a prayer that she starts talking about anything to pull my attention from how close she is.

"How fucked up is it that the first thing I thought when you called me is that I won't be alone for Christmas?" She laughs to herself and picks up the wine glass off the little table in front of us. "I mean, I knew that I would be since it's how this whole job was supposed to work out but... kind of feels like I wished this on you."

She tries to hide her hopes with a joke, but I know she really feels this way. I can feel it.

"Drea, why didn't you just ask me?"

*Always running from us. Always denying.*

As she should be.

"Because..." She searches in her wine glass for a few more moments, trying to find an excuse. She tilts the glass back and finishes off her wine. "It would have been pathetic and inappropriate."

"Why?"

"Steph likely wouldn't want her boyfriend to be sharing a room with me." She swings her legs off the couch. "I wouldn't," she murmurs.

I freeze. "Wouldn't what?"

"I wouldn't want you to be in a room with any other woman. Especially not one in tiny shorts and a tank top... and one bottle of wine down!" Her head tilts toward the bottles on the counter and the one we had sits empty with the second one already open. "I mean, I wouldn't want my boyfriend in this situation... You know?"

"Why not?" I hedge.

"Because. How could I trust nothing to happen?"

My eyebrow raises."Is something going to happen?"

"No?" A question and not a statement.

"So, why are you worried about Steph?"

"I'm not."

"You've talked about her more than I have. I would say that you're pretty worried."

"I have not." She stands and goes to fish another bottle of wine from her bag. Rushing to the kitchen, she gets the bottle opener from the counter, stabbing it into the cork much harder than necessary. She already has another one open. Either she's had too much or she just wants something to do instead of having this talk. Her tolerance is far too high for it to be the former.

Holding her hand still on the bottle, I say, "I don't think so. You started this conversation... again. We're gonna finish it. And I need you to be somewhat sober." She tries to wiggle out of my hold, but it only makes me cage her closer to the counter. My dick is fully hard now that her ass is pressed tight to my body. I lean over her, whispering in her ear. "Why is it that you can't be trusted in a room alone with me?"

Her breathing picks up and she drops the bottle opener. It hits the surface with a clatter but I don't budge.

"Tell me. Be honest." I rasp, restraint hard for me to hold onto.

"I-I am not the one in a relationship. You tell me."

I could clarify that I'm also not in a relationship, but I don't. What good will that do when she would still fight tooth and nail to deny any attraction to me when it's clearly there?

Placing a hand on her waist, I slide it around to her soft stomach. My fingertips grazing over the waistband of her shorts. "Is it because I could touch you just like this and hold you close to me with no interruptions?"

She says nothing but I see the pulse in her neck thumping faster and faster.

Using the hand on her middle, I bring her body as close to mine as I can manage. She arches, just slightly, and the soft give of her ass on my dick makes it jump.

My other hand cups her tit and even with my big hands, I know it'd still spill over if she weren't wearing this bra. I slide my hand up her chest to grip her throat. Not tight enough to cut off her air, but enough to feel her heartbeat increase. Leaning down to whisper in her ear again, I admit, "Having you in my arms like this makes my dick weep but I won't take anything further until you give me the word."

I release her and walk back to the sitting room. If I didn't, who knows where I would have taken this. I'm tired of the games and the denial but I'm also not a fucking monster. I don't want her to regret me. I want her to make the decision to cross that line with me on her own.

I don't want to talk about Steph either.

I want to talk about Drea and Tony.

Us.

This is the conundrum of being the good guy.

Drea's cheeks are flushed when she meets me in the sitting room again. "Ant?"

"Yea?"

She balls her hands into the hem of her shirt, nervously twisting and untwisting it. Her bottom lip caught between her teeth. "What if it is me that can't be trusted?"

# Chapter 23

## Drea

What if it is *me that can't be trusted?*

The answer is obvious. I can't be.

I've held him at arm's length for one reason.

He means too much to find out that he's just like the rest. And that's not fair, to him or to me.

Years of denying something that has been true all this time. I have been waiting for a man just like Anthony. He *is* the man that I've waited for. None of the men I've dated could ever compare to the standard that he has upheld and raised the bar for time and time again. All of that couldn't be more apparent than with him being here now.

Closing my eyes, I utter, "I can't lose you, Ant."

I don't even have to ask for support or for him to be there because he already is. He always is. I can trust my heart, my life, my daughter's life, in this man's hands. He has always been there for me.

"You won't," he responds with certainty laced through his words.

I made this pact with him and he honored it for years. Never complained about how dumb I was to still try looking for someone else. Men may still be shit and untrustworthy and all the criticisms I've found and proven with the bums I've been dating. But, I could shake myself for being so blind and untrusting of Ant.

"Our pact... it wasn't for nothing. I—"

"It means everything to me. What we agreed to—I'd never go back on that for anyone. When we said those words to each other, I knew that you were the one for me. What we want is the same, Drea."

Why had I been so stupid?

I shake my head. My heart is still trying to beat right out of my chest. This can't be true because I am a smart woman. I am empowered and resourceful. I... "What about your girlfriend?"

I don't care about Steph. I should feel bad about that but I don't.

I know this man. If he wanted to be with her, truly wanted her, then he would be.

But he's here—with me. Not her.

"What about her?" Maybe red flags should be sparking but still no sense of alarm is coming about. *He's for me, not her.*

I squeeze my eyes closed again. "I can't lose you over something so insignificant as lust."

With his big hands on me, I was at his mercy.

And still, he gave *me* the choice. Never crossing the line if it's not what I wanted.

Even my body knew that I wanted to. Each time I'd pull a toy out, I'd imagine it was him. I'd call his name. It was his body, his heart, I craved, that I came alive for. Even though I hadn't had it yet.

I wanted to.

"That's what you think this is? Lust?" He leans forward, elbows resting on his thighs. "Could I wait for you? Commit to you finding your way to me as something so fleeting?" He shakes his head. "Maybe for them. But for me? This is everything I've wanted and more. There are no other options if you're here. I don't know how else to say it."

"Try. Please? You are too important to me to cross this line for anything less than what we both deserve."

He looks between my eyes, taking in my vulnerability laid bare for him. The *thunk, thunk, thunking* of my heart in my ears. It pulses stronger and stronger with each step I take, traveling from my heart to the sensitive area between my thighs. All I can think at this moment is: Tony looks too good sprawled in that recliner. I had ignored so much of what made him beautiful because he always felt too good to be true.

Too perfect to be mine.

Maybe I was wrong.

I finally release my tank and take the final step toward him. "Say something," I plead again.

"I don't want to say the wrong thing and have you play with my feelings." I stand in front of him now. His eyes never stray from mine. "If I act on this... If I show you what more I want from you, I'm not taking it back. I refuse to only have parts when I find out what it is really like to finally have all of you."

"Okay," I respond. The butterflies in my stomach kicking up a fuss at the power of his conviction.

"I will mean everything I say and do." His calloused hand brushes along the outside of my thigh, raising goosebumps along my skin. "I won't let you regret me for doing just that."

"I'm saying yes, Ant." I push my way between his legs, making space for myself and all my hope too.

He rises from the overstuffed chair, easily. Hands sliding up my thighs to find my hips, walking me back to the couch. My knees hit the cushions and I drop to sit. His hands never leave me.

Tony looms over my body, blocking the light from above us. He's never used his size to intimidate me and I, somehow, never took into account how truly big this man is. *He is no ant.* His shoulders span farther than I can see with our eyes still on each other. I close mine for a moment to catch my breath. The scruff of his jaw brushes along my collarbone before his soft lips meet the heated skin of my neck. My hands press to his chest, not pushing him away, but searching for grounding in this moment.

*This is really happening.*

His heart beats under my hand and I press more firmly to feel it.

The breath catches in my throat when his teeth nip at my sensitive neck.

All this teasing is too much and I want more.

I need to have more than he's giving me.

I'm falling, falling, falling into the emotions burning brightly in his eyes.

With both of my hands on his jaw, I bring his mouth to mine. Our lips meet and I hear the reverberating click of my heart opening and emptying its contents out to make more space for him. Tony kisses me tenderly and with all the restraint of a man who respects me.

But I don't want the respect.

I want him to ravage me because I need to ravage him.

Maneuvering myself up onto my knees, I take control of our kiss. I demand the security of his words with his actions. Years of self-doubt and denial leading to this moment between my best friend and me.

When my tongue dips into his mouth, he softens to let me take what I need. As good as I give, he takes. He takes and takes everything that I give him in this kiss. His hands squeezing, grabbing, holding everywhere he can reach.

I'm inflamed under his attention. He spares no inch of my body when he finally lays us down on the couch.

My tank top is askew and my shorts are practically nonexistent with how they've ridden up. I can see the faint red shapes of where his hands have grabbed ahold of me and I flush at the visible evidence of his desire.

He looks me over as I lie here. The claw clip in my hair digs painfully against my head. I pull it free and feel a little cheesy about letting my hair down like this. I avoid his gaze for a moment, all the while reprimanding myself for feeling self-conscious now. He leans over me again, heat rolling off his skin, between my legs. "Look at me," he says.

The fire in his ebony eyes practically cackles. I begin to say something, but he speaks again. "You are the sexiest woman I've ever had the privilege of laying my hands on. If you can stay out of your head long enough, you'll be the sexiest woman I've ever had my dick inside of too."

I blush more fiercely and Tony kisses my flushed skin from my chest to my neck. I'm turned on in a bad way. I can't even press my thighs together to get relief, but I feel how wet I'm growing. I'm afraid I'll soak these little shorts before I get to see him.

He drops to his knees, turning me so my legs hang off the couch. Kissing and licking my thighs until I'm downright squirming.

"Touch me. Please," I beg. "I need you here." Spreading my thighs, wide enough for his big body to fit fully between them. I don't hesitate to ask for what I want because it's been so long since anyone has made me feel like asking was an option.

But for Tony, I want to give him my all.

With a fist on his chin, he swipes a thumb over his bottom lip. Assessing me. "I've waited to hear you say that, but the first time I put my mouth on you, won't be on this couch."

He picks me up like I weigh nothing. I'm shocked, to say the least, but I wrap my arms around his neck, giggling as he carries me to the bed.

I land with a bounce when he drops me. Ripping his shirt over his head, I catch sight of a different one.

Tucked into the waistband of his jeans is the dark crown of his very erect penis. I squeeze my thighs together for real. My eyes widen. I may have bitten off more than I can chew with this impressive man. That part of his body matches the rest of him perfectly. Big, big, big. The tight broad head is already shiny and taut with need. I lick my lips in trepidation. It's an anaconda. I don't even know if my hand can fit around it.

He notices me staring and chuckles. "You won't be getting this tonight. There's no way you could fit me right now." I pout, but he chuckles again, kissing my thigh. "Don't worry. We'll get you there."

I shiver with his dark promise. I haven't been stretched over anything that big... ever.

He crawls onto the bed and up my body to kiss me again. The hard length of him present and hot against my stomach. How could I have been resisting what Tony can surely give to me?

His kisses are rough and desperate as I take a chance to admire the cut lines of his back muscles down to his narrow waist with my fingers. I've never been able to explore him more than a cursory glance before. Now, I make myself familiar with all the gifts his hard labor has given him. His ass in these Wranglers should be a goddamn sin. I grab onto him with both hands to pull his body closer to mine.

He resists with ease, breaking our kiss. My hands still cup his tight ass and he chuckles at me again. "I don't think I like these chuckles very much," I huff.

Smirking, he says, "I don't think I like you trying to rush me when I have all night."

"I'm not," I say, chin up. He raises an eyebrow, eyes trailing over my body and back to my face. "Okay, maybe a little bit," I admit.

"You're rushing the wrong things." His finger catches in my top and tugs. "Take this off." I do what he says. "The bra, too," he adds.

It's awkward to unhook the bra under him, but he reaches around to help me. He gets impatient himself, ripping it off me. Both of his hands cup my breasts and he sighs in relief. "I knew they'd be too much for my hands. I'll never be able to keep my hands off these perfect titties now."

His head dips to kiss and nip along where they spill over the tops of his hands all while he pinches my already hard nipples between his finger and thumb. "God, you are such a tease."

"Don't like it huh, Boss Lady?" he retorts.

I would have responded with something smart, but he catches a nipple between his teeth. I moan and buck my hips to no relief. "That feels so good. Don't stop," I beg. My hands hold onto his head to keep him close to me. His warm tongue flicks over the sensitive peak, back and forth, lazily working me up and up. The cool metal from the chain around his neck tickles my body as it dangles there while he works.

He hums against me and switches to the other nipple giving it the same attention. I press him more firmly against me until his face is buried and he licks, sucks, and nips at me with more fervor. "So, so good. Keep doing that." I count in my head before I release my hold on him and he sucks in a breath, smiling, going right back to the other nipple and I do it again.

My core clenches tight and I writhe along his leg between mine.

Easily, he breaks my hold on him and meets my lips again. He sucks my bottom lip into his mouth and our eyes catch. The emotions swirling in his gaze light a new fire in me.

"You're so fucking sweet. I need to get a taste of you for real." He moves to the end of the bed, fingers in the waistband of my panties. "Take these off, Drea."

# CHAPTER 24

# Drea

TREPIDATION BEATS IN MY heart like a drum. Years of placing value on *the deed* made me feel like opening myself up to anyone was a step that had more value than I could comprehend.

A prize.

No one is worthy of winning it more than Anthony.

He looks up at me through hooded eyes from the foot of the bed. It takes a few tries, but I manage to wiggle out of my shorts and panties before he helps me pull them down my legs.

"You know, I was twenty before I even shared a bed with someone..." The words bubble out of me as I try to fill the charged air with something. Anything to tackle the nerves I have about all of this. I'm naked and exposed in more than one way. I trust him, I do. But I also know that I can't go back after this.

Ant pauses at the foot of the bed with me there, naked, and him, still in his jeans. On his knees, only his chest and shoulders are visible as I look down at him on my elbows. "Why?" He finally looks up from my body and asks. I take a much-needed breath. Stalling is all this is. Why am I *stalling*?

"After I got pregnant, I didn't want to end up in that situation again. It's not that easy to find another partner in Alpenglow when you've got a toddler at home." He stands from the floor to lean on the edge of the bed. I sit up fully and make space for him. I would expect to feel at least a little self-conscious with my nudity but I don't. After years of loving on myself and discovering that my body is more than a lure for sexual attention, I can't. The reverent way Ant's eyes roam over all the details and dimples he couldn't see before bolsters my confidence more than his words did. And that's saying a lot because he's only ever had encouraging words for me. I continue, "Especially with the gossip. Couldn't escape it. So my girls helped me. I went out with Clo and Mel one night in Denver and..." I huff a laugh. "You know how that all turned out."

He nods, a finger starts gently running over the skin of my ankle and I shiver. "We don't have to do anything you aren't comfortable with Drea. I have patience in spades. Want more, I can and will give you more. Want to just cuddle and watch something, I'm fine with that too. But I'm not letting you go back on what we both know is next for us."

A little breathless, I say, "What's next, Ant?"

"Us. We. You and I are what's next." He doesn't look up at me, instead talking to my calf that he's running his finger over. Watching the goosebumps he elicits and running another rough finger over them. It feels more intimate than his hands on my breasts. The restraint I've never been shown before. Everything is my choice, and I can go at whatever pace I choose.

My breathing picks up and my heart races in my chest.

*This man is perfect.*

I slide down the bed again to rest back on my elbows. He raises up on his forearms to make space for me. Like this, my pussy sits right below his face. I shiver at the first puff of air from his lips as he takes me in. I'm open and presented for him. Still wet from everything we've done so far.

His head ducks to rest his nose at the hair above my opening, just taking an inhale of me. "How is it that you smell like baking all the time? Vanilla and cinnamon follow you everywhere." His eyes meet mine and the hunger is back. I bite my lip, forcing myself not to close my legs.

"My body wash..."

"Makes me so fucking crazy. Please tell me this is consent because I want to bury my face in this pretty little pussy until I pass out."

I nod my head, "Yes. I—" I don't manage to get the next words out before his arms wrap around my thighs to pull me even closer to his mouth. With them on both sides of his head, his breath is even warmer on my slit. Just that slight increase in air pressure in my center makes my legs shake in anticipation.

His hand reaches over my thigh, simultaneously holding me open and in place for him as his broad shoulder keeps that space for him. With a thumb and his index finger, he spreads my lips apart. "Already swollen and soft, baby. I love it." He continues the spreading motion and it feels so good as my inner lips part for him as well.

My fingernails scrape along his scalp as he takes his time perusing my center. I keep my mouth shut so I don't go on rambling about my failed sexual encounters before him. I can't bear for him to stop and nothing else matters when he's here with me like this.

With his other shoulder keeping me spread wide for him, I don't dare clench my thighs when his index traces a finger around my opening now. His burning gaze meets my own fiery ones to praise me. "God damn, D. This pussy is fucking weeping for me. Can I taste you now?"

I can only nod in my concentration of not bucking into his mouth. I'm burning with my need for him to keep touching me. Burning in my desire for him to get what he wants from me.

Ant's finger dips inside me and I clench around it immediately. He grunts when my walls tighten for that brief moment before he's removing the finger to slowly slide it into his mouth. His eyes close as he hums his approval of my flavor. "Just as sweet as I knew you'd be. I need more."

This is the moment when my soul leaves my body... Just one pass of his warm, wet tongue has my insides quivering. It's been so long that I barely register the whispering from my own mouth as I hold on for what it's worth.

Don't get me wrong, toys are a blast. And I do mean, an absolute riot. But nothing could ever beat a finger, tongue, scruff combo.

"Ant, please don't stop." There's a slight rocking of my hips to the rhythm of his finger in and out of me. Not big enough to truly fill me, but large enough to clench around.

"You couldn't pay me to stop. You're so tight, baby. I can barely fit my finger in this little thing." Even with his finger and face attached to me, he never hesitates to praise me. *I'm gone for this man.* What he makes me feel is too much.

My head falls back to the pillow behind me when he swirls just the tip of his tongue around my clit until my swollen bud is sensitive and throbbing. Not a drop of my ongoing release goes to waste with his finger moving in tandem with his tongue in and out of me as I shudder and shudder until I break.

"That's right, D. Show me how you'll squeeze this big dick when I give it to you. Show me how good it'll feel." That's it. That is the very end of my leash. Vision going black, jaw clenched to hold back my scream, and fingers gripping the sheets for dear life.

This is what I was missing.

*This man is all I was missing.*

He's suddenly there. Kissing me, holding my waist, my sides, my breasts, anything he can reach. "You're so beautiful, Andrea." He's got his dick in hand, jeans discarded somewhere, using my release to stroke into his own. When his cum paints my belly, he groans into my mouth. I'm delirious with the smell of sex in the air and the heat of his body against mine. "You're so beautiful, baby."

His eyes are as sincere as ever. The heat has banked, but the admiration burns brighter than ever as he slowly kisses down my neck and chest to take a nipple into his mouth again. Rough fingers play at my needy clit again. His palm covers the bud as he enters me. This time two fingers stretch me that little bit wider. It's delicious and, oh my god, it's not long before I'm coming again with his cum still on my stomach and his mouth suckling softly at my clit. I'm beyond bliss as another orgasm rips through my consciousness.

When he's certain that I have nothing left to give him, he cleans his face and mouth in the bathroom before he crawls up the bed to clean me too. I'm half dead as the full effect of my two orgasms come to pass. Sleep sounds so good when he wraps the blanket around us and then his arms around my body. He's still naked as I am and it feels good with him at my back.

The heat in the room has come down to something much more comfortable when he turns the lamps off beside us. The large window to the other side of the bed shows the snow still softly falling like we're inside a snow globe. The reality of what just happened between us feels like a dream more than reality. I could never in my mind have imagined he knew how to do all of that with his tongue.

Denial and waiting.

That's all that has been between us for years and I feel cruel. To myself and to him. And for what? Every sign has pointed to him being the one for me and I ignored them.

"Promise me you won't leave," I say into the darkened room.

He buries his face in my hair, breaths coming slowly as he settles to sleep for the night. "I can't go anywhere in this snow. It's late."

I don't know if he's being purposefully obtuse or if he doesn't know what I'm asking him. With whatever strength I have in me before I pass out from this extremely long and emotionally draining day, I clarify, "I can't lose you, Anthony. Tell me that you won't leave me."

I know how desperate it sounds, but I don't care. I don't care about anyone else in his life. I refuse to say her name and ruin this moment that's between us. It has to be me or I need to create separation now. At this moment, he feels like mine and getting used to that is not good for me if he'll leave. Now that I've bared more than my soul to him, I need to know that he will still be in my life.

"Please," I whisper.

His lips meet my shoulder and I snuggle deeper into him. "Your name has been tattooed across my heart for as far as I can look back. You'd have better luck erasing that, than you would in keeping me from you. Never lose me, if I have any say in it."

The breath I was holding, slowly rushes out from between my lips. His big paw slides up and over my thigh to my hip, to my waist, and finally gripping my breast in a hand. Lips never leave my skin.

I'm wearing those hugs I love so much from him right now and I don't want to go to sleep any other way again.

A gasp breaks free when I feel him harden between my cheeks. I test the width and length with what becomes an insistent presence behind me. "It can't be that big," I whisper in disbelief.

I feel his smirk against my skin as sure as I hear it in his voice. "Is," he grunts. "Ignore it for now. I told you, you're not getting it tonight."

My thighs clench and it only serves to squeeze the stiff ridge of him tighter between my ass cheeks. "I—

"Drea. Go to sleep."

I want to say something smart back, but I really am tired.

He didn't say never. He said not tonight. And the promise of that soothes my mind and I fall asleep in his arms as the snow continues to come down outside.

# CHAPTER 25

# Drea

I FEEL LIKE I'M floating on a puffy little cloud as I check on the rest of my desserts the next day. Breakfast service isn't very busy as it seems most people are sleeping in for Christmas. The four-tier layer cake had held up well and only one small nick needed to be fixed. As it's Christmas Day, it'll be the big special reveal for their dinner tonight. It's ready to go and so am I. I pack all my things as best I can and get a few things for breakfast before I leave.

If I were at home, I'd already be up making cinnamon rolls for Mireya to wake up to. I won't be making anyone's breakfast this year. And the freedom of being able to grab something on my way out of the kitchen feels like a blessing more than the sorrow I predicted it would be when I packed for this trip. As I haven't gotten a call from her or my Mom yet, I'd have to guess that they're also sleeping in.

Normally an early riser, Ant was surprisingly still asleep when I left the room. I am ready to relax and unwind from the stress I've held onto for the past couple of weeks. What better way to release stress than to find out just how big that anaconda really is. Might have to change my business card to also add snake charmer, I think to myself, as I grab the food I ordered and thank the staff before I leave the kitchen for the day.

I'm downright bouncing with impatience to get back to my hotel room. The snow has been steadily coming down outside and there is no end in sight to the freak storm that came out of nowhere.

Can't say that I'm upset about it. A white Christmas always feels like magic.

Sometimes, divine intervention is the only way to get through to people.

It's me. I'm people.

I've had a whole lot of men in my life for a short time. They didn't deserve any more of my attention than I had given them. Now, I think about how different my life could have been if I just let Ant assume the role that he had already carved out for himself.

He could've been mine.

We could've been an us.

I could've filled the loneliness with someone who knows me better than I know myself and encourages me—supports me—with his whole heart.

That cowboy is in my room right now, waiting to spend this holiday with me.

Fair to say, this is my Christmas miracle.

My phone vibrates in my pocket and I think it's Ant's impeccable timing, but it's a different special person in my life. I smile when I answer the call.

"Merry Christmas, Mama!"

"Merry Christmas! Are you having fun?"

"Yea. We just woke up. Grandma's already making tamales for abuelo."

"Just him? Save me some?"

"Not a chance. I think I'll be lucky to even get some. Dad hasn't had them in years and I don't think 'buelo even wants to part with the ones he's getting."

"He definitely is lucky…" I trail off as my thoughts take me to the idea that he'll have my daughter at the cabin by this time tomorrow.

"Where's Ant? I want to tell him Merry Christmas, too." I freeze for a bit before I remember she knew he was coming here when he dropped Milli off before.

"He's still sleeping, I think. I just finished last-minute checks and I'm headed back to my room. I'll tell him to call you." I have no idea how to approach anything about Ant and me with her just yet, but that is not a can of worms I will be opening right now.

"Okay. I got Milli some Christmas pajamas. She looks so cute with Quito! They're a matching set."

"I have to see that! I want to FaceTime later. Don't forget!"

"Okayyy. Love you, bye."

"Love you."

When I reach my door, the sound of Christmas music greets me over the slam of the door behind me. Following the sound to the bathroom, I'm greeted with a pleasant sight. Tony sits in the spa tub singing along to *Please Come Home for Christmas*. His voice isn't as buttery smooth as Rodell Duff's but the sentiment and timing is too good. I feel a renewed wistfulness for my Christmas miracle in my heart.

Ant stops singing when he catches sight of me in the mirror.

"Don't stop on my account," I say.

He laughs and the water ripples around him. "I'm in a merry mood."

"I can see that." I wiggle my foot out of the non-slip clogs I wore to work. "Can I join you?"

He nods and reaches for the drain to let some of the water out for me. Then his eyes trail over my body as I remove each piece of clothing. Walking over to the tub, I run my fingers up my thighs to my chest. Squeezing my breasts together by the time I'm in front of the fragrant water. It's humid in the bathroom from the hot water and I love how the combination of that warmth mixes with the heat of his heavy gaze.

There's something winter-y about the smell of this room though that I can't place. "Left little holiday gift bags at the doors. It's a bath bomb." His head tilts toward the bathroom counter where I see the gift bag he was talking about.

I raise an eyebrow. "And you helped yourself?" Chuckling, I question, "What if I wasn't here to enjoy this bath with you?"

Ant shakes his head. "Not possible. When I called room service to get breakfast up here, Olivia was all too happy to let me know *my wife* was already headed upstairs with our breakfast."

I've never been mistaken for someone's wife before. There's a little spark of something in my chest as I think about the possibility of a commitment on that level. All of that thought process comes to a halt.

"Olivia?" I practically sneer. I do not like the sound of another woman's name on his lips.

He just laughs as if my sneer is the cutest thing he's ever seen. He stands from the tub, water sluicing down the hard lines of his chest and abs and strong legs. His dick already bobs hard for me. Whatever my imagination pictured, I was still off by a few sizes. He doesn't pay it any attention, instead holding his hand out toward me to help me over the edge into the water.

He sits first and I sit in front of him with my back pressed to his chest. His massive length squished between us. I reach back between us to give him a tug.

Ant's hand stops mine. "Ah-ah. Not yet, Boss Lady."

I sigh. "Fine," I say begrudgingly. I relax into his embrace and sigh again. But this time it's not in frustration. I have the weight of the weekend zapped from my mind. He knew a bath was all I needed. Really all I needed was him. His arms wrap around me as we settle in this position. Christmas music softly playing in the room.

After a while, he lathers up my loofah to wash my body. I relax into his touch as the soap covers my arms and chest. We switch and then it's me soaping up his form. We rinse off and my skin's heated from more than just the casual exploration of each other in this tub big enough for a king.

For a moment I thought we were moving too fast. That couldn't be true because it's been too long since we haven't moved at all. This bath is intimate and sensual in a way that I would expect to be awkward but for us, it feels just right. Like a part of our story that we had skipped before and are watching back in recollection. So much of my connection with Ant feels this way. Like I missed him when I had him by my side all along.

Fluffy robes are next for both of us as we sit across from each other at this miniature dining table. My legs brush along his and neither of us pulls away. Our matching smiles hide something that can only be the promise from last night. I'm downright giddy as I bite into one of the cinnamon rolls I brought us for breakfast.

Ant breaks the silence, wiping his mouth with a little paper napkin. "You gonna tell me what you're smilin' so big about?"

"You go first," I giggle.

"Smilin' 'cause you're smilin'," he says.

"Well, that is not why I'm smiling," I reply, and his brow lifts. "I'm smiling because of my Christmas miracle."

"What?"

"Yea. I got a Christmas miracle and I'm very ready to see more of it." I look, not so surreptitiously, toward his crotch from where I sit across from him. Now I can't help my giggles as he puts the pieces together.

He stands from the table and walks the half a step over to stand behind me. Whispering in my ear he asks, "Where are you going to receive this Christmas miracle? Here?" He braces a hand on the table over my shoulder. I turn to kiss the arm that's been exposed to me from his sleeve catching on the fluffiness of my own robe. With a smile on my lips, I turn to face him with a kiss so sweet from our cinnamon rolls and the hint of what's in store for us.

"Come on, Boss Lady. Let me see what the big guy got you for Christmas."

I follow him to the bed, letting the robe drop as I stand there in front of him. He lets his robe drop as well.

Biting my lip, I let my fingers trace over his body and he does the same to me. My hands freeze over his chest where I can feel his heart beating. For a second, I have this urge to apologize to it, to him.

That feeling dissipates when Ant says, "Bring me the biggest toy you brought on this trip."

I choke on air for a moment, unsure if I heard him correctly or if my mind is just playing tricks on me. "Huh?" I stutter out.

"You can't get this," he motions to himself  "until I know you won't hurt yourself on it. Show me how much you can take."

Looking at his hardening length between us, I gulp and scramble over to my duffel. I search quickly for the smaller zippered bag that holds a few of my favorites and lube. If I was going to spend the holiday alone, I was prepared.

The rabbit toy I pull out is a long-time favorite of mine. Looking at the purple length and girth of it, I bite my lip at how drastically unprepared I am for the mammoth Ant is packing.

"Okay, so this is the only one that could even come close." Close is a generous descriptor.

When I turn back to him on the bed, his strong thighs and toned body are in perfect display for me on the bed. My God, he was blessed in every way. His hand lazily strokes over his length as I walk back to the bed.

He looks from the toy to me and then back to the toy. "It'll have to do," he says. "I'll make it work." Patting the bed next to him, he makes space for me to lie down as well.

That sweet kiss from earlier completely burns away as he takes my mouth with something more urgent and heated in mind. His hands roam over me until he reaches my sides to pull me on top of him. I rock, uninterrupted over his length, feeling all the delicious veins and hardness against my sensitive lips.

Just as I'm getting close enough to clench around nothing, he holds me up to slide down under me so that my pussy is right over his face.

"What are you—" Then I cry out at the first lick over my pussy until he's doing that sucking thing to my clit again.

I can't stop my thighs from squeezing his head tight as the tightness in my lower belly increases. I'm approaching my climax again when I realize I've had him under me for maybe a little too long.

"Fuck, Ant, I'm—"

He presses my thighs back to the side of his head, "If I wanted air, I'd tell you." He growls into my sloppy center, voice rumbling through my body like electricity. Even though his voice is a little muffled, he says, "I want you to soak my face, baby."

With his desires, I give him exactly what he wants. I let go as I come on a cry that I muffle with a hand over my mouth. Rocking and rocking over his busy tongue. I feel like I might pass out, his mouth is definitely part of my miracle.

But I want him inside me.

As if he can hear my thoughts, he flips us so that I'm on my back.

"Fuck, yes. You're wet enough to not even need this," I see him still covering the toy with the lube. I can't believe this is my life. He looks into my eyes and I nod. We're doing this.

First with his fingers. One then two, then with just the tip of my toy. I nod again, biting a finger as he notches the purple tip a little farther. I understand that he wants to take his time but I'm losing patience. I move against him, pushing the toy inside me as far as it will go. He watches my pussy carefully as he slides one finger inside of me with the toy. "Oh, God. That is..." I murmur when the little flexible ears of the toy bob against my swollen clit.

"Still not enough." He says. Licking his lips, he removes one of his fingers. My eyes grow wide and I watch him rub another finger through my wetness to ease another finger inside me as well. Two of his big fingers plus my toy make my toes curl and uncurl at the stretch.

I cry out. "Oh. Oh. Oh my God. I'm going to come, babe."

"I know, baby. It's still not enough." I scratch at his shoulder, nearing my climax and all at the same time still wanting more from him. I start to move on his fingers and the toy to get more from this invasion. He smiles big and wide like he just won the lottery. "I'm gonna turn this on and try to get another finger in. Okay?"

I nod, unable to speak words being this close to the edge.

The moment the toy begins to pulse in a deep *thrum, thrum, thrum* on my G-spot, I dig my nails into his shoulder for real. My leg curls around his head, pulling him in closer to me. I'm not in control of my body at all when he moves the toy back and forth. The third finger goes in with minimal resistance and I begin to cum harder than I ever have. "Oh, fuck," I cry out. Stars burst and dance behind my closed lids and I thrash, trying to hold on to this feeling.

"Eyes on me, Drea. Recognize who's making you squirt like a damn water hose all over the bed."

# CHAPTER 26

## Tony

WET.

This woman told me that she was getting a Christmas miracle but as my body and her thighs glisten with the release that keeps coming out of her, I knew she was wrong.

The only one getting a miracle right now is me.

They say that patience is a virtue. I am being rewarded. Let me be the first to confirm.

Lapping up every drop I can get to from her quivering thighs, I murmur praise into her skin.

As I've asked her, Drea's eyes never leave me. I can feel them on my skin even as I focus on my task of cleaning her with my tongue.

"I-I've never done that before," she exhales. Winded and blushing hard.

"I want you to do it again," I growl with more command than I intended. Something about seeing her undone in this way makes me feral.

Remember what I said about patience, it has definitely worked in my favor. As I pull this toy from between her legs, I know she's ready for me. There's just one problem.

I don't have any condoms.

Not one.

It's been years, five long years since I needed one.

Drea sits up, concern and something else on her face when she catches me in my thoughts about it. "What? What's wrong?"

"No rubbers."

There's a large wet spot on the bed that she kneels around to come to where I stand. Even on her knees, she's still level at my jawline. Here I stand with my dick hard enough to hammer a nail and the woman of my dreams naked and ready in front of me.

There's nothing I can do about it.

"No rubbers," she repeats back to me.

I look into her eyes and try to piece together what she could mean. My mind is hearing a statement but it could be a question too.

"Baby..."

"No rubbers." She shakes her head. Arms coming around my shoulders to lace her fingers behind my head, pulling me close. "Neither of us has been with anyone else in years. I just want to be with you. We've had time between us. Labels between us. Expectations between us. I just want you between my legs now."

Even hearing those words from her lips, I'm stuck for a moment more. I've never had sex without one. Ever. *Wrap it up* is so ingrained in my brain from my Pa and my brother that it's not crossed my mind. Especially not with a woman I'm not married to. A fact that burns in my heart because I would marry her right now, today if she'd say yes. I never thought that at thirty-eight I'd be experiencing a first quite like this but for her, I would try anything. "You don't have to do that, Drea. I'll find—"

"I'm on birth control. The only thing you should be finding is your way inside me before I lose my mind." She presses us closer together and the heat from her center produces another growl from my chest.

"It's whatever you want, Boss Lady," I smirk, carrying her farther up the bed.

I hook her calves under my arms, spreading her wide for me again. My dick already stands at attention. I flex my hips and the head of my dick meets the warm, wet skin I've been dying to feel this way. I love how she whimpers and wiggles. But I'm determined to take care of her.

I value this woman. I value her enjoyment.

The last thing I want is to ruin her good time because she's not been prepped enough. Just in case, I pour more lube into my hand and smooth it over my shaft.

Her heels dig into the back of my thighs, urging me closer.

When the tip slips inside her, her back arches, I might bust right now with how tight she still is. Sweat breaks across my forehead and I wipe it with the back of my arm. It'll take strength not to go off early.

The first slide into her is unlike anything real. It's unreal how perfect she feels with just the tip in. The warm grip of her around me was better than anything I'd ever felt before. My dreams and my fantasies would never have known how wrong they were. It had been worth all the prepping and stretching because even still she's so tight I have to take my time. Each inch that disappears between those swollen brown lips has my spine tingling more and more. My mind instantly clears all comparisons because nothing could ever be as perfect and right as moving inside of Drea.

"Ant. You're so big. I don't think I'm gonna last baby." She gasps out, back arched, heels digging into my thighs. Even as she complains of not lasting, she's still asking for me.

"You're taking me so well, baby. You were made for this dick. Come now or hold on for the ride. It's yours to do what you want."

If being with her felt natural, being inside her was that feeling of pulling up in the driveway with the porch light already on, beckoning you. You know? Like knowing someone was there waiting for you to come inside. The first smell of something good cooking in the kitchen and that first feeling of your toes sinking into the plush rug after a hot shower from a long work day. Being inside her feels like coming home.

Her moans pick up as my pelvis meets her clit with a bump. I repeat the movement hitting her clit over and over. I'm as deep as I can possibly be but still, I want to be deeper. I want her to feel me under her skin and beg me to stretch her sweet little pussy every time she gets that itch.

I do my best to fit as much of her tits in my hands as I pump her full of me. I want to watch her lose it all over what I'm doing to her. The flush up her body, each bounce of her big tits, the way she grips onto the sheets, the soft "O" of her mouth, and even the sweat sliding down her curves.

My tongue trails over its path to her neck and she explodes. Her release, gushing from her as she squeezes my dick so tight I lose my vision for a bit.

"Just like that." I lean back and rub over her sensitive clit, slowing my thrusts until she's panting and squeezing my length again. "Look at this mess you're making for me, baby. I fucking love it." I fucking love you.

But we both know that. I'm not gonna be the one to say it right now. She is my future and soon enough I'll have all the time in the world to tell her how much she has always meant to me. I'll take my time in showing her that too. I can't stop what I'm doing at the moment though. She wants me and wants this dick, badly. It's in her eyes, pupils blown wide.

"On your knees," I say, sliding my dick out and running my hands over how slick she's made me.

She's moving to her knees and I get out of bed. I need to see this in full view. Drea looks over her shoulder. "Where are you going?"

"Nowhere." Good luck getting rid of me now. "I just need to see you open and perfect for me just like this." She drops her face into the bed to laugh or giggle or something but I couldn't care less. It puts her juicy ass on display for me like she is presenting me with the best present I've ever gotten for Christmas. "Merry Christmas to me."

"Merry Christmas to us," she says into the sheets. I'm back on the bed now, guiding the head of me into her opening. Her breathing picks up and I know I've got her right where I want her.

By the time she registers just how deep I am, I've already picked up the pace. Slamming against her plush ass and watching how the jiggles can't catch up with the speed I'm going.

Like I said, perfect.

The sheets are muffling her cries of pleasure but I want to hear them all. I gather her soft hair around my fist and she supports herself on her hands. "Can I hold you right where I want you, by your hair like this baby?"

"Y-yes, she cries. "Fuck, yes. Please, please, I need— Yesss..." she says when I grab onto this hip I've been fantasizing about since the first time I saw them. It fits in my hand like they were made just for me. It's a new angle where I can control how I hit that spot inside her that makes her little toes curl.  I pound into her over and over and she comes again, pussy fluttering over my dick and I can't hold it anymore.

Each spurt of my cum inside her is met with the throbbing of her aftershocks and I'm certain I've never felt as good as I do right now. I pull her into me and roll us onto the bed so that I'm spooning her from behind. Our sticky bodies pressed close and breaths still coming harshly

I'm slow to pull out but the second I do, I know I'll do anything, be anything that I have to in order for her to allow me inside her body again.

Drea's phone chirps and she reaches blindly for it on the nightstand. "I can't believe it's not even one yet and I'm already done for the day."

She flops back onto the bed and I lean up on an elbow over her, "You're done?" I ask.

Her little grin lights up my soul as she pretends to consider it. "Well, maybe not for the whole day but I did promise Reya that we'd call her later." I bring her hand to my lips, kissing over each of her soft knuckles. "FaceTime... So, we should probably not look like...You know? This," she adds, gesturing to our naked bodies.

"Make a good point. How about a compromise instead?"

"I'm listening..."

"I'll let you shower after," I raise an eyebrow, "you let me between these thighs one more time."

Her brows pinch. "I don't think you know what a compromise is. You're supposed to be making a claim for both sides, not just one."

"You're right. I'll let you shower after you squeeze my head between these thighs again. Don't think I was being clear enough before."

"Ant!"

"What?"

"That's for me. What about you?"

I shake my head, kissing her fingers again. "If you only knew how many times I wished I could be in this exact position, you'd see how tasting you, just how you are right now, was more than generous on your part."

# CHAPTER 27

# Tony



THE SNOW HAS FINALLY stopped.

While Drea spends time drying her hair and getting ready to leave the room for the first time today, I look up stuff for us to do since I won't be leaving her side until I have to. At some point yesterday, I was able to check on Milli who is still with Mireya. M&M are getting along good, which I had no doubt about since my dog seems to love Mireya more than me sometimes. She shared what presents she got from everyone and I'd say it was a better Christmas than I can ever remember having.

*For more than one reason.*

The resort has a heated outdoor sitting area where they will bring you a meal while you get a beautiful view of the trees and slopes behind. We can spend the day together doing something outside of this room and it'll be nice. Don't get me wrong, I've thoroughly enjoyed everything that's happened inside this room, but I know we could both use a little fresh air and give room service a chance to clean.

Drea leaves the bathroom glowing in her robe. "You are so beautiful," I exhale. She looks like a dream with her light brown hair and twinkling eyes. Her lips still look thoroughly kissed with how plump they are right now. I'm across the room, grabbing her around the waist and pressing my lips to hers before I can stop myself. Her warm little hands are on my chest as I take her lips with mine.

"Ant," she breathes. "I need to get dressed or else we won't leave this room today." Her breath hitches when I make it down to her neck just exposed from her robe. "Ant…"

I pull away, knowing she's right. "Alright. Get dressed. I'm gonna cover my eyes."

Her brows bunch into a little V on her forehead. "Why?"

"Want us to leave, right? Seeing you naked again is not gonna get us out of this room."

She swats me out of the way, laughing at my antics. "I'll be fast," she promises and we're out of the room and headed to the scenic sitting area before long.

I didn't actually expect it to be too warm when we were outside after the snow. Living in Colorado for as long as I have, it should not surprise me to be surprised by the weather. And yet, this past storm was the kind of surprise I'm glad I received. We sit on a love seat that has us close and snuggling under a large heating lamp near the glass railing.

It's warm enough that we're both able to remove our coats. I'm in the henley and jeans from my car that I'm still grateful I packed. I didn't actually put any extra boxers in there. An oversight I'll have to remember to correct when I throw another set of clothes back there.

Drea's tan sweater tunic looks fuzzy and soft over her dark jeans and little booties. I can't help running my finger over the soft material on her thigh. Just one day ago, I'd be fighting the urge to touch her and now I feel more than comfortable with the touch and know that she does too.

When I stop to drink some of my coffee, she places my hand back on her thigh to continue my ministrations. "That feels good," she comments briefly before carrying on with her description of what happened before she drove up here.

It was a stressful mess that she pulled off with only a little help from me. And it was small. The perfectionist in her wants to be able to do everything for herself.

"What you did in checking on me and then driving several hours to the resort to help me out... made everything better for me. You can't know how much that means."

"Love for you to think of me as the hero, but you would have made magic happen anyway. I saw everything you brought when I was in the kitchen. What you did is incredible, with or without that one tray of cake," I tell her. It's the truth and I wish she could see that she is enough even when she thinks she's not.

She blushes and squeezes my hand on her thigh. "Thank you," she says in a small voice, looking down at our hands.

We talk over our breakfast about nothing and everything with the incredible view and cozy feeling of rightness between us. I'm not ready to face the real world that's behind us in Alpenglow Ridge. With luck, we've managed to avoid any conversation that could bring us to the awkward reality we were in just before the trip.

It can't be awkward now that the thoughts I had, of being buried between her legs or fucking her pussy into the shape of my dick, are simply memories. Some of the best memories I have. Nothing either of us has to feel ashamed of.

I can only hope that we'll continue to make more of those memories now that we crossed that line. When our food is done, I pay the tab and we get bundled up again to find something else to do. I see a clearing in the trees just below the sitting area and ask one of the servers about it.

The path is shoveled clean to the frozen pond that is just visible through the trees. Snow sits in fluffy clumps on the branches around us. The needles on the trees have the same frosty covering. It's just Drea and I on the path making the moment feel even more special. She holds onto my arm with both of her mitted hands as we walk side by side. It's romantic even in the daylight. I might not be the most slick motherfucker, but this is pretty damn smooth for a day date. I didn't even plan it to be this way. For us, it just seems like everything is falling into place.

When the trees clear and the pond comes into view, we both gasp at how stunning the view is. Crystal blue frozen water spans out in front of us. Some areas are snowier than others, but there is a distinct layer of ice underneath. There are poles wrapped in festive ribbons and bows with lights strung between them in red, green, and white. It looks like something right out of a Christmas card. If I were a smart man, I'd tell her right now that I love her with all of my heart. Probably should drop to one knee. I never claimed to be a smart man. If I were, I'd have a ring on me at all times so I'd be prepared to lock this in and let everyone know she's mine. That I'm hers.

I still have time.

"Wow," Drea says, pulling me from my thoughts. "I'm so happy we got to see this."

"Me too. The woman said frozen pond, but I wasn't expecting it to be this..."

"Fancy?"

"Yea... or empty with how it looks." It's so nice out here, I'd expect everyone to at least come and see it on their trip. I guess none of these cops are too keen on the views outside of the retreat.

Drea shrugs, pulling us closer to a dip in the snow piled up on the side of the pond."Well, Christmas was yesterday, it was probably busier then."

"You're right. Missed that because you were insatiable."

She bumps me with her shoulder, "Me? I don't remember it that way."

Leaning into her side, I whisper, "Remember you begging me to fit my dick inside your tight little slit."

She shivers. "Stop that Ant or I'll make you go back to the room right now."

I chuckle at her teasing. "Oh no," I feign dismay, backing away from her. "What a horrible idea. Please don't make me go back there." I hold my hands up in front of me as she tries to grab me.

Somehow, I end up tripping and falling backward and she comes tumbling down with me. Snow flies up around us and we're both covered by the time we stop laughing.

She hovers over me with her hands on my chest. My heart beats wildly under her touch. Looking from my eyes to my lips, I meet her in the middle and kiss her like the starved man I am. My tongue slips into her mouth and claims what was always meant to be mine. She moans when I take her bottom lip between my teeth for a soft nip.

I sit up so that she's straddling me. I could care less that my jeans are getting soaked through with my coat not protecting my ass on the hard ground. My hands find their way to Drea's ass and hold her even closer to me. The heat from her hot little core blazes even with our layers between us and I'm questioning if I could maybe slip inside her out here with no one catching us.

My fingers are searching under her tunic and coat to land on the button of her jeans when my phone rings.

I stop for a moment and consider not answering, but I've got all the time in the world to be with my girl now. I can get on and off the phone in no time to get back to what we're doing. Drea kisses my neck, swirling her tongue and making me question whether I want to answer this phone again.

I fish my phone out of my pocket and see it's Mireya calling. I'll always have time for her. "What's up?" I ask when I answer.

"Ant," Mireya whispers. "You have to help me." I hear the tears in her words and freeze.

"What do you mean? What's wrong?" Now, Drea freezes. Her head pops up, concern already in her features.

"I-I don't know where I am. I ran. I just ran with Milli and we're hiding."

"Ran? Why did you run? Reya, what's going on?" Drea climbs off me and we're both standing, listening to the call as I put it on speakerphone. "Drea's here too."

"Some people came and grabbed Dad. They grabbed him and he's in the trunk of the car. I-I don't know what to do. They t-took him!" She sobs in the line and my heart breaks just that little bit more. "I h-heard a gunshot. They t-took him."

"Fuck!" I shout. "Do you remember our winter survival course? Hide and stay hidden until you hear us. Okay?"

"My phone doesn't have service past the trees. Ant, I'm scared."

"It will be okay. We're coming for you. Just hang tight. Stay with Milli." I'm grabbing Drea's hand and pulling her back down the idyllic little path. "Drop a pin and we're gonna come get you. Don't use your phone. Save the battery."

"Okay. Please hurry," she whispers.

Goddamn. What did Colton get them into?

# CHAPTER 28

# Tony

A BLUR. THE NEXT twenty minutes of us gathering all our stuff from the room and checking out is a blur.

The car is silent as I see Drea freaking out in the passenger seat. She watches the little dot as we get closer and closer to her daughter.

There's a chasm spreading between us that only I know the origin of.

I've held on to these secrets for far too long. Now, someone I love is in danger because I kept my mouth shut. "Drea, what do you know about Colton?"

She blinks. I glance over to her from the road, "He's from Harmony Hill. We spent a lot of time together as kids. His grandmother, mom, and my mom are good friends—"

"No. Not that shit. Like, with how he makes money. Outside of the police department. Know anything about it?" God, I pray she does because I don't know if I can shatter all of her innocence about him in one swipe. Goddamn.

Her brows pinch. "I know that he used to sell a little weed when we were in high school, but he's a cop now."

Her tone implies that she doesn't know anything about what he's been doing recently. "Not used to." I huff out a breath. Feeling both frustrated and angry that I had to be the one to tell her all of this. "Yea... A cop. A sheriff. What difference do you think that makes?"

She raises her hand from her leg for it to flop uselessly back into her lap, clearly frustrated too. "It makes all the difference! That's illegal. He can't possibly be doing anything he's sworn not to do."

I tap the steering wheel a few times. The silence stretches between us as I debate how much to tell her. What *can* I tell her? "Just because he wears a badge, doesn't make him an upstanding citizen."

"Will you just tell me what that means? What the shit does that have to do with my daughter hiding in the forest right now?" Her brows pinch even tighter as she considers me.

"It's my fault," I admit.

Drea frowns and I hate it. "Anthony... Tell me what is going on!"

"Do you remember when I brought you to Colton's house after your beater kicked it on the side of the road?"

"Kind of... Yes. What about it?"

"Blue and I showed up with you and Mireya. Reya played with Milli out back and Blue was in the house with Colton and all his 'goons.'"

She nods her head, motioning for me to continue. "What about it?"

"Blue came to town looking to get me to come back home. Go back to the boot. I turned him down like I always do. But we ended up at your baby daddy's house."

"Don't call him that," she snaps.

"Drea. I need you to pay attention. What I call that dumbass is not important."

She huffs, crossing her arms over her chest. "Okay. He was talking with Blue..." She's too agitated to stay in one position, her arms whipping up into the air, then flopping into her lap between her thighs. "What about it?" She repeats.

I sigh. "Do you know what Blue does? What my family is known for?"

This deeper frown is devastating. She looks at me for a long time. I don't know if she suspects or has ever heard anything about it. It certainly was not from my mouth. "No," she responds after a while.

"The Duponts move the most weight of legalized substances into states that have not legalized them yet... that would have been my fate if I had stayed but I didn't."

"Legalized substances? What?" She punches my arm. "Like what?"

"Weed, mostly. But they started adding mushrooms, hallucinogens... that kind of thing. I can't be sure but it stands to pass."

"What does this have to do with Colton?"

"It has everything to do with him!" I slam my hand on the wheel and I hear her gasp. "If I had not introduced those two that day, everything would have been different."

"What do you mean? What do—"

"He's a part of all of this Drea. He's allowing all this weight to move out of Colorado to Louisiana undetected and undeterred. He's overseeing it. Allowing the runners to get past state lines."

She shakes her head in disbelief. "He's just a sheriff in a tiny town. He's a cop. He can't be doing that."

"I don't know exactly how it works, but what business would another cop have in stopping a sheriff's truck? They don't care about that. Or better yet, how would it benefit them." I shake my head. "All I know is that it has gotten bigger and bigger. Who knows exactly how big because I'm not in that shit. Tried my best to stay out of it."

"And my daughter is missing..." Drea trails off and I see the first tear fall before she begins hitting me in earnest now. "You knew Colton was doing this shit and you still let him take my daughter into the middle of the woods alone? How could you not say anything?" More tears fall and I reach for her face to wipe them. She smacks my hand. "I can't even get a hold of him! I don't know where my daughter is!"

I focus on the road again. The highway has been cleared but it's still dangerous to drive in this weather. I exhale a deep breath. "You know I care about Mireya. Drea, you allowed him to be a part of her life long before I met her. Who am I to tell you what your kid can or can't do? I don't know what happened to Colton or who took him. All I know is that Blue has been to Colorado more than once in the past couple of months. That is not a good sign for him."

"Your brother... I've had him in my home. Cooked for him. Now, he might have done something to the father of my only child. What could happen to Colton?"

"I don't know," I admit, feeling as defeated as ever. I fucked up in not telling her. I fucked up.

"What do you mean you don't know? This is your brother!"

"I'm not a part of that operation. Don't know enough about it. I never wanted to. I came to Alpenglow to escape all this bullshit. I wanted no part in it. Knowing anything could incriminate me, incriminate you."

She shakes her head. "My daughter is missing. Ant, we have to find her. I don't know what I'll do if I lose her."

"We will. I know we will. I'm sorry, D."

"I can't believe I trusted you and this is what happens!" I open my mouth to apologize again, but she holds up a hand. "I don't want to hear your excuses. I don't want to talk until my daughter is safe in my arms again. That is the only thing I have time for." And just like that, every wall we climbed, every line we crossed, every bit of progress the two of us have made, disappears and I'm back to square one. My hands tighten on the steering wheel.

The only person I should be mad with is myself.

The car is silent again until we pull into the driveway for Colton's family cabin. There is only one car, Colton's, when we park. Drea is out of the car and marching over to the cabin as soon as we stop.

I'm right behind her until I hear something coming from Colton's trunk. Taking a chance, and maybe a stupid one, I open it.

He's shivering in only a tank and boxers. His wrists and ankles are duct taped and so is his mouth. He looks barely conscious with bruises marring his light brown face where he isn't bleeding. "Fuck. You are in a bad way," I comment. I don't have my knife or anything on me so I pick him up and carry his shivering body to the cabin. Drea is already standing in the kitchen on the phone with who knows who right now. I drop Colton onto the couch and go to the kitchen to search for scissors or a knife.

"He better know where my daughter is," Drea says. "I updated the girls about us being here. They're on their way. I can't believe this is happening." She holds her face in her hands and I rush over to her, refusing to let this space exist between us even though I am part of the problem.

Before I reach her, I hear an unfamiliar voice in the cabin. "Who the fuck are you?"

I turn around slowly.

"Hands up," he barks. "I'm gonna ask again before I start shooting. Who the fuck are you?"

"I'm Tony." I keep my hands up in the air. "We just came looking for the girl that was here. We don't want any trouble." Though trouble has already found us and it's my fault.

"That so?" He questions. I nod and he cocks the safety off his gun. "Funny. Why is Colton not in the trunk where I left him? Looks to me like you do want trouble."

Colton is still laying on the couch in the living room behind us but I'd like to kick his ass right now. Drea stands half behind me and I can feel her shivering with fear, or adrenaline maybe, against my back.

"Listen. Don't want anything to do with what you and Colton have going. Okay? We just want to find his daughter and leave."

"Put the fucking gun down, Thane." A skinny woman with blonde braids walks around him in the small cabin space. "They clearly don't know any-thing. It's fucking Tony. If you shoot Blue's brother, you're guaranteeing bullets in our heads too."

I watch the woman as she looks in the kitchen before she gets close to us at the back counter. I put an arm around Drea behind me. "Where is Mireya?"

She flashes me a smile that is meant to be friendly but appears sinister with the glint in her dark eyes. "I think we got off on the wrong foot. I'm Kitty. This is Thane. We work for your brother." She takes another step in our direction. "I don't know anything about a girl. We're only here for one reason. Something went wrong with the package we were supposed to be delivering and now we just want to talk to Colton about that. You don't need to get involved or even remember who we are. Probably best that you don't." She pats my chest and I take a step back from her. She immediately reaches behind her for a small gun and it's aimed at my chest before I can blink.

"This is not our business. Trust me, we want nothing to do with it," I rush out. Unarmed and with too much on the line, placating is the best I can manage until we get out of this alive. Each second we spend here is another second that Mireya needs us to stay alive.

"Perfect. Just tell us where Colton is and we will be on our way."

I feel no loyalty toward that prick. Ultimately, he got us into this mess. "Couch," I say and she backs out of the kitchen to the living room. Thane is right behind her with his gun still trained on us.

I hear the dull thud of something meeting flesh and the rip of duct tape. "I didn't sign up for this shit." Colton groans and falls to the floor. "Where is the girl?" Kitty asks.

"Don't... Know..." he wheezes between coughs. "Not... Here..."

Another thud and I feel Drea rush from behind me, "What do you mean Mireya's not here?" Thane steps out of her way, amused at the fury on her face when she charges up to Colton. I'm right behind her. She tries to grab for him, but I hold her back. I know she's upset right now but I don't want her to do something we will all regret. Time is of the essence and if he doesn't know where she is then we need to try and find her ourselves. "You piece of shit. How could you let this happen to our daughter?"

"D, c'mon. He made his own decisions. We need to find Mireya and fast." I still hold her in my arms when I turn to the small woman in front of us. "I don't care what you do with him. We don't want any part of it. Like I said, just want to find the girl. If you're done with us, then we're going to do that."

She considers me. Her eyes flick to Thane behind us for a moment and then back to me. "Thanks," Kitty says, "Be on your way, and don't come back. We're watching." For someone so small, I know there's no leeway with this woman.

I back us out of the front door to the cabin and Thane closes the door behind us.

Once outside, Drea takes one look around at the trees past the clearing. "She could be anywhere," she cries.

"We'll find her. Our friends will be here to help us look."

"But not the police?"

I shake my head and she nods, "You're probably right. I don't know. I just wish I could find a clue about where she's gone."

"First, you have to try to calm down. Know that she's going to be okay. Mireya is smart and capable. We will find her."

Snow has covered the ground and made it hard to see exactly where anyone had been in the wooded area. We call out to her, hoping that we'll get to her before something else can.

Using what I can remember from our winter survival course that I helped Reese teach at the Ranch, Drea and I look through the woods and make note of where we are. It's tense and each minute that passes feels like hours as the cold starts to affect both Drea and I.

There's a small voice coming from the west and I follow it. "Mireya. Hang on, we're coming." I call, moving quickly through the branches, breaking them if necessary to reach her.

At first, I don't know what is happening but I feel something brush my pant leg and double back. "Mireya?"

I start digging at the snow-packed tight against the fallen logs. She managed to make a shelter with packed snow that kept her hidden and away from the elements. Milli whimpers when she sees me and the both of them are shivering.

She only has on a sweater and jeans with her leather boots. It's almost nighttime now. Hours out in this kind of weather could have been much worse had she not found shelter. Taking my coat off, I grab her out of the little hole and wrap her up.

"A-a-a-nt. You found me. M-m-ma?"

"I'm here baby. I'm here." Drea turns to me, tears streaming down her face. "Let's go. We need to go." She scoops up my dog and we make our way back out of the unforgiving weather.

By the time we get back to the cabin, an ambulance is already there. I carry the girl in my arms over to the truck, shocked to see that Colton is already there.

He looks badly beaten and his leg is being wrapped.

One of the EMTs rushes to help Mireya and starts assessing her. Drea is right by her side.

I give them space while I hold my dog who has held up far better than Mireya. In my arms, she wiggles about until I let her down and she goes to stand at Drea's side.

My sights are set on the grown man who really caused this mess. I don't have much time before the EMTs will be making everyone clear the area to head for the hospital. Colton looks even worse than he did when we left him. He's already talking by the time I reach him. "Thane tried to cross Blue. I suspected but didn't know quite how. He was gonna divert the package, to who knows where, but I thought going to the cabin would keep me out of it. He found me, beat me, and shot me in the knee to keep me from going after him. Has my phone and wallet too."

I ignore his pained expression and the evidence of his beating. "Where is he now?"

"Left. Drove off as soon as he got what he wanted."

"Which was?"

"The location of the package. I was gonna have someone else run it or I would tell Blue exactly what happened. But I couldn't. I'm not willing to die over this shit."

"Yea," I growl ready to dismiss him completely and get my brother on the phone.

Our friends comfort Drea as she watches the EMT work on Mireya as much as they can. She needs to get to the hospital. Drea looks around and when her gaze lands on me, I nod. "I'll be there as soon as I can."

She takes in my words and gets into the back of the ambulance with her daughter. I watch them get her stable and turn my attention back to Colton. "This ends today or you're done seeing Reya. I don't give a shit about what you're doing behind closed doors, but I do care about those two. Your greed and ignorance almost cost her life and yours."

"That's rich coming from you. You're as much a danger to them as I am. Blue has plenty of enemies and they're only growing as he gains more territory."

"That doesn't have anything to do with me. I'm not a danger to them." Even saying the words aloud makes me doubt their validity.

He shrugs, looking pained when he turns on his gurney. "You can't know that."

The EMT moves me out of the way as they roll Colton in too. I'm still in my head when the lights and siren sounds of the emergency vehicle charge down the driveway and onto the street.

# CHAPTER 29

# Drea

I KNEW THIS WOULD happen. He was too good to be true.

I sit on the side of my daughter's bed, her hospital bed. It's been hours and finally, I've been able to see her again. They were confident that she wouldn't need to be intubated because Milli was able to keep her warm in their little shelter out in the woods.

I'm stuck between feeling like the worst mother and the worst person for not seeing all that I learned about Colton from Ant. He kept all of that from me and I don't know how I ever trusted either of them.

All that I thought Ant was and I was still not able to protect me or my daughter from his mistakes.

Men are all shit.

No exceptions, whatsoever.

Mireya is sleeping in a hospital bed as the machines beep and whir around her. My sweet girl who trusted him most. She called him when she needed help. A fact that was not lost on me.

We both trusted him.

A knock at the door pulls my gaze away from my daughter's peaceful face.

Ant's large body takes up the entirety of the doorway. He ducks inside the room. I feel his familiar presence like a change in the warmth of the room. It brought me comfort before, but now I don't know exactly how to feel. I want to be angry. I want to fight for the ignorance I had before now.

When we were perfect.

When everything made sense between us.

He moves closer to the bed, taking in her condition. There's pain and regret on his face as he looks her over. It tugs at my heart, but I won't be sucked into his emotions. My own is too fierce and feral right now with my daughter in the hospital for his secrets.

I clear my throat, "Can I talk to you?"

He faces me fully and I feel like I've been hit by a truck. His handsome face still shows the full range of emotions he's feeling with all his vulnerability lining his eyes. "Yea. What's up?"

Shaking my head, I say, "No. Let's go out for a bit."

His brow furrows but he pats Mireya's arm before following me. I hear his heavy boots behind me as we make it outside the hospital.

I find a clear spot under the alcove off to the side of the emergency room. In the warmer months, I'm certain this is likely a garden or something. Now, it's covered in snow at all heights. Taking in a lungful of the cold air, I say what's been on my mind. "I think we should forget all about the past couple of days."

He flinches. "Forget about it?"

"I just don't think this is going to work." I shake my head and cross my arms over my chest. "I have to think about Mireya and what's best for her."

His jaw ticks and he just stares at me for a bit. We look at each other but I refuse to break the silence first. I can feel the tears singeing my eyes uttering the few words I already have. My emotions are so high with everything that has happened in the last seventy-two hours.

"Why would we do that?" He asks in a voice that is too soft for how I feel. Hearing that hurt could make me change my mind. I can't do that. I won't.

"I just—I don't think I can trust you anymore."

Now he really looks affronted. "Trust *me*?"

"Yes. You kept all of this from me." I gesture around me at nothing in particular. "My daughter is in the hospital. I had a gun pulled on me." I huff. "My daughter is in the goddamn hospital!" Repeating it louder now as the dam on my control slips.

"How is that because of your trust for me?"

"Anthony—"

"Wow. Anthony, is it?" He nods a couple of times as I chew my lip. "How am I in trouble? None of this is because of me."

"Your brother is some big gang lord and you never thought to tell me that. You never thought to tell me that Mireya's Dad was also connected to this. You never did. You never planned to. I was always going to be blindsided by what you're hiding from me."

"I was protecting you from the truth. Having that knowledge could be deadly if the wrong people found out you have any idea of what is going on here."

"I don't care. You knew my daughter would be implicated. I have to look out for her."

"No."

"You can't say no. Ant, this is my only daughter. She is the one thing I refuse to budge on."

"Your one thing? Drea you have a list longer than the encyclopedia about what you want and need. I've been there for you more than anyone else *ever* has. Do you really put so little faith in me?"

"I shouldn't have put faith in *anyone* but myself. Definitely not in someone who's not even committed to me." I throw my hands up into the air. "Speaking of truths you've blindsided me with, you have a whole girlfriend likely worrying about you."

His jaw ticks again. "I don't," he bites out.

"Excuse me?"

"Steph and I aren't together anymore. I ended that."

I blink. "What? When? And you kept that from me? Why?"

"I don't know," he grumbles. "There never seemed like a good time to tell you."

"Never... a good... time." I punch a fist into the air. "You are not the man I thought you were. What could have happened if... if any detail were different. With anything! Had I known what you clearly knew about Colton..." I stop talking when my throat gets too clogged with emotion for me to continue. It's too much. Everything is too much for me to deal with right now.

"Drea. I can't be held responsible for what Colton and Blue have going on. With Steph, I get it." He reaches for my hand, but it sits lifelessly in his. I don't grasp it back like I always do. I'm so unsure of everything right now. "That's not my life. I left all that behind me when I came here. I would never knowingly put Mireya in danger." He blinks a few times but I can still see his eyes turning glassy with unshed tears. "I love that girl more than I have a right to. I know that. But you have to see that too."

"That hurts more than anything else. I thought that you could protect us both from getting hurt but you didn't."

The blaring of ambulances cuts into our conversation and I take a step away from him. A commotion of staff moves around to get the gurneys out of the vehicles. I notice right away that one of them is Mack Stewart. I gasp when I see the state of his leg and it's a miracle that I could even recognize him with the gross angle of his nose and gauze there. The flannel was a dead giveaway though. It's the same one Reese bought all of us for Christmas last year in mustard yellow and navy blue with the Mason Ranch logo on the breast pocket.

I'm dialing Reese before I even think about it. She was already on her way to the hospital for me and Mireya, but now she's in hysterics. She passed the scene of the accident with his truck and another. She chatters animatedly but I hear nothing when I see the other two gurneys.

It's Kitty and another body that's covered completely. She looks unconscious for sure. I have no idea who is under that covering but I'd bet anything that it's Thane.

The roads aren't safe even when shoveled and salted. If they're from Louisiana like they sounded, driving in this kind of weather had to be foreign to them. I can only hope that Mack survived their reckless driving if they did in fact get into an accident with each other.

"Drea, let's talk about this when everything has cooled down." I forgot that my hand was still in Anthony's. I tug it out of his grasp. "We should go back into the hospital with Mireya."

"No. There's no *we*. I don't want to talk about anything right now. I want space and I want you to give it to me. Can you do that?"

His lips press into a thin line, but he nods before walking off to his car.

I watch him go and it's not until he pulls out of the parking lot that the tears I was holding onto fall.

# CHAPTER 30

# Drea

THE DOORBELL RINGS AND I peer over my shoulder towards it. Sighing, I use my forearm to swipe hair out of my face, only to realize there's already flour on my arm so I've just got flour on my face now.

Reaching for a towel instead, I wipe my hands and forehead to rush over to the front door. *Maybe Ant is here to talk.*

Looking out of the peephole, I smile and open the door for Mel, Reese, and Clo. "If this is going to go the same way the conversation at Mel's house went, I'd rather not."

Clo has the decency to look a little chastised. "We might have gone a little hard that time."

"Honestly, how are we expected to be anything less, when we don't have you to be the voice of reason?" Reese says, hugging me on her way into the house behind Clo.

"I'm not included in that," Mel says when she enters last.

"We know," the three of us say and laugh.

Mel puts her hands up. "Just want to make that clear."

They all follow me into the kitchen and I know when they've made it in because their chatter stops abruptly.

"You've been busy huh, Drea?" Reese tilts a bowl towards her, looking at the contents.

"Busy? No understatement could be more understated." Clo looks for a place to put her huge purse down but there aren't any surfaces for her things. "Did you book another event without us knowing?"

"No," I say, looking around the kitchen with fresh eyes.

"Riiight..." Reese drawls. "So, umm, walk me through what exactly is going on here and I'll save my assumptions for later."

I clear my throat. "I'm just making a few things." Pointing toward the far left counter, I just walked away from. I say, "Tortillas, fresh. Obviously. Can never have too many. I've got about a hundred so far but I figured I could take some to the shop and use them for a menu item... or something."

Gesturing to the mixer that is still whirring on the island, I tell them, "I'm making more of that maple meringue since it's such a big hit. Timer is almost up on that. Maple is just warming on the stove now. It's gonna go inside the choux puffs that are cooling off in the oven right now." All four trays. Not that they asked, or that I'm going to volunteer the information either.

"I have a couple of pork shoulders in the pressure cooker right now. Pulled pork will be good to stock the freezer." Looking over to where Mel is inching, I say, "No need to check in there. I'll send some home with you all." She doesn't stop though and the three of them gasp at how full my freezer already is with the food I've been cooking almost non-stop since I got back from the hospital with Mireya.

Mel cringes and closes the freezer door. "Okay... Drea, I've never seen that much food in your freezer. This is an industrial-sized one, right? I'm scared to even look in the fridge."

"I'm not," Reese says and yanks the fridge open. Another round of gasps. "Where are you going to possibly put all this food, Drea? We haven't even finished the tour of counters yet and you're still making stuff."

"Well, the double chocolate cake..." I look down at my hands. "I'm just waiting for the puffs to cool so I can bake them off."

Clo puts a hand on my arm, "That's six pans of cake over there. Are you really making six pans of double chocolate cake?"

Still talking to my hands, I whisper, "I can't stop." It's Chloe who hugs me first, but it's not long before Reese and Mel join her in embracing me. The tears fall and I let them in the arms of the women I know have my back. Reese drove me back to the resort so I could get my van after leaving without it. When I got Mireya settled to rest upstairs in her room, I came into the kitchen. The Christmas decorations, specifically the garland I'd decorated and hung on the window in my kitchen, reminded me of him. And thoughts of him in my kitchen brought on all types of memories between us. All of them were good and that hurt even worse.

I was hurt and I can't take back those words. Was I hurt about him keeping Steph a secret from me, both dating her and then breaking up with her? Yes. It hurt to think that he couldn't share that with me. That I wasn't his safe space like he was for me. Should I have pushed him away because of that? Probably not.

We needed to talk about it.

Everything with his brother just feels overblown now. I wish I had known but it also made sense to me why he wouldn't tell me about whatever criminal activity his brother was involved in. I should have been grateful for that ignorance. But now that I know, I have so much respect for his choice. How he escaped that life and chose a better future for himself. I'm more angry that my poor choice, of the Colton variety, dragged him back into it. I don't know how that's affecting him. I still can't believe Blue runs some criminal empire. He always seemed like a chill guy. But I suppose you don't just go around telling people you're the don...

At the end of the day, none of this was his fault and I don't think that I can't trust him. If it weren't for him, I don't know if my daughter would be alive right now. He is still the best guy that I know and I'm lost without him.

*I miss him so damn much.*

"If I stop working for even a second, I'll have to think about everything that happened and I don't want to."

"Mireya is fine. She's sleeping upstairs and CJ told me that she's even texted him a few times." Reese rubs my back. "What's wrong? Tell your girls who we need to beat up."

"Reese, look at the pattern," Mel says. "These are all his favorites. I'm guessing but I know I've almost lost a hand about the chocolate cake, at least. Is that what this is about?"

"You miss him," Clo says simply and I cry even harder.

"I do," I blubber. "I miss him so much."

"Then get him back," Reese says softly, rubbing my back.

"I told him that I couldn't trust him. I—"

"Now tell him something different. You two need to talk. Emotions were high. There was a lot happening. You can apologize and talk it out." Mel says.

"Some of this cake would definitely smooth things over too. I have also almost lost a hand because of this shit." Clo adds, handing me a tissue from her purse.

"You think I can fix this?" They all nod.

"I think you can work together to fix what broke between you two," Reese says.

They stayed for a while longer, helping me clean up the kitchen and figure out where all this extra food could go.

I finish baking and frosting the cake before I shower and get ready to leave.

Clo is the first to give me approval since she is the one who picked out my outfit, whereas Reese picked out lingerie. Mel gave me a hug and I felt so much better with all of us leaving the house together.

"Update us. Tomorrow, of course. I don't need that heavy breathing on my line. I've got kids," Reese says before she pulls out in her SUV with my friends and food in tow.

In front of Ant's house, I can already see that he's not home. Only his work truck is in the driveway. There are no lights on in his house.

Looking over at the chocolate cake, I breathe in deeply and try to calm down. He's just at Taylor's or something.

Then my phone lights up with a call from Reese. I accept the call immediately.

"Honey? Are you over there?"

"Yea. I'm parked out front. I don't think he's here." I hear the hope in my own voice and it feels pointless because I know she doesn't have anything good to say from the tone she took.

"No... He's not there. Milli is here with my parents. Tony went to Louisiana yesterday. Didn't say when he'd be back."

# CHAPTER 31

## Tony

THERE'S A KNOCK AT my door and I get up from the couch to go see who it is. Milli is hot on my ankles when I look through the peephole. I was hoping it'd be Drea but no. It's my brother. I reluctantly open the door for him and he comes in, rubbing his bare hands together. He couldn't have been out there longer than a few minutes. Guess I really have gotten used to the winters here. Nothing like how it is in Clayton.

"I just got back from the hospital," he announces, though I haven't asked him any questions.

My mood is sour and salty since I've been sitting in my house thinking about everything I've been through this past week. "For what?"

He scrunches his eyebrows in a way that is so similar to mine. Oddly enough, I am the more sinister-looking of the two of us because of the cuts on my eyebrow from being a clumsy kid. "Colton and one of my others were there. I had to try and get the stories straight. Your name came up in both."

"So what? Said one of your others. What about that Thane guy?"

He shrugs a shoulder, "He didn't make it. Dead men can't tell any more stories."

I shudder. "Did you—"

"Be real, T. You think I'd off somebody in a public hospital? This ain't that. I like my life in the free world just as much as you."

I roll my eyes. "Look, I don't know what you'd do."

"I know." He sits on the couch next to me. "What do you know about that Mack dude?"

I shrug a shoulder. "Good guy, I guess. Works on the Ranch. Lives right next to it, actually. What about him?"

"He was in the room with one of my runners like some kind of bodyguard. Didn't matter anyway because she was useless in terms of information."

"What does that mean?" I ask, then pause. "Wait, she?"

"Yea, she. Kitty."

"She was the woman Thane was with when we got to Colton at the cabin. She was holding a gun, kicking Colton's ass just the same."

"I bet. I brought her in myself. Saw potential. But now… I don't know. Too many things aren't lining up and she can't even remember me." I could care less about his criminal dealings. I'm already too close. I don't know anything and it still cost me everything.

I turn to my brother, "Why are you here?"

"I came to check on you." He puts a hand on my shoulder but I shrug him off.

"You see me and I'm alive, so you can go now."

"What's the big deal? She's just some woman."

"She's not *some woman*. She is the best woman I've ever met. You wouldn't know what love looked like and you definitely wouldn't know what I'm going through. I'm all fucked up waiting for her to let me back in."

"So why the fuck are you here then? She needs you. You lose her and then what? You just mope around here."

"Look. She doesn't want her life entwined with us."

"Mmh. Sounds like giving up to me." Blue looks thoughtful for a moment and I don't know what will come out of his mouth next. "I need your advice." That is not what I expected.

"I don't know if I'm the best person to do that."

"Nah, just be real with me. I think you can give me… perspective."

"Hmm"

"You got out. I always thought you were making the best choice for you. No bullshit. It really made me respect you. This life, this life is not for everybody. I'm not gonna lie to you and say that I don't love it. I do. But I wonder... when I get ready to settle down like the simp you are for Drea, will I have to give it up?"

"I don't know, man. Look at what happened to Ma. Gone because of whatever shit Pa was into. This girl, whoever she is... She'll always have a target on her back."

"But that's the thing. Pa was moving shady. He wasn't doing what we do now. The operation doesn't even look like how he had it. If he were here, he'd be proud."

"It's even more dangerous. I've only caught a glimpse and I almost lost my life."

"Ack. Kitty would not have let that happen. Thane was dumb as shit. That got... out of hand. As much as I believe in solving the problem myself, karma did it for me."

"My employee did it for you." I had only seen Mack briefly before I went to see Mireya that day. His leg was already... fucked, no other word for it. He's lucky if that thing heals right.

Blue holds his hands out in front of him. "An accident is an accident. One less drop of blood on my hands."

I shiver, thinking about what amount of blood *is* on my brother's hands. "Whatever." I get up and grab two beers from the fridge, handing one to Blue. "What else do you want?" AKA *how do I get rid of you?*

"How can I find someone in this crazy world? Is it even fair?" I sit back down on my couch, but Blue perches on the armrest.

"Nothin' fair about life. You could lose someone just as easily to a car accident as you could to a bullet. If she knows you, then she'll know that." I swig some of my beer and set it on my knee. Picking at the label on the neck with my thumbnail, I tilt it one way and then the other. "Bruh, you're a risk no matter how you play it."

"You're right."

"Should I be worried about some woman in your grasp?"

"Yea," he says simply.

I sit up straight on the couch, setting my beer on the coffee table. "What the fuck? Who?"

"Probably best you don't know at this point. Life's a risk, remember?"

Shaking my head, I finish my beer and go to grab another. Before I leave, I grab some pretzels from my pantry too. "I'll take your word for it." That's four beers down and it's not quite two in the afternoon. At this rate, I'll sleep like a baby when I break open the brown. Time flies by much faster when I'm two sheets to the wind. My heart can't hurt if I'm too drunk to see straight. It'll take more than this to get there though. Normally a benefit of being as big as I am, but now I'm gonna have to try hard to get smashed.

"I guess as a heads up, I'll let you know. We're taking Colton back with us when he's discharged today."

"You what?"

"He knows something. Thane's gone and Kitty was only in so deep before she lost her memory. Without what Colton knows, we don't have the information needed to nip this shit in the bud."

"I thought you said it wasn't that."

"It's not. I don't need a camera crew or audience. Can't have anybody thinking I've gone soft. I'll get the answers I'm looking for or find out who has them."

"Fuck." I already know what this means. "Give me your word that you're not going to kill him."

"Why?"

"He's Mireya's Daddy. It would devastate her to lose him after everything that's happened."

"So, what?"

"I can't let you do that."

He laughs, a cruel sound. "Let me? Lil' bro you don't *let* me do shit. If I want him, I'll snatch him. Simple."

"C'mon, there's gotta be another way."

He scratches his chin. "Oh, there is..."

"Shit." I rub a hand over my face, already exhausted with what I know is coming for me.

"Welcome to the family, T."

# CHAPTER 32

# Tony

I'VE BEEN BACK TO Louisiana many times since I left the first time. There should be no difference in returning now, but there is.

As I stand in this warehouse so far off the highway and main roads surrounded by Blue's men and women, it's clear that I'm in far over my head. They grabbed Colton as soon as we arrived but I got to casually stroll behind my brother as he led me into, what I imagine is his primary workplace.

This seedy warehouse is as seedy as you could picture a warehouse would be. There are guards on every corner and nothing out in the open for you to know what's going on. It's all closed doors. Less a comfort than it would seem. Unless escorted, you couldn't find your way out. It's a maze of treachery. I trust my brother not to turn on me but I could not say the same is true for the man I brought here.

The room we're in now is wide open with nothing in it except a drain in the middle. A large hose is curled on the wall and two large rolling carts sit right next to it. One guess on what is inside either of them. Colton sits, cuffed to a chair, just at the center of the room though I doubt he could get far with the full leg cast he has on. "This was not my plan. You have to believe me," he cries.

Blue's mouth lifts at the corner in a sinister way that would make me reconsider if I were in the same position Colton is right now. "It's easier for me to just get rid of you. Tell me why I shouldn't."

"I told you. I was moving the new stuff this weekend. Twice as much, as we discussed. I had all the sheriffs in Breck. I even had my ex as an alibi if need be." Blue flicks a look at me but focuses back on Colton. He's sweating in the chair under these bright ass lights. I'm not sure he even knows where we're standing. His mouth doesn't stop moving though. "I switched with Alex because I suspected Ethan—Thane—was doing something shifty. It didn't feel right."

There's a long silence where my brother cleans his nails with a very large Bowie knife. It's gratuitous but no one would question the actions of Blue. I've never truly seen him at work before. This is not the boy I grew up with or even the man who slept on my couch when he was in town. If I saw this version of Blue on the street, I'd cross to the other side. And that's saying something because I'm no punk otherwise.

"So where is the new stuff now?" Blue asks in a tone too casual for the consequences of his answer.

"If he hasn't gotten to it, it's still where I left it. I'd be bringing it now if I wasn't taken." Colton shoots a look toward me. I glare back at him. It was not my choice to take him. More importantly, he had a far better experience with me as opposed to coming here in the trunk of someone's car for almost a full day of travel.

"How can I trust that's true? Could be another setup. Who are you going to take out next?"

"It's not. I swear. I'm not that dumb or that smart. I didn't even know Thane was dead until Tony told me. I never had malignant intentions. Please..."

"Oh-ho-ho. He's pulling out the big cop words. You sure you aren't wearing a wire or some shit?" Blue had his men make sure of that before he even came into the room. I know he's messing with this guy.

"I-I'm not. Please. Ask Kitty. I was never working with Thane."

My brother stands from the table he was leaning on and walks closer to where Colton is strapped down. The lights cast harsh shadows on his face. "Great plan." Colton sighs a breath of relief. Blue turns to me, "Let's ask the woman who had brain damage and can't remember anything about what happened that day."

Colton pales. "She what?"

"Was admitted soon after you were." Colton furrows his brow. "Didn't know that? Awfully convenient that Thane is dead too."

Now, Colton looks a bit green. "I told you, I didn't know he was dead. I—"

"Now I have a package missing and a dead runner but you managed to survive."

"Tony, please. Tell him how you found me. I was ambushed—"

"By a small woman and a dumbass. Both of which don't have the package that they supposedly *intercepted* from you."

The chair rocks for a moment as Colton tries to free himself, pointlessly. "I don't have it. I never crossed you. It wasn't me. It was Thane. It's still where I left it! Please, believe me."

The steps Blue takes to walk behind Colton can be heard from anywhere in the warehouse, it's so quiet. His men respect him and that's made clear by how smooth his operation runs. When he speaks, it's just as clear. "Except it's not."

Colton's mouth hangs open before his head drops in defeat.

"So, where is it? Last time I'mma ask nicely."

"I don't know." It comes out as quiet as a whisper.

I don't know what to think. I didn't think Colton had it in him to make such a dumb decision but even I am shocked.

Blue turns to me again, "What do you think is worse? A few more gunshots or drowning?"

I shrug, jaw tight because I feel like I just brought this man to his death. I tried to do what was best with my back against the wall but I still failed. Whatever Blue chooses, I don't want to be here for it.

Blue slowly runs the knife in his hand along the edge of Colton's face. Two of his men waste no time to flank him. "I think drowning. It's long but hey! Much easier for us because the gators will take care of you real nice. Much less cleanup for us. If I were you, I'd sing like a fucking canary to not end up as gator chow."

"Call Aaron." He mutters, sweat running down his face and darkening the t-shirt he's wearing.

"I'm sorry. What was that?" Blue asks.

"Aaron. He was the only other person who knew. He probably moved it again after everything happened with Thane and I ended up in the hospital."

"Just thought of that did you?"

"It was the contingency protocol for anything like this. He knows the danger we're all in if this shit goes topside. I have a family. He has a family. We all have people who would suffer if this ends badly... I didn't know if he did. I still don't but that's the only other reason why it would not be exactly where I said it was."

Blue nods to one of the guys to his left and he pulls out a burner phone. Colton gives him the number and Aaron picks up after a couple rings. "I'm at dinner right now. This better be good."

"I don't care if you were getting your dick sucked. Where's my fucking green?" Blue snarls.

"Blue? Oh. I thought you were... Can I talk to Colton? He's the only one who has this number..."

"Tell him where the goddamn package is, you idiot!"

"Geez. I just wanted to make sure you were okay, piece of shit..." He tells them where it's at. A storage facility on the other side of Harmony Hill from his house. Blue ends the call before Aaron can continue yapping.

"This was your lifeline. You better hope everything checks out."

◆•◆•◆

ALMOST NINETEEN MORE HOURS until I can be back at my house and far from the events of the last two days. Irritation was twenty-four hours ago. Now, I'm irate.

I would like peace and quiet. Unfortunately, I won't be getting that with the bane of my existence riding in the passenger seat of my car.

"You vouched for me?" Colton asks just after we cross Louisiana state lines.

I grunt in agreement. Not particularly happy to drive him back to Colorado. It's a long drive and I'd prefer to not talk at all.

"You're an alright guy," he says.

"That really means less than nothing coming from you," I gruff.

"Fair. But, I mean it all the same."

My patience is thin and I still haven't gotten a chance to process exactly what I've been complicit in happening all because of him. "Do you think I care?"

"I don't. I don't." He shifts in his seat. "It's just that I was thinking Drea must be lucky to have you looking out for her. I'm not even your friend and you saved my life this weekend."

"Saving your life cost me the people you didn't even think about when you started working with my brother."

"What?"

"Your shady shit, which is beyond illegal, fucked up everything I had going with Drea. We were happy until you did whatever this was."

"How is that my fault? I'm the one with the busted leg and I don't know if my face will ever look the same after Thane and Kitty were done with me."

"Who cares about your face! What about Drea? Mireya? Your alibi? Why the hell did you get her that event?"

"Oh, that."

"Yea... that."

He shrugs, "We were moving heavy this week. I saw an opportunity to clear the path for us to get out of Colorado with ease. Every sheriff and deputy sheriff who would have been in the way of transport was too busy getting fat on the sweets Drea makes. None of them would have even thought about work. Plus, if they asked, I'd say I was with her and Mireya for the holiday. After how big the check was for this event, I'm sure she would've backed me up." The nasal quality of his voice, from too many hits to the face, annoys me even more as he explains himself. "Drea's always had a soft spot for me. Even when we were kids. In high school, I'd keep the joints burning at their parties in AR and that kept my pockets pretty heavy. She was always telling her friends she knew a guy. I was lucky to be *that guy*. It's unfortunate she got knocked up so quickly but I like Mireya. So, here we are. I'm not sure how she knew to bring Blue to my doorstep, but now my pockets are even heavier than ever. "

God. I knew there was a reason I hated this guy so much. He's a garbage person who was happy to use Drea for whatever she was useful to him at the time. I regret ever helping him in any capacity. The urge to kick him out of the car and make him walk the rest of the way is strong.

Drea may not want anything to do with me now that she knows the truth but I'll never stop caring about her. It was my mistake to think that this man didn't deserve every consequence coming to him, dealt by Blue's hand. Colton will never put their lives in danger like he did at the cabin for as long as I'm standing.

"I meant what I said before. Don't come around Drea or Mireya again. You're a shit person and they deserve better." He opens his mouth to speak but I talk louder. "I may have been born a Dupont, but I'm nothing like him or you. Those two are my priority and if it comes to picking my loyalty to the family name or them, I'm picking them. Every. Time. That means if I even hear you trying to reach out to them, I'm coming to break your other leg. One of these days, you're gonna screw over the wrong person and I won't let your bad decision affect them ever again." Looking over at him, I demand, "Understand?" He grits his teeth but nods his head. "Nah. Say that shit right now."

"I understand."

"Good. Now shut the hell up for the rest of this drive or I will leave you on the side of the road."

# CHAPTER 33

# Drea

IT'S THE NEXT DAY and we're all back at my house. I'm proud to say that I haven't baked anything. But I'm not proud of how many of the things I had already baked are in my body right now. I don't even want to think about it or I'll barf.

My girls are here and I should be grateful that someone has come to check on me. Again, I wish it were Ant but it's not. Tomorrow is New Year's Eve and I still haven't heard from him. I don't even know if he's back from Louisiana yet.

"He may have said that he and Steph are over but I'm sure he's running to repair whatever it was with her now."

"He could be in Louisiana for all sorts of reasons." Reese postures with all the hope she can muster in her voice.

"But he didn't tell me. Or Mireya. I only know because you said something."

Reese cringes just a little. "Maybe I shouldn't have said anything."

"Reese!" Mel and Clo yell in unison.

"What? I didn't know he wouldn't say anything." She sighs. "This is Tony we're talking about here! You can't assume the worst of him. He's a good guy."

"I know that," I mumble, squeezing a pillow closer to me.

"Well, why are you crying then?" Clo asks.

"Because I lost my best friend."

"Oh come off it. You two banged like bunnies..." Reese sits up on her side of the couch. The movement barely jostles me but I flop back on the couch like the hopeless thing I am right now. She doesn't acknowledge my dramatics and keeps going. "Like it was your Christmas present from Santa. You can't lie to us anymore and say he's just your best friend."

"True," Mel confirms

Clo claps her response, "True!"

"You all don't understand," I say, still lying on the couch with my safety pillow in my arms.

"Do you love this man?" Reese asks.

"He—"

She shakes her head, restating, "Do you love Tony, Drea?"

"Yes." Now that he's gone I can admit that. I loved him more than as a friend. Who knows for how long but there is no denying that I have deep feelings for this man who has been by my side all this time.

Reese places a hand on my arm and I finally sit up on the couch. "Then make it right with him."

Clo is next to come sit on the couch at my other side. "You mean more to him than Pantsuit Barbie!"

"I thought we agreed not to call her that anymore," Mel says.

"We didn't. You did," Clo clarifies.

"Call him," Reese says.

There's a quiet moment between the four of us with all their eyes on me. What she's suggesting is simple enough. A week ago, her statement would not have felt like a dare. But tonight?

"I can't."

"Can't or won't?" Mel asks softly.

I squeeze my eyes shut, wishing I could go back to a week ago when everything was how it was before. But that's a lie. I loved being with Ant. I loved waking up next to him and having a piece of him that no one else could have. I loved every moment of our time together... until I didn't. "It will be weird. I was awful to him. I threw stuff in his face that he didn't deserve. He deserves more—"

"Ah-ah. I'm gonna stop you right there because we've already had this conversation. I love you, I really do. But I'm drawing the line. You are amazing. We've covered that. Tony has been in love with you in every stage of your life. Through every horrible fling, you've had. Through all the ways you've sidelined him," Reese says.

"Endured all the teasing from us because we all knew he wanted you even though you were adamant about ignoring it," Chloe says.

"And he still wants to be here for you. Don't assume the worst, Drea. Call him and tell him your truth." Mel adds.

I agree with them but I still can't call. When they leave I lie in bed, thinking over what I would say to him. It needs to happen in person. He deserves that much.

I know Ant. Even if there were some surprises that I learned recently. He loves me and I love him. He will come for me and I will be here waiting for him when he does.

# CHAPTER 34

# Tony

KNOCKING ON THE DOOR at eleven-thirty, I feel just a little less confident in my plan than I did when I got back to my house finally. After a shower and a shave, I bolted out of the door. I texted Mireya and she told me that she was spending the night at the Mason-Whitfield's house which suited me well since Milli was with her. I've never been more thankful that they get along so well. I know my dog hasn't missed anything with me being gone.

Drea, the beautiful queen that she is, answers the door in another dress I've never seen before. It's shimmery and black, clinging to each one of her dangerous curves before it hits the ground. She can't be wearing heels since she's looking up at me in her doorway. Her hair is done and she has makeup on... maybe she's going somewhere or has just come back. I don't know and I don't care.

"Can I come in?" I ask after a few moments of us taking the other in. She doesn't answer but steps out of the way to let me inside the house that had always felt like home. I take my hat off and put it on the hook she hung for me.

I follow her to the couch and she sits, curling her feet under her. Instead of sitting next to her, I remain standing. She gives me a curious look at first but then her lips curl at the corner. "Sit. What are you doing?"

"I'm here to apply," I say.

Her face holds a squint of mild skepticism but she asks, "Apply for what?"

In the quiet drive back to Colorado, it gave me time to think about what I really wanted in life. I'm thirty-eight and not getting any younger. Drea wanted space and I think she's had enough of that. I can't let her go without at least trying to fix what I broke between us. Without trying for her again.

"First," I hold up my index finger. "Wanna start with, I'm a cake person and so are you. Not partial to pies or cookies but that's not important. I'd like both a slice and the whole cake because I love strawberry cake. You have double chocolate, I'll take that too."

"Okay..." she says but there's amusement on her face at my seemingly random declaration.

"Second," I hold up my middle finger too. "Don't want a situationship. I'm not that kind of guy and never want to find out what that kind of life is about. I value connection and purpose. I believe that it was my purpose to stand beside you and show you just how important and significant your presence is in my life. You could never be swapped out for another woman and I make do. If I can't have you, there is no other woman, living or dead, who could have that position."

Admittedly, it's awkward to just be standing here doing this, but I'll be uncomfortable if it means she knows everything I have in my heart for her. Her eyes are misty but she says nothing so I continue.

"Third," I add my ring finger to the ones I'm holding up. "Would never tell you no, if that was something you wanted, and I hope like hell it is, but I want more than to find the nearest fuckable surface to have you on. The times I have spent with you are some of the best memories of my life. And I hope to make many more... with the inclusion of the ones we make on the nearest fuckable surface, in any given room, at any given time."

Drea laughs quietly but moves to the edge of the couch. I can't believe it's been five years since I first heard her tell me these words. A conversation between the two of us that changed my life in every way possible.

"Fourth," holding up my last finger, I say, "Pleasure to me, actual me, not metaphorical me, means Andrea Montoya. I was happy to just have conversations with you. I was happy with just the smell of you in my truck or the smell of your house on my clothes at work. I was happy with the sound of your laugh across my skin when we watched those videos on your phone. I was happy with the opportunity to taste anything you made first because you valued my opinion. I was happy spending my nights here with you and Mireya and Milli together. You were the one for me long before I ever had the pleasure of knowing how you sound when you come or what you looked like with nothing on. If you will ever have me that way again, I'd come to you on my knees and show you that pleasing you pleases me very much.."

Drea stands from where she was sitting. A tear falls, but I catch it with my thumb. She holds my hand to her face and I make my final point.

"And last, I want to make a different pact. Hopefully, this one will be less painful for me, but the jury is still out on that." I chuff a laugh, feeling more nervous than I was before with my other four. "I promise to love you and keep you for as long as I live. I'll never keep anything from you and put your safety and the safety of Mireya before anything else. I promise to be your best friend for as long as you'll have me." I drop to one knee in front of her, taking her soft left hand in mine. "And if you'll have me, I'd like to apply to be your man, your only man, from now until my last day." Pulling the chocolate brown ring box from my back pocket, I open it and present the ring to her. "I love you more than words can say, Drea Montoya. Will you marry me?"

"Yes, Ant! God, yes! I love you so much. I want all of this too." She wiggles the finger in my hand and I slide the ring onto the third one. I hold my breath but it's a perfect fit. She looks at the ring with her hand over her mouth.

Standing from the ground, I scoop her up in my arms and carry her to the bedroom. Laying her gently on the bed, I cover her with my body, kissing her until we both need air.

I'm unbuttoning the button-down I wore over here when I notice she's giggling while looking at the ring on her finger.

"What you laughing at? Hurting a man's pride here." I had to stop at a jeweler in Denver on my way here just in case there was any chance I could have this woman again. Colton sat in the car as I chose the ring that made me instantly think of the woman currently giggling on the bed. An oval cut center stone with a cushion-shaped halo all around called to me when the man brought out the options available. Guessed on the size and it fit her perfectly. Life is just not that cruel. It looks good on my fiancée's hand.

"I was just—" she giggled some more, "thinking about how you are the latest man I have ever met." She breaks off into more giggles.

Now, I'm more confused. "What?"

"I've been waiting here all night for you. Took a shower, did my hair and makeup. There's even dinner waiting for us in the kitchen. And you get here just in time for the ball to drop. You're always so late," she falls back onto the bed. It takes me a second, but now I know Mireya must have told her I was in town long before I made my way over here.

I look at the time on my phone, "We've still got ten minutes," I complain. "Late is better than never."

"If you weren't over here by midnight, you would have gotten a very angry guest at the start of your new year." She laughs again, but I'm on her now, running my hands up her slinky dress to find out what she has underneath.

There's a side split that opens to reveal her sexy legs. I pull the lace black thong down her legs and put it into my mouth, smelling and tasting her before I've even got to her yet. She gasps as I spread her thighs open for me with my shoulders.

"You look so pretty spread open like this for me," she leans up on her elbows to get a better look at what I'm doing. I lean over her hot lips, running a finger through the wetness already spilling out for me. "Let's see what comes first, Boss Lady. You or the new year."

I couldn't tell you which one it was, all I know is that we brought in the new year both getting what we want.

# CHAPTER 35

## Epilogue - Drea, Six Months Later

"I'VE NEVER SEEN A group of people throw more parties than your friends," Ant grumbles from the bathroom. Fresh out of the shower, I can smell the body wash he prefers still in the air.

"There are lots of things to celebrate in life," I remind him

"If I had let it slip that I was trading in the Charger for an SUV, you all probably would throw a party for that too."

I walk into the bathroom, where Ant is putting product in his curls now that he's growing his hair out again. I turn to give him my back so he can zip up my sundress.

After reminiscing about how sexy he was with the long hair and beard, I noticed he had begun letting his time between haircuts linger more and more. He looks good with or without the hair, but being able to pull on it when he's between my thighs certainly has its benefits... for both of us.

Spinning back to face him, he whistles long and slow. I try to be quick in getting out of his grasp, but he already has me pinned against the sink with his hips. "Were you planning on going somewhere, baby?"

There's mischief in his eyes as they roam over the flouncy dress I've chosen. "I was..."

"Nah, you aren't," he says, hoisting me onto the sink before I can get another word in.

Only in his athletic shorts, I know exactly what's on his mind. Sliding me to the edge for easy access, he pulls his impressive length out over the stretchy waistband of his shorts.

My legs wrap around his waist. "People are going to be here in a little while! We do not have time for this, Anthony."

"Boss Lady," he nips at the sensitive swell of my breasts above my neckline. I should care if he's leaving marks that could be seen later but I don't. My toes are already curling with his erection hardening between my thighs. "They can wait a few minutes for me to make my wife come."

He cups me over my panties and I moan before giving him as stern a look as I can manage while still looking up at him from the sink's edge. "Just a few minutes. We have to be quick."

"Quick." He agrees around a smirk. "Only because I'm gonna take my time with you all night." I don't get a chance to respond before his fingers are at my clit. "Mmm, you just came in here so wet for me and you thought I'd let you leave like that?"

"It's your fault," I whimper, riding his hand, searching for more already.

His smile stretches his cheeks. "Let me make it better then, baby." I spread my legs even wider for him. With two fingers inside me, he asks, "Can you take all of me now?"

Each time he fills me, it's a stretch. I don't know if I'll ever get used to how big he is and I love it. "I want it all right now, Ant."

"That's what I like to hear," he says, lining himself up at my opening. I don't wait for him to guide me. Instead, I take what I want. Sliding down his length until I'm fully seated. My man loves when I use his dick like my own personal toy.

His gaze burns into me as he exposes my breasts over the neckline of my dress. His thrusts are slow and measured while he suckles a nipple into his mouth.

My head falls back and his hand is there to grab the back of my neck as he finds the spot that both of us like. Then, he's increasing the pace, faster and faster. Strong thighs meeting mine as I try my best not to scream out his name with people moving around the house.

"Ant. Anthony. Fuck, oh—I'm gonna come. Please don't stop."

"Never," he says, moving his hands to my waist, getting impossibly deeper. "That's right, Drea. I want it all." He pounds my pussy so hard that products start to wobble and fall off the counter but I don't care.

My orgasm takes me to a place of absolute bliss as he follows right behind me. We crest that high together, eyes locked and breaths coming fast. Neither of us gets a chance to catch our breath before our lips and tongues are tangled together.

So insatiable and hungry for each other and I don't see that slowing down any time soon.

A knock at the bedroom door makes us freeze.

"Uhhh... Just a minute." I call from the bathroom.

"If you two could keep your hands off each other long enough to close the bathroom window, that'd be nice." Reese's voice comes from the other side of the door. She laughs and adds, "You better be glad it was just me and Clo out back instead of the rest of your guests for the evening. Get cleaned up and help us already."

I take a look to my right and sure enough, the bathroom window is still open to let the steam out from our earlier showers... And the part of the yard where they're setting up is directly outside of it.

"Oh," I whisper. Ant looks over his shoulder and starts laughing deep from his stomach. I smack at his chest and he slowly slides out of me. Both of our eyes are glued to the mixture of our releases following close behind. He kisses me again before grabbing a towel to clean us up.

"Worth it," he says, smacking my ass on the way out of the bathroom. He takes a few minutes to get dressed and we're finally leaving the room to help everyone get ready for the party.

After the new year, Ant moved out of the rental and into the house with Mireya and I. Impatient as ever, we got married at the courthouse and had a big feast thereafter. It was actually pretty perfect. All that was important to us was the presence of good food and good people. That's exactly what we got.

Mireya was overjoyed at being able to keep her dog with her all the times but probably a little more happy with being able to finally call Tony, Dad. Look, there were few times that I saw him cry. When she slipped and called him Dad on a phone call after school, he was a mess over it. That night at dinner he asked her about it and she just shrugged saying, "About time. Easier for all of us, right?" She played it off like it wasn't a big deal, but the three of us know how long we waited to be a unit just like this. Not a dry eye or smile-less face was in the house that night.

*Life really can be sweet sometimes.*

There was a big commotion over which hand would get his rental next. Chandie was so sick of the bickering that she let Cammie have it, much to many's dismay. Poor thing, she relented to sharing it with someone and I think Ellis drew that straw. Ant thought it was all hilarious because he suspected that having Ellis and Cammie in one house would be a disaster and she'd likely move out anyway. Time will tell though. He saw them bickering outside of it, even getting his last boxes out.

There's some hooting and hollering from our friends when I make an appearance in the yard. At this point, Mel, Tyson, Taylor, Mack and his new girlfriend had arrived. "Will you guys quit?"

"Will you guys quit?" Clo giggles from where she's arranging all the toys.

Mireya had been in a mood for months and avoiding the Mason-Whit-fields house. Eventually, that all simmered down. Thank goodness because I was seriously worried about my girl. CJ and Mireya practically grew up together, it was not like them to spend so much time apart. Through it all, Mireya had Ant to confide in since she felt more comfortable talking to him about it all. I did not love being on the outside of it but I was so grateful that she had someone she could let in, that she trusted. Ant, eventually, relayed to me that it was just a crush that had gone very strange with not only the closeness of our families but also hormones running a muck. Now, they seem to be back to normal and spending time with each other again.

She's happier and that makes me happy too. Her and CJ went with Cory to pick up the little one we had been waiting for.

It's been a long time coming, but we couldn't be more excited. Ant might be a little bit huffy over the pomp and ruckus I'm putting on for our new addition, but I think the little girl is worth it. We greet the rest of our guests and friends as they join us and mingle as we wait for our guest of honor.

Finally, Cory arrives with pink balloons tethered to the SUV. My daughter hops out of the door, struggling to hold the crate to everyone's ooo's and aww's. CJ's behind her to support the weight and they place it down where Reese and Clo have made a little pedestal.

Mireya opens the door and I swear everyone holds their breath as the little one takes her time sniffing around the edge of the crate. With an adorable pink bow around her neck, the little chocolate lab puppy gallops into the yard and straight for Ant. No need for planning, she already knew what to do.

There's a twinkle in Ant's eyes as he takes the adorable ball of fluff into his arms. "Come here, sweet girl," He coos, holding the little dog under his arms to get a look at her. She yips and her little puppy teeth nibble at his hands as she wiggles there.

"I've been calling her Maple." I bite my lip while he thinks the name over. Then the realization dawns in his eyes.

"Very cute, Drea." Now, we're both thinking about maple meringue and that one fateful day where he nearly caught me doing you know what. My cheeks heat but since we still have guests all around, I need to change directions in this conversation.

I turn to the crowd, saying, "Alright everyone, let's wish Maple a very happy Gotcha Day! It's time to cut the Adoption Day Cake!"

Our friends take their turns coming to pet the puppy and welcome her into the family. Eventually, Milli comes over to greet her sister with a little help from Mireya. They're fast friends playing with all the new toys Maple's been gifted.

"Now you have even more M's. But it might get confusing if you call for M&M and the wrong pair comes in," I giggle. He chuckles with me and pulls me in for a hug. I sink into it. There is nothing better than his big bear hugs. Now they always smell like him and our laundry detergent.

**THE END**

-

Thank you for reading Whisk til Peaked!
Read the other standalones in the series HERE!

<hr>

WANT TO SEE MACK fall hard for the Southern girl that came crashing into his life? Preorder **Roped on the Ridge** HERE and keep reading for a sneak peek at their story...

Roped on the Ridge Link

# Thank You for Reading!

Thank you for joining me on this journey through Whisk til Peaked. Your time and support mean the world to me, and I hope you've fallen in love with the characters and their story as much as I have!

## Share Your Thoughts

If you enjoyed this book, leaving a review is one of the best ways to support authors like me. Reviews help other readers discover stories they'll love, and your voice matters! **Leave your review on Amazon or your favorite review site!**

## Keep the Love Going

Whisk til Peaked is part of the Alpenglow Ridge series. Dive deeper into the world of Alpenglow Ridge with these other books in the series:

**Saddled with Finesse**: Can their unexpected kiss ignite a love strong enough to overcome the shadows of her past and give him the fresh start he's been searching for?

Tropes: Returning to hometown, Single Dad, City Boy/Country Girl, He Falls First, Close Proximity

**Verse to Acclimate**: Years after heartbreak tore them apart, a broken small-town girl and country music's rising star must face the scars of their past to find out if love is worth a second chance.

Tropes: Second Chance, Best Friend's Brother, First Love, He Falls First, Mutual Pining

**You can find all my books on my website: www.zeakayleighgalan.com**

## Stay Connected

Want to be the first to hear about new releases, exclusive content, and special offers?

**Sign up for my newsletter at www.zeakayleighgalan.com/news**

## A Special Treat Just for You

Keep reading for an exclusive sneak peek at the next book in the Alpenglow Ridge. Get ready to meet new characters, revisit familiar faces, and fall in love all over again.

Thank you for being part of this journey. I can't wait to hear what you think!

With love and gratitude,
Zea Kayleigh Galan

# *Sneak Peek*

## KATHRYN

Beep. Beep. Beep.

*What's that sound?*

Beep. Beep. Beep.

*Where am I?*

Beep. Beep. Beep.

*Why am I aching all over? My head is killing me.*

I blink my eyes open. Vision blurry and unfocused. It's like sand has crusted them closed and each blink hurts with the lights so bright around me. I squeeze them closed. This feels like the worst hangover.

My throat is terribly dry and I cough to get relief.

*Where am I?*

I wince at the feel of something on my arm. Not on... in. Tentatively raising it, I panic. Why are there so many cords attached to me?

The beeping increases with my racing heart and two women come to my side with navy-colored scrubs on. "Kathryn? Calm down, sweetie. It's okay," one of them says. "My name is Amana and I'm one of your nurses here. They just lessened your sedative so you might feel a little disoriented waking up."

"Where... Am... I?" I struggle to croak out.

"Rita, grab her that water." Turning to me, she says, "Kathryn, you're in the hospital in Harmony Hill."

Rita is back with a water cup, holding the straw out for me. I drink slowly and it feels better immediately. My head is still killing me though. "What's Harmony Hill?" I ask.

Amana's eyebrows pull together. She looks to Rita and they both look back at me. "Harmony Hill, Colorado. You were in a car accident on a county road not far from here three days ago. You came here with a concussion and minimal damage to your person. A few stitches but no broken bones. Does that sound familiar?" Amana asks.

"No," I feel myself frowning. "I've never left Louisiana..."

Rita speaks up next as Amana scribbles something on a clipboard. "Don't worry about that too much. The doctor will be in to see you shortly. Just hang tight, okay?"

I nod, but it's not okay. They leave the room and I look at my surroundings. How did I end up in Colorado?

Trying my hardest, I attempt to recall what I was doing yesterday. No, she said three days ago. How am I here right now?

Looking down at my arm again, I see the IV taped there, but it's everything else that confuses me. What are these tattoos? Little patchwork pieces of art span the length of my arm... no, both my arms.

There's whispering coming from just outside the door that's rising in volume.

"I'll just be a second," a voice says before a man comes into the room on crutches.

He comes over quicker than I would expect for someone on crutches, but I don't recognize him. In a long-sleeved flannel shirt and, oddly enough, exercise shorts with a work boot on the foot that's not in a cast. He's kinda goofy looking with the big smile he has on his face for me. I don't know why he's so happy. There's a large bandage on his nose and deep purple bruising under both his eyes. He got into a fight with someone or something and it doesn't look like he won.

But those eyes. They stop my heart for a second. I've never seen eyes this color before. Even from the distance he stands, they're striking. They look like... like a chlorine pool that's sparkling in the summer sun. Clear and inviting, even with the bruising and bandage.

He smirks a little and waves toward his face, "Oh, this? You should see the other guy." Then, he winces. It's boyish and kind of adorable. "I-I didn't mean that..." He takes a step back from me and I watch him make space between us. "I'm sorry for your loss."

"My... Loss?" I say, my voice feeling like razor blades.

"I don't... I'm messing this up. Let me start from the beginning." He clears his throat and runs a hand through his hair. It's light brown and a little greasy but longer in the back where the front is only long enough to flop onto his forehead. "I'm Mack," he says. His smile is big, imperfect, and happy. It's infectious. I smile, despite my circumstances.

"Kathryn," I respond.

"I like it..." he gives me a sheepish look... "Of course, I already knew that since I've been awake longer than you have. I've been in this room more times than this but they said you woke up so I had to see you."

"See me?"

"Yea. See you."

"Why?"

His face turns more solemn, great clouds over his perfect blues. "To apologize."

"For my... loss."

He nods slowly. "I was in the truck your SUV came in contact with when you hydroplaned across the ice on the county road. The EMT managed to get you and me out of the vehicles but your friend... He didn't appear to be wearing a seatbelt... He didn't make it."

Nothing he's saying makes any sense. Ice? Is it winter? Clayton has never had ice on the roads. But I'm not in Clayton. I'm in Colorado. How random and... "What friend?"

He shifts his weight on the crutches and maneuvers over to the chair to the left of my bed. There's already a bag there. I don't recognize it but there are so many things I don't recognize. I'll just add that to the list. "Sorry, my pits were starting to hurt." He stretches out his leg that has the cast and hands me the water bottle the nurse brought in for me. "Do you need help with this?"

I tentatively take the water bottle, but it is heavier than I expected. He never truly let go, so it's easy for him to help me move it closer to my mouth and drink. "What friend?"

He sighs. I get the feeling that he doesn't like to be the bearer of bad news. That sigh told me everything I needed to know so I brace for whatever it is he'd say next. "His name was Ethan Davey. Does that name mean anything to you?"

All at once, memories of a brown-haired boy flick through my mind. Us at five learning to ride bikes together. Then, us at sixteen trying our first beer. He always had a rebellious streak but he had a heart of gold. What I remember most was his hugs. So many hugs. "Ethan," my voice breaks and tears roll hot and heavy down my cheeks.

Mack puts the water bottle down and picks up a crutch to hop on his good leg, closer to the bed. He uses a tissue to clean my face and when I open my eyes again, it's his blue ones peering down at me with all the understanding a friend could have.

I don't have any memories of this man who's at my bedside. Is he my friend? I don't know why he's the only one here or why I'm in Colorado, to begin with. There are too many feelings that sit heavy on my chest.

Ethan is gone.

*How did I get here?*

"I'm so sorry, Kathryn. Driving on the ice can be dangerous even for us natives too. I wish I had better words to say, but I know nothing can replace the loss of a loved one... I know that better than most." He looks down at the bed for a time. Bracing his arm on one side of the bed, he hugs me with the other free one. He smells like fresh cut grass, earthy and familiar, and leather as his warmth envelops me.

He moves back to the chair and picks up the bag, throwing it over his shoulder. Surprisingly there's a brown cowboy hat behind it that he plops on his head next. It's a little dirty and crooked but it suits him. "Well, I'll let you get your rest. I think the doctor will be coming in soon." His sparkling eyes, a little dimmer than before.

Then, he's walking over to the door. He's... leaving, taking all the sunshine with him. "Mack," I say with a scratchy voice. He turns back around to face me. "Will you stay?" He blinks. "Please?" I ask.

The corner of his mouth lifts. "Of course."

---

WE'RE GOING BACK TO Alpenglow Ridge for Kathryn and Mack's story: **Coming Early 2025!!!**

**PREORDER BOOK 4 HERE!**

# Acknowledgements

Drea and Tony have been so special to me since I first began to think about Alpenglow Ridge. You might remember them from Saddled with Finesse as side characters that seemed to have a strong connection that everyone could feel. To me, I held them close because I could recognize how important their bond was. Intimacy is one thing that I really enjoy writing and I knew that for this couple, it was not ignited or built on lust alone. They are more than that in my mind. But as you saw, they are very, VERY hot when that lust builds! As my first slow-burn couple, I was right there with you hoping and wishing for them to take that next step. Normally, I say that I write these stories for me, but Whisk, I wrote this one for them.

This story could not have been possible without the support from my best friend and husband, Bryan. He is the reason why I even have the courage to share these stories and who listens to me ramble about these characters like I'm gossiping about our old friends. I love you so much, mi rey.

Thank you Gram! Dare I say, my biggest supporter! I'm so grateful for your faith in me and my words.

Many, many, many thanks to my BETA team! You have no idea how much you help me. Your feedback is always, always appreciated! Thank you Abby G, Faith H, Jessica N, Karime G, Melanie H, Sabrina M, and my other BETAs!

A big thank you to Shaye, Lindsey and Good Girls PR who helped in so many ways to make this book possible. Your expertise and efficiency was such a blessing with this release.

Thank you to every ARC reader who read and reviewed this holiday story! You all are rockstars. I'm so grateful for your time.

To my author friends, your encouragement means so much to me. I never thought I'd be here, standing where you've stood. Thank you for including me in us.

Thank you to YOU, the reader! You are the reason why I write these tales. Never underestimate your power and worth. I hope that you enjoyed your time in Alpenglow Ridge and that you will come back to learn more about this little mountain town... and stay a little longer for more stories from me.

Never miss a new release by signing up for my newsletter: www.linktr. ee/zeakayleigh

# Also by Zea Kayleigh Galan

**Alpenglow Ridge**

Saddled with Finesse
Verse to Acclimate
Whisk til Peaked
Roped on the Ridge

# About the Author

ZEA IS A PASSIONATE storyteller who brings romance to life with heartfelt emotion and unforgettable characters. A lifelong lover of love stories, she weaves her background in anthropology into crafting tales where swoon-worthy heroes fall hard for their strong, relatable heroines.

Living in the picturesque mountains of Colorado with her husband, daughter, and a spoiled, posh cat, Zea draws inspiration from her surroundings to create warm, vibrant settings readers want to escape to. When she's not writing, she's indulging in her other loves: cooking, hiking, designing clothes, or curling up with a romance novel and a plate of sweets.

Zea is dedicated to connecting with her readers and invites you to join her on this journey of love, laughter, and happily ever afters.

Want to be the first to hear about new releases, exclusive content, and special offers?

Sign up for my newsletter at

www.zeakayleighgalan.com/news

www.instagram.com/zeakayleigh

www.facebook.com/zeakayleigh

Signed Book Shop

www.ingramcontent.com/pod-product-compliance
Lightning Source LLC
Chambersburg PA
CBHW032249310726
48973CB00008B/2354